SIX STEPS TO HAPPINESS

SUZIE TULLETT

BOMBSHELL

BOOKS

Print ISBN 978-1-913419-13-4

ALSO BY SUZIE TULLETT

For Day
My fourth little angel

1

Ronnie checked the kitchen clock, realising she had just enough time to pour herself a glass of wine before her pizza delivery landed. She giggled as she decanted, raising the glass in a silent toast. Putting it to her lips, she savoured the taste with a smile, at the same time imagining the evening ahead. With a bit of luck, that night was *the* night.

Intent on drinking every drop, she didn't bother putting the bottle back in the fridge. There was no point to-ing and fro-ing from one room to another when she didn't have to. Instead, she took the bottle with her as she headed into the lounge and positioned herself in the window – a large bay that gave a one-hundred-and-eighty-degree outlook, the perfect vantage point, one of the lower windows open so she could also hear the van.

Keeping her attention on the street, anticipation bubbled inside of her. Looking first left and then right, Ronnie felt like a naughty teenager as she wondered where her delivery had gotten to. Having opted for a barbecue prawn and salsa verde pizza, straight from Bello Italiano's gourmet range no less, its cost made it seem even more delicious. "Where are you?" she asked, her eagerness fast becoming impatience.

She took in the houses that made up Holme Lea Avenue while she waited. Within two mirroring rows of semi-detached properties, she and Nick had lived at number six throughout their married life. They'd bought it for a song, such was the state of it back then, and Ronnie couldn't help but smile as she recalled the old blue bathroom suite, the various floral wallpaper designs and the accompanying patterned carpets, all of them migraine inducing. And the kitchen... How she ever dared cook in there was still a mystery.

Over the next few years, however, they'd lavished a lot of love and a serious amount of cash on the place, turning it room by room into a home they were both proud of. And unlike the neighbours who'd come and gone over the years, Ronnie couldn't imagine living anywhere else. Holme Lea Avenue was where she'd built a home, and raised a daughter. It was where Ronnie belonged.

She pondered residents past and present. Some she'd been saddened to see go, others she'd more than happily waved off. Ronnie felt her pulse quicken. Then there were those who refused to move no matter how hard the encouragement.

Her spirits lifted once more when she at last spotted the Bello Italiano vehicle and, downing the contents of her wine glass, she excitedly topped it up again in readiness. She watched the driver pull up and check what she assumed to be a worksheet before getting out of the vehicle, pizza box in hand. "Let the fun commence," Ronnie said, as the unsuspecting chap headed for the house next door.

"Hold it right there," her neighbour, Gaye, called out, the woman's voice loud and clear as she appeared to greet him.

Pizza man paused mid approach and glanced around, as if checking it was him she was talking to. "Excuse me?"

Watching them, Ronnie appreciated her behaviour was childish, but it gave her a sense of power in an otherwise uncontrollable situation. And it wasn't as if she hadn't tried to do the mature thing; she'd knocked on Gaye's door a few times hoping to discuss the matter. She'd even written a long heartfelt letter about why next door should move on to pastures new. But the longer she and her letter went ignored, the more Ronnie's rage stewed and she had to let it out somehow. Not only that, after what Gaye had done, her own actions didn't compare.

Ronnie sneered as she took in Gaye's attire – grey linen trousers, a smart white shirt and long floaty cardigan, all finished off with clearly expensive jewellery. Moreover, unlike every other mere mortal on the planet, despite it being the end of the day, her hair was perfect, as if she'd just stepped out of a salon. Gaye appeared the picture of respectability.

Ronnie sniffed. "Funny how images can be deceiving." She glanced down at her own clothing. Ronnie knew she looked like a sack of potatoes in comparison. "Still," she said, returning her attention to Gaye, "at least I can wear my integrity with pride."

Watching her neighbour turn on her charms, Ronnie rolled her eyes. "Here we go," she said, at the same time recalling the number of delivery guys who'd already fallen for the woman's over-the-top smile and pathetic lilt.

"I'm sorry, love," Gaye said. "But I think you've had a wasted journey."

Ronnie looked from her neighbour to pizza man and, narrowing her eyes as she took in his demeanour, she again dared to hope that that night was *the* night that Gaye would crack. Unlike his predecessors, pizza man appeared unimpressed by the woman's charade; standing his ground, he seemed immune to her excuses. "Ha!" Ronnie said, delighting in the fact that Gaye's act wasn't infallible after all. "This is more like it." Ronnie sipped on her wine as she continued to observe them. Gaye fluttering her lashes, pizza man failing to notice; it was the best entertainment Ronnie had had in years.

Pizza man thrust the box of barbecue prawn and salsa verde into Gaye's hands before fixing her with a no-nonsense smile. "So, what will it be: cash, cheque or card?"

"Fantastic," Ronnie said.

Gaye's patience really began to slip. "But I don't want it," she replied, trying and failing to give the box back. "I didn't ask for it."

"Really? Because someone did." Pizza man held out the receipt for her to inspect. "This is Holme Lea Avenue, isn't it?"

Ronnie smirked. "You tell her."

Gaye looked at the piece of paper. "Yes."

"And this is number eight, is it not?" Pizza man pointed to Gaye's house while Ronnie continued to snigger.

"Yes. But..."

"No buts, lady. And I don't have all night."

It was all Ronnie could do to stop herself cheering.

Gaye appeared lost for words as she stared at the chap in front of her.

"Not so clever *now*, are you?" Ronnie wondered which card her neighbour would play. Would she grit her teeth and hand over the cash? Or tell pizza man what was really going on? Either way, Ronnie wasn't budging until a decision was made and neither, it seemed, was pizza man.

Gaye clearly struggled to control her outrage as she took another look at the receipt, her eyes widening as they rested on the amount due. "How much?" she asked, her voice rising a couple more octaves.

A burst of laughter shot out of Ronnie's mouth and, mid-sip, so did a spray of wine.

"What can I say? Quality costs," pizza man replied, a response that made Ronnie laugh even more.

Gaye, however, continued to appear less than amused and taking a deep breath, she turned, before coolly striding back towards her front door. She stopped halfway up the path and, still holding the pizza box, gave Ronnie a long cold stare. *Finally, a reaction.* It seemed Ronnie's patience was paying off. She knew she was supposed to feel intimidated but considering their history, Ronnie didn't care how the woman looked at her. She simply smiled as she stared right back and, taking the opportunity to further incense her neighbour, raised her glass in salutation.

Gaye fumed as she stormed inside, while Ronnie waited for the woman's next move.

"What the...?" As a police car pulled up behind the Bello Italiano vehicle, Ronnie couldn't believe what she was seeing. Her jaw slackened and she stood there open-mouthed. "Well, you certainly know how to cross a line," Ronnie sneered, forced to acknowledge that calling 999 was nothing compared to what Gaye had already done. "Of course you do."

Watching the attending officer disembark and head for number eight, Ronnie swallowed hard. She took in his thick padded stab vest, police radio and utility belt, home to handcuffs, a baton, PAVA spray and goodness knew what other incapacitating accessories. As if that wasn't scary enough, it wasn't only his uniform that commanded respect, the guy was a giant, his whole mien exuding authority.

Ronnie looked from him to pizza man, wondering what to do for the best. One inner voice telling her to intervene and admit that she was the one who'd ordered the damn food, another insisting she stay put.

Ready to do the right thing, Ronnie placed her glass down on the windowsill. However, knowing that confessing would put an end to her antics, she hesitated, reminding herself that someone had to make next door pay for what they'd done and if not her, then who?

With her feet refusing to move, Ronnie continued to observe, easing her guilt with the fact that pizza man himself didn't seem to care. She watched his chest swell as he took a deep intake of breath, his accompanying expression full of disdain. Placing his feet hip width apart and folding his arms across his chest, he appeared to settle into his stance, ready for the long haul. "Ooh, you're good," Ronnie said, admiring the man's attitude. If Gaye wanted a battle, it looked like she'd got one.

"Evening," the approaching police officer said.

Reappearing at her door, Gaye raced down her garden path, immediately launching into a string of complaints and talking at such speed that Ronnie struggled to make out her words. Even as Gaye's voice got louder, every sentence remained indistinguishable thanks to the woman's non-stop screeching. Ronnie winced, convinced that if her neighbour didn't calm her pitch down and soon, it wouldn't be long before everyone's ears bled.

A door opening opposite caught Ronnie's eye and despite some earlier rainfall, Mr Wright, watering can in hand, stepped out into the open air. He smiled her way and Ronnie gave him a wave. She liked Mr Wright. Unlike his wife who'd become quite cold towards Ronnie of late, he had proven himself more than understanding. Pretending to turn his attention to his hydrangeas, he seemed to keep one eye on the flora and one on the noisy goings on.

Needless to say, he wasn't the only one showing interest. As Ronnie glanced up and down the street, it seemed Gaye had attracted quite a few spectators. Many of Ronnie's usually discrete neighbours had opted to come out from behind their curtains and, like her, stand in full view. Mrs Smethurst a few doors down had even appeared at her gate. Ronnie smiled.

Seeing everyone like that was more than she could have hoped for. Gaye was going to be the talk of the street. Again.

Refocusing on the commotion, it was obvious Ronnie wasn't the only one to notice the growing interest; the police officer had clocked it too. He took in the audience, before at last putting up a hand to silence Gaye, an action the woman clearly didn't appreciate. Halfway through her sentence, Gaye suddenly froze, glowering at the interruption. Unlike pizza man who didn't even try to hide his smirk.

"Ha!" Ronnie said, smirking along with him.

"If we could take this inside, madam," the police officer said.

"But..."

He gestured to the neighbours. "Unless you want everyone knowing your business?"

Ronnie laughed. It was a bit late for that.

Surprised by so many onlookers, Gaye stood there wide-eyed. Flushing red, she certainly didn't look comfortable being such a source of entertainment and she clearly regretted losing control. She suddenly flicked her head high, as if trying to regain some respectability.

Talk about optimistic.

Ronnie gulped a mouthful of wine. "It's going to take a lot more than that, love."

Without another word, her neighbour turned and strutted back up her garden path.

"Would you mind waiting here, sir," the officer said to pizza man.

Pizza man nodded, seemingly happy to oblige, while Ronnie topped up her glass in readiness of the next instalment.

2

R onnie checked the time, having watched all her neighbours disappear. No doubt fed up of waiting, they'd retreated, one by one, back behind their curtains. Mr Wright's hydrangeas had had their fill of water and those like Mrs Smethurst, who'd clambered for a glimpse of the action from their garden gates, had shut themselves away again. Something Ronnie thought fair enough; in their view, sitting in front of the TV with a cup of tea had to be better than standing in the cold. She gave a final check of the street. Only she and pizza man remained.

Ronnie's impatience grew as she wondered what was going on inside number eight. Surely it didn't take that long to read a woman her rights for wasting police time? Then again, she knew from experience that Gaye was good at milking situations for all their worth and Ronnie easily imagined the woman's smarmy voice, protesting her innocence as usual. Of course, the elusive *boyfriend* would be backing Gaye up every step of the way, making out the *rufty tufty* delivery man was the real villain of the piece. After all, to say otherwise meant owning up to their own wrong doings, something Ronnie felt confident they'd never do.

She considered finishing off the contents of her wine glass so she could put it against the wall to listen. Not that there was any point, Ronnie reminded herself. No matter how many times she'd seen it in the movies, that tactic never worked. Glasses, teacups, mugs, plastic beakers... Ronnie had tried and failed with them all.

Finally, she heard the sound of number eight's door opening, and Ronnie immediately stood to attention. Her heart raced. That police officer had to have seen through Gaye's charade and Ronnie struggled to contain her excitement at the prospect of her neighbour getting locked up for the night.

"Thank you for your understanding," Gaye said.

Ronnie cocked her head, puzzled. *Understanding? What understanding?*

Her confusion deepened when the police officer stepped outside, allowing Gaye to close her door on the whole episode. Ronnie's eyes narrowed. "And what are you doing with that?" she asked through the window, spotting the pizza box in his hands.

She watched on, helpless, as the officer headed down the path towards pizza man. She fumed. Clearly it was of no consequence that her neighbour was a lying so-and-so and had just wasted precious police man-hours. The two men talked in hushed tones, leaving Ronnie not only wishing she could lip-read, but wondering what the hell was going on and continuing to stand aghast, she felt tempted to bang on the window and insist the police officer did his job. Gaye had to have committed some sort of crime. Surely her earlier display warranted an arrest for a breach of the peace.

Discussion over, pizza man shook the police officer's hand before returning to his delivery vehicle and going on his way.

Ronnie pursed her lips; she'd had such high hopes. If anyone could have met Gaye head on, Ronnie had been convinced it was him; another reminder that images could be deceiving.

Disappointed, she waited for the police officer to climb into his car and drive off into the distance too, realising that yet again she had no choice but to accept defeat, that there wouldn't be a *For Sale* sign going up next door quite yet. But much to Ronnie's surprise, the police officer didn't move, he simply stood there, looking down at the pizza box he still held. After a moment, he straightened himself up, before turning his attention to Ronnie. She froze as he stared her way. "Oh, Lordy." Taking in his expression, he clearly knew what she'd been up to.

Her mind raced as he walked towards her door. However, try as she might, she still couldn't come up with an alibi for the time of the pizza order. She knew she should go and speak to him, but the nearer he got, the scarier he looked, and Ronnie couldn't bring herself to move. She picked up her wine glass, pausing for a second before downing its every drop. "You can do this," she told herself. "Remember, you're the real victim here."

Placing her glass on the windowsill and shutting the window, she smoothed down her clothes, wishing to God she looked a tad more respectable as she headed back through the lounge and into the hall. She hesitated at the front door, steeling herself as she opened it, suddenly stopping when she found herself face to *chest* with the policeman. She swallowed hard, her eyes slowly moving upwards until they finally looked into his. "Officer," she said, her voice cracking. If he'd seemed tall and intimidating from a distance, the man was positively terrifying up close. "How can I help you?"

"I believe this is yours," he replied, holding out the pizza box.

Ronnie took in his sternness and with panic rising, wondered if that was a trick question, a ploy to make her say something she might later regret. She looked from him to the offering, and praying her blushes didn't give her away, made sure to keep her hands by her sides. Her antics might not be those of a master criminal, but Ronnie wasn't stupid, she knew acceptance would be an admission of guilt.

"May I come in?" he asked.

As tempting as it was to refuse entry, Ronnie knew better than to risk any further trouble, and her heart pounded as she stood aside, her hand gesturing down the hall to the kitchen. Following him, Ronnie told herself to play it cool. Guilty or not, she'd seen enough crime shows in her time to know anything she did say could be taken down in evidence and used against her. For her own sake, she had to remain silent.

Watching the police officer scan his surroundings, she saw his eyes settle on the Bello Italiano takeaway menu she'd left sitting on the kitchen counter. *Oh, bugger*, she thought, as he placed the pizza box down next to it. She felt the colour drain from her face. It was the exact evidence he needed to slap on the handcuffs and lead her outside, humiliating her in front of all the neighbours. Worse still, in front of the two next door. Ronnie pictured herself being paraded out, the both of them smirking and rubbing their hands with glee. As if they hadn't put her through enough.

"I take it you know why I'm here?"

Having incriminated herself already thanks to the menu, Ronnie didn't want to look any more foolish by denying it. But as sure as damn it, she wasn't going to admit to anything.

"And I suggest you also know harassment is a criminal offence?" The police officer stared at her, his eyebrows raised in anticipation of an answer.

Ronnie, however, remained steadfast.

He shook his head at her continued silence. "As much as I appreciate you're having a hard time..."

Ronnie flashed him a look. That was putting it mildly.

"The way I see it we have three options. One, I can arrest you."

Ronnie's back stiffened. After everything she'd been through. *You mean you can try*, she thought, ready to go down with a fight.

"Two, I can give you a formal harassment notice which stays on record for a year..."

Ronnie scoffed. Having never had as much as a parking ticket, the very idea that her name be kept on file somewhere was ludicrous.

"Or three..." The police officer pulled out his notebook and a pen and began writing. "You can sign this."

Suspicious, Ronnie eyed the notebook and pen being proffered. Something else she'd learned from her TV viewing was to never sign anything without first getting it checked by a lawyer.

The police officer sighed at Ronnie's lack of co-operation. "It simply says that next door have agreed not to press charges."

Ronnie almost spluttered. *How bloody kind!*

"And that I've given you a verbal warning telling you to cease and desist."

Ronnie snatched the notebook and pen from his hand.

"Your signature, should you choose to add it, is an undertaking that states, yes, you're going to leave them alone."

Ronnie rolled her eyes as she looked down at the transcript. Despite what he'd written, he had to know how unfair the situation was. Anyone with half a brain could see that *she* wasn't the baddie, her neighbours were. She took in his signature, *PC Shenton*, a name she wouldn't forget in a hurry, before returning her attention to the man himself. Hoping to spot even a glimpse of understanding, much to her frustration none was forthcoming.

"It's up to you," he said. "I don't mind which course of action we take."

Ronnie glared in response, but the last thing she wanted was to spend the night in a jail cell. "You're all heart," she said, realising she'd no choice but to scribble her name in the notebook and give it back.

"Twenty-five years," Ronnie suddenly added, as she watched him check over her signature.

PC Shenton looked up from his reading. "Sorry?"

"To the day."

He appeared confused.

"They left that bit out, did they?" She plonked herself down at the kitchen table. "If they're going to paint me as some kind of lunatic, you may as well know why."

PC Shenton shifted on his feet, clearly uncomfortable with her attempt at full disclosure. But Ronnie didn't care about his unease. As far as she was concerned, her neighbours had given their side of the story, so it was only fair she gave hers.

"That's how long we were married. Exactly twenty-five years." She sighed at the absurdity of her situation. "We weren't much more than school kids when we met. Bloody kids when we tied the knot. Now look at us."

She recalled the evening he left.

Unlike her, Nick hadn't wanted a big celebration. After months of putting in extra hours at work, he said he didn't have the energy for anything fancy, and not being a party animal at the best of times, much preferred a quiet dinner at home, just the two of them. Naturally Ronnie was disappointed, twenty-five years was, after all, a milestone. But instead of feeling sorry for herself, she set about organising the perfect evening. She bought champagne, cooked his favourite meal and even sprinkled the dining table with heart-shaped sequins. And while Nick was upstairs getting changed after another day's grafting, she set the mood with a romantic playlist and numerous candles.

"Oh, Nick," Ronnie said, her heart leaping when he finally appeared in the doorway. She took in the suitcase at his side, packed and ready to go, all the while asking herself how she could have doubted him. Excitement enveloped her. No wonder he hadn't wanted a party, he'd secretly been planning to whisk her off on a celebratory getaway.

Throwing her arms around him, she froze, suddenly confused. His whole body felt tense; it was like hugging an ironing board. She stepped back, his hard expression telling her everything she needed to know. The only person going anywhere was him.

Ronnie shook herself back into the present. "Who does that, eh? Who leaves their wife on their actual wedding anniversary?"

Unsurprisingly, the police officer didn't have an answer.

"And if that's not bad enough, for the bloody woman next door?" Ronnie played with her wedding ring, twisting it around her finger, first one way and then the other. "She calls herself Gay with an *e*, for goodness sake. That's how she introduces herself." Ronnie feigned laughter, mocking herself more than anyone else. "It was no doubt going on for a while and I was just too blind or stupid to see it." She fell silent, before lifting her gaze. "So, tell me. What am I supposed to do? How does *anyone* handle a situation like mine?"

PC Shenton's expression softened. "I'm sorry. It must be difficult."

Ronnie smiled an empty smile. At least he had the grace to look like he meant it. "Some of us aren't the wallowing type," she carried on. "Despite what happens in the movies, ice cream and break-up songs don't always cut it."

3

A ccording to the cookery book, Ronnie's cake mix should have been smooth and creamy, not the lumpy mess she found herself faced with. Staring into the bowl and then at her recipe, she couldn't understand what had gone wrong; she'd followed its instructions to the letter. Ronnie knew she'd never been what anyone could call a natural baker, but what she lacked in skill she more than made up for in enthusiasm and never one to give up, she plunged her wooden spoon back into the mixing bowl and stirred even faster.

As her arm began to ache, she recalled some of the more memorable homemade cakes that had gone wrong over the years. The unicorn that ended up with less of a horn and more of a phallus sticking out of its head; the princess that looked anything but regal thanks to her boggly eyes and menacing smile; and then there was the so-called Minnie Mouse... The reason cake-making duties were taken away from Ronnie. She didn't think her daughter would ever get over the nightmares after that particular cake fail. When it came to Ronnie's baking, expectation versus reality couldn't have been further apart.

Thanks to Minnie, Ronnie only ever encouraged her inner Mary Berry when she was stressed. During difficult times she found baking therapeutic, all that egg cracking, whisking, and beating were perfect for getting rid of negative energy. She looked around at the state of her kitchen; flour, spilt milk and eggshells covered almost every surface. Still reeling from the previous night's pizza shenanigans, it was no wonder she'd spent the morning producing enough dodgy cake to feed a small country.

The sound of the front door opening and closing caught Ronnie's attention and she stopped stirring for a moment, frowning at the unexpected interruption. She wasn't anticipating any visitors.

"It's only me," a female voice called out.

Recognising it as belonging to her mother-in-law, Bea, Ronnie relaxed in response. "I'm in the kitchen."

Entering the room, Bea stopped, suddenly grabbing the door frame in exaggerated horror. She took in Ronnie's efforts. "You're baking."

"I am."

"Again."

"I keep telling you it's either that or crafting a couple of voodoo dolls." The number of times Ronnie had looked at her sewing machine and felt tempted.

Putting down her mixing bowl and wooden spoon, she smiled at the sight of her guest still clinging on for dear life, Bea's colourful attire and dry humour never failing to brighten her mood. Wiping her hands on a tea towel, Ronnie cleaned up some of the mess off the table. "And to what do I owe the pleasure?"

Bea took a seat, careful to avoid the dusting of flour in front of her. She fiddled with the numerous bangles adorning her wrist. "Oh, you know. I was passing."

Ronnie paused and knowing a fib when she heard one, folded her arms tight across her chest. "He rang you, didn't he? About what I've been up to?"

Bea didn't answer, which was an answer in itself.

"So, he's sent you round to give me a good talking to, has he?"

Bea laughed. "Something like that."

Ronnie noted the glint in her mother-in-law's eye. "Meaning?"

"Nick wasn't the one to ring, Gay with an *e* was."

Ronnie scoffed. "Why am I not surprised?"

"I suppose *I* shouldn't have been really. That woman does have more neck than a giraffe. Of course, I told her where to go. That I wasn't in the business of telling Nick's *wife*, the mother of my *only grandchild*, what to do."

Ronnie bit down on her lip, trying to disguise her amusement.

"Although I can't say it went down too well."

"I bet it didn't." Ronnie turned to make some tea, at the same time imagining Gaye coughing and spluttering down the phone at Bea's response, something she'd have paid good money to see.

"And neither did telling her it was Nick who needed to sort his shit out, not you."

Ronnie spun round again. "Bea!" She put a hand up to her mouth, doing her best not to laugh.

"I know, I know, I shouldn't have sworn, but someone had to put her in her place. And it's not as if your tactics are working, is it?"

Ronnie's smile faded. As grateful as she was for the loyalty, she had to acknowledge the difficulty in Bea's predicament. Her mother-in-law shouldn't be forced to take sides when it came to either party; the reason Ronnie had kept her antics to herself. Besides, Nick was Bea's son, her flesh and blood, and Ronnie respected that. "I'm sorry. No-one has the right to try to put you in the middle of this, least of all Gaye."

"My dear, it's that son of mine who should be apologising. We wouldn't even be having this discussion were it not for him."

Unable to disagree, Ronnie got back to making the tea, before carrying a couple of mugs over to the table. "Well, thank you," she said, placing them down. "But in future, please don't feel you have to stick up for me. I'm a big girl and I can fight my own battles." She took a seat.

"Really? Because the last I heard you were almost arrested."

Ignoring the fact that her mother-in-law had a point, Ronnie felt her hackles rise. She still couldn't believe she was the one who had ended up in trouble. She thought back to the previous evening's events, and while it was a resolve best kept to herself, felt determined to get rid of them more than ever. Ronnie took a deep breath. She just had to decide how.

"I thought you weren't here to talk about that?" Ronnie said, putting on a smile.

"I'm not."

"Then why are you here?" Ronnie took a sip of her tea. "I mean it's lovely to see you, but you don't usually pop round at the weekends." A voice interrupting from out in the hall immediately diverted her attention.

"It's only me."

Ronnie's face lit up. "Willow?" she said, putting down her mug. "What's she doing here?"

Ronnie's daughter appeared in the doorway. "Oh, Lordy," she said, suddenly stopping. Taking in the sight before her, Willow's eyes went from the flour, to the eggshells, to the spilt milk, before resting on the discarded mixing bowl. "Things can't be that bad, can they?"

"Don't you start," Ronnie replied, laughing. She got up from her seat, holding out her arms ready for a hug. "You should have called," she said, pulling back. "To let me know you were coming."

"Why?" Willow raised an eyebrow. "So you could bake a cake?"

Ronnie shook her head. She and Willow might be the image of each other, but her daughter had definitely inherited Bea's sense of humour. "Come on, sit down," Ronnie said. While Willow took the seat next to Bea, Ronnie grabbed another mug from the cupboard and set the kettle to boil again. "I'm so pleased you're here." If anything was going to take her mind off her woes it was a long overdue catch-up with her daughter. "How are things going with Jonathan?" She handed her daughter a fresh mug of tea.

Willow rolled her eyes. "They're not."

"What do you mean?"

"I mean we're not together anymore."

Ronnie sighed. Jonathan had seemed like such a lovely chap. Then again so had Richard, Leon, Simon... the list went on.

"He got too clingy. And you know me, I like my own space. I'm not into all that lovey-dovey stuff."

"That's because you've yet to meet *The One*," Bea said.

"*The One?*"

"Don't worry, he's out there somewhere."

Ronnie giggled. The last thing her daughter looked was worried.

"And what if I'm not looking for him?" Willow asked. "What if I'm quite happy as a singleton?"

"Oh, you'll still meet him," Ronnie replied.

"And when you least expect it," Bea added. "You'll be out and about minding your own business and bang! you'll find yourself staring into someone's eyes, suddenly feeling a bit hot and bothered. Your heart will be racing, and you can forget about stringing a sentence together. You'll be far too tongue-tied to say anything that makes sense."

Ronnie saw the wistful look in her mother-in-law's eyes. She knew Bea was thinking about Nick's dad, Eric, a man Ronnie would have loved to have met. She'd seen photos, of course, and heard stories that proved he was every bit as kind and gentle as Bea and Nick described. She reached out to Bea with a comforting hand. Why were the good ones always taken too soon?

Bea pulled herself out of her reverie. "You mark my words, young lady. Before you know it, it will be love at first sight."

Willow let out a laugh. "Don't hold your breath. Anyway, I'm far more interested in what's been going on around here lately."

"What do you mean?" Ronnie asked.

"Duh. The policeman who came a-calling."

Ronnie stiffened. "You know about that?" Her shoulders slumped in disappointment. "Of course you do. Why else would you turn up out of the blue like this?"

Realising that, like Bea's, her daughter's visit wasn't purely social, Ronnie's good mood was ruined. She wondered what Nick thought he was playing at. It was bad enough him and his floozy trying to coax Bea into doing their bidding, but for Nick to get his daughter in on the act too, it was unforgivable. "Whatever your father and Gaye with an *e* told you," she said, addressing the issue head on, "I'm not losing it, I'm not hormonal, in fact I'm not anything except angry. *Very* angry, in fact. Which I think, under the circumstances, I'm entitled to be, don't you?" She looked from Willow to Bea, taking in their wide-eyed expressions. "What?"

"Dad and Gaye didn't tell me anything," Willow said.

"They didn't?"

"No."

Ronnie frowned in confusion. They had to have done. "So if it wasn't them, who was it?"

4

S omeone had told Willow what Ronnie had been up to
and Ronnie wanted to know who.

She waited for one of them to answer the question,
but both her daughter and mother-in-law appeared as uncomfortable as each other. Neither would look her in the eye, let
alone speak, and Ronnie's patience was running a bit thin. She
watched Willow steal a glimpse at Bea. "Well?" Ronnie asked,
feeling like a teacher dealing with two naughty school children.

Bea shifted in her seat. "It was me."

Ronnie stared at her aghast. "But why?"

"Because I'm worried about you."

"And after listening to that little rant, so am I," Willow said.

Ronnie again looked from one woman to the other, her frustration rising all the more. So what if she'd pulled a few pranks
on next door? As far as she was concerned, everyone was
making a fuss over nothing. She got up from the table, heading
straight for the discarded mixing bowl, and picking up the
wooden spoon, frantically stirred the cake mixture like a mad
woman. "You've no need to be," she said, her hand working the
utensil at double speed. "I assure you. I'm absolutely fine."

Willow and Bea appeared to exchange a glance before Willow got up from her seat and approached. She took Ronnie's baking apparatus from her and laid them down on the counter. "Mum, no-one's saying you're wrong for wanting revenge."

"Revenge?" Ronnie replied, as Willow guided her back to the table. "Whatever gave you that idea?"

She and her daughter sat down.

"Don't you?" Bea asked. "Because in your shoes I bloody would."

"No. I don't," Ronnie said. To be fair to herself, even after the previous night's events, when PC Shenton had arrived on the scene, revenge had been the last thing on Ronnie's mind. She caught Willow and Bea sharing another look. They obviously didn't believe her.

"Then what do you want?" Willow said. "Because from what you've been up to, it certainly looks that way."

Thinking about it, Ronnie had to appreciate where her daughter and mother-in-law were coming from. After all, she had been doing her best to make next door's life a misery. She just wished Willow and Bea could understand her position in return. Having tried everything else, resorting to mischief hadn't exactly been a choice; thanks to Nick and Gaye, she'd been left with no alternative. "I want them to move," Ronnie said. "Leave Holme Lea Avenue to start over somewhere else. Instead of shoving what they've done in my face every day."

"And are your antics working?" Willow asked. "Are they packing their belongings as we speak?"

"Or are they digging their heels in, ready for the long haul?" Bea added.

Ronnie sighed. "God knows what those two are thinking."

Her daughter reached over and gave Ronnie's arm a gentle reassuring rub. "You need to start concentrating on your own future, Mum."

Ronnie couldn't believe what she was hearing. "But that's what I'm doing."

"No, love," Bea said. "You're not."

Ronnie looked from one to the other, aghast. Surely they didn't think she should be the one to up sticks? "*I'm* not going anywhere, if that's what you're suggesting. This is my home. And I can't simply sit here and do nothing."

"No-one expects you to," Willow said.

"Really? Then what *do* you expect?" Ronnie felt her irritation continue to grow. After everything Nick and Gaye had done, she couldn't understand why she was the one being lectured.

"Mum, you were nearly arrested. You can't possibly expect us to sit idly by while you build up a criminal record. Because that's where you're headed if you don't stop what you're doing. Having rung the police once, they'll do it again, and you might not be so lucky next time."

"Who says there'll be a next time?"

"You tell us?" Willow asked. "Will there?"

In Ronnie's opinion, Willow and Bea were talking to the wrong person. Rather than going on at her, they should've been round at number eight, telling Nick and Gaye that selling up was the least they could do after the hurt they'd caused. She wanted to scream that, yes, she planned on harassing them for the rest of her life if that's what it took. But looking at the troubled expressions coming back at her, she couldn't say it, she'd clearly caused enough worry. "No," she replied instead, her voice curt. "There won't."

"That's what they all say," Bea said. She turned her attention to Willow with a knowing expression. "I told you we should have stepped in sooner."

Stepped in sooner! Anyone would think Ronnie was some wretched drug addict the way her mother-in-law was jabbering on. An addict in need of saving. Ronnie stared at first Bea and then Willow, her eyebrows raised in disbelief as realisation dawned. "Please don't tell me this is some sort of intervention."

"That's one way of putting it," her daughter replied.

Ronnie scoffed, they had to be kidding. "So, what's next? You ship me off to some rehabilitation centre for spurned women?"

"Not exactly," Willow said.

"What do you mean, not exactly?" Goodness knew what the two of them had in mind.

"When I was about fifteen, I saw this thing on TV." Willow got up from her seat, collected each of their mugs, and went to put the kettle back on. "Which for some reason, even after all these years, I've never forgotten. It was on one of those daytime shows." She giggled, turning her attention to Bea. "I was meant to be at school but couldn't be bothered going."

Ronnie cocked her head, her thought processes momentarily diverted. "Sorry? You skived off school?" That was news to her. "When? Why?"

"Relax, Mum, it's not as if it did me any harm. Anyway..." Willow got back to the matter at hand. "This woman, a journalist I think, was being interviewed. She was nine months pregnant and her husband had left her six weeks previous."

"When she was due to have a baby?" Ronnie asked. "What is it about some men?"

"And you think you've got it bad," Bea said.

"Exactly," Willow carried on. "But the funny thing was, the woman being featured was fine. She claimed it only took six weeks to get over him, and that was that."

"Rubbish!" Ronnie said. It had been more than two months since Nick's departure, and she couldn't imagine ever getting over the shock. "Unless she underwent some form of intense counselling or something."

"I can't actually remember the ins and outs," Willow said.

"But I don't think so. She certainly didn't mention anything like that."

As her daughter handed everyone their fresh drinks, Ronnie shook her head. She couldn't help but question what any of this had to do with her. "And you're telling me about some random woman because?"

"Because it's thanks to that interview that we have a plan," Bea said.

"A plan?"

"Yes." Her mother-in-law smiled.

Ronnie took in the two women before her. One, an individual so averse to commitment, the word didn't actually appear in her dictionary. The other, so devoted, she'd never been able to move on from her dearly departed's death. Not quite the relationship experts Ronnie would have chosen. In fact, she'd have laughed had the situation not been so ridiculous.

"Except instead of giving you six weeks to sort yourself out," Bea added. "We're giving you six steps."

"Steps?" Again, Ronnie questioned their qualifications.

"Yes," Willow said. "And we guarantee that come the end of them, Dad and Gaye will be a thing of the past."

"Whether they live next door or not," Bea said.

Bold statements, indeed, thought Ronnie and made with such sincerity she wasn't quite sure how to respond.

"So, are you up for the challenge?" Willow asked.

Ronnie scoffed. "Let me get this straight. By taking part in this plan of yours, you're telling me I won't only be over my *twenty-five-year* marriage, I'll no longer give a damn that my husband..." She turned to Bea. "Your son." She turned to Willow. "And your father... has shacked up with the woman next door?"

"Yes," both women replied.

"You really think life's that easy?" They might have had faith in what they were saying, but Ronnie had never heard anything so absurd.

Willow and Bea nodded emphatically. "Yes," they said again.

Taking in their confidence, Ronnie didn't know whether to fear or admire their conviction. More to the point, she dreaded to think what their six steps entailed. She watched Bea reach into her handbag, pull out an envelope and place it in the centre of the table. "And that is?"

"Your first step," Bea replied. "Should you choose to accept."

"Jesus," Ronnie said. She shook her head at them both, before drinking a mouthful of tea. "And everyone thinks I'm the one losing the plot."

5

R onnie leant against the kitchen counter, a mug of tea in her hand. She yawned, tired after spending the night tossing and turning, thanks to the weird dreams playing out in her head. *Dreams?* she considered. *Nightmares, more like!*

She could still feel the fear as she pictured herself, stood alone and scared in a courtroom dock, her fate sealed when the presiding judge put on his black cloth cap ready to announce his verdict. All eyes on her, Ronnie tried to protest her innocence, only to find her voice failing over and over again.

"Guilty!" the judge declared.

Ronnie grabbed the dock's handrail to steady herself. Cheers from the public gallery rang in her ears and she looked up to see Nick and Gaye applauding her downfall and hugging each other in celebration. Willow and Bea sat nearby, motionless as tears streamed down their faces. If only Ronnie had listened to them. Even the police officer and pizza man were there to bear witness, the two men neutral in their response, as if Ronnie being dragged off to prison was all in a day's work.

Ronnie shuddered, bringing herself back into the present.

Anyone would think she'd committed murder. The previous few days had clearly messed with her subconscious.

She moved to the kitchen table and took a seat, at the same time eyeing the envelope that Willow and Bea had left behind. Still unopened, it teased her, willing her to peek inside.

Resisting the temptation, Ronnie knew her daughter and mother-in-law meant well. But as for insisting it only took six simple steps to get over a twenty-five-year marriage, she found that downright preposterous. Ronnie let out a hollow laugh, forced to ask herself what would she know? Looking back, if someone had suggested Nick would one day leave her for the next-door neighbour, she'd have called that preposterous too.

Ronnie knew one thing was certain, if her previous night's sleep was anything to go by, she couldn't carry on the way she had been doing. Picking up the envelope, she toyed with it, wondering what she had to lose.

Running her fingers along the seal, she tried to guess what was inside. Maybe a spa pass to give her some much-needed rest and recuperation? she fancied. Or even better, they'd booked her a holiday and she was holding a plane ticket in her hands. Ronnie couldn't think of anything better; a good dose of sunshine, sand and sea, not to mention a bar's worth of cocktails, would go a long way to soothing her recent state of mind. "Sod it," she said, putting her thumb under the corner and, going for it, she ripped open the envelope.

Ronnie's pulse quickened in excitement as she imagined herself jetting off to some far-flung golden paradise and she paused, savouring the moment, before pulling out a folded piece of paper. Not sure what she was looking at, Ronnie opened it out. Her heart sank, dreams of any kind of R and R vanishing in an instant. There was no spa, no holiday, no gift of any kind. Merely a note containing three little words instructing her to act. "How could you do this to me?" she asked. Staring down at step one, she read the words again: *Join a gym.*

Ronnie tried to fathom Willow and Bea's reasoning. But while she knew the obvious benefits to be had from regular exercise, she couldn't for the life of her figure out what any of them had to do with her marriage breakdown. Continuing to stare at the note, Ronnie sighed. The last thing she wanted to do was join the Lycra brigade and start pumping iron. She leant back in her seat and, glancing down at her belly, pinched the skin on her waistline. Surely they weren't trying to tell her she was fat?

She sighed again. Of course they weren't. Neither Willow nor Bea had ever been backwards at coming forwards; if they thought she needed to lose a few pounds they'd have come out and said it. *Or would they?* Ronnie pondered. She hadn't exactly been herself of late. Under the circumstances, one mention of her weight and she'd have probably reached for her nearest bake and thrown it at them. Only to later regret the waste of a good cake.

Disappointed, she tore up the piece of paper, telling herself that the mere idea of a six-step plan was stupid to begin with. However, staring at the shreds, she suddenly felt guilty. Her daughter and mother-in-law were only trying to help. Besides, Willow and Bea were right, she did need to move on, and for her own sanity as much as everyone else's. She gathered the pieces into a neat little pile.

But the bloody gym.

～

Having searched the garage, the vacuum cupboard, the bottom of her wardrobe and every other cubbyhole she could think of, Ronnie dragged a set of stepladders up the stairs and onto the landing. She panted as she opened them out and, staring up at the loft hatch, insisted there had to be a pair of trainers in there somewhere. Even an old pair of Willow's would have done if Ronnie could find them, because she had no intention of buying any.

Taking a deep breath to gather herself, she couldn't believe what she was doing. Unable to remember the last time her feet had left *terra firma*, any job involving ladders had always been Nick's responsibility thanks to her fear of even the slightest of heights. She gripped the sides of the ladder, already starting to sweat as she dared herself to place a foot on the first rung. "You selfish so-and-so!" she said of her husband. "How could you do this to me?"

She wondered what other delights she had in store as a single woman. Thinking about it, much of their domestic life had inadvertently settled into *his* and *her* roles, both of which *she'd* now have to tackle. Not that they lived like throwbacks to the 1950s, they'd simply fallen into a routine. Him taking charge of the DIY, her of the kitchen, forcing Ronnie to question how, in the twenty-first century, that had happened. On the plus side, she supposed taking on her ex's responsibilities couldn't be that difficult. Recalling Nick's inability to change a loo roll and put a toilet seat down, swapping a tyre or papering a wall had to be a doddle.

As Ronnie began her slow ascent, her legs felt as wobbly as the ladders. But in between squeals, she refused to be beaten, she would climb those rungs if it killed her. Considering that a distinct possibility, her heart picked up pace way faster than her feet. However, thinking about the number of times Nick had laughed at her fear, his mocking expression served to spur her on.

At last she reached the top step, but it was a small consolation. With her knuckles almost white thanks to holding on so tight, her hands refused to release their grip. She looked up towards the loft, knowing that to have any chance of getting in there she'd have to let go at some point; that wooden board wasn't going to move itself out of the way. Trying to summon up the courage, she maintained her grasp with one hand while letting go with the other.

Her palm shook as she reached up and struggled to manoeuvre the board to one side. The ladder jolted, but despite her panic, Ronnie refused to give up. Instead she cursed, wondering why Nick hadn't bothered to fit a proper opening, one that included a staircase and a door. She wondered why she hadn't simply gone out and bought a pair of trainers.

She gave the board above her head a huge push and it popped out of position. Managing to slide it over, she continued to feel precarious and had to brace herself before stepping onto the top plate, something she knew she shouldn't really be doing. Making sure not to look down, she grabbed at the sides of the loft opening before the ladder got the chance to fold under her weight. However, not the most agile of people to begin with, as she huffed and puffed, hoisting herself up took more effort than Ronnie expected.

She groaned and her legs flailed all over the place before she finally managed to haul herself in. "At last," she said, wiping her forehead as she slumped down on the floor. Ronnie tried to catch her breath and while a part of her felt pathetic for struggling like that, another part felt proud. Everything considered, it was a miracle she'd gotten into the loft at all.

After a moment, she glanced around at the numerous boxes and bin liners surrounding her. She didn't have a clue what any of them contained, only that they each represented a time in her married life. She pulled one of the boxes towards her and, remaining seated, opened it up.

Taking out a little metal figure, Ronnie smiled at the holiday souvenir, her mind instantly transporting back to happier times. Delving further, the box appeared to be crammed with treasures picked up on their travels. There was a hand-painted boomerang from Spain of all places, that Willow had insisted she have; a gold plastic Eiffel tower from a weekend in Paris; and a set of four ornate ceramic tiles from Morocco that Ronnie had known would be perfect for the bathroom. Ronnie ran a finger over the pretty blue and terracotta design and, questioning why they'd never gotten around to fitting them, she wondered how something so precious could be discarded like that. She sighed; they'd been tossed aside just like her.

Setting the tiles down, she looked around again, a lump forming in her throat. It saddened her to think there'd be no more trinkets, or boxes, or bags to add to the collection, that that room and what it contained in that moment would forever be the sum total of her and Nick's life together, like some sort of time capsule.

Wiping tears from her eyes, Ronnie told herself there was no point in crying, she simply had to get on with the job at hand and find those elusive trainers. She readied herself to start searching. However, rising to her feet, her gaze automatically drew to the hole she'd minutes before climbed through. A rush of nausea enveloped her and she plonked herself down on her bum again.

Shuffling herself out of harm's way, she questioned how she'd ever get back onto the landing below and could already see the newspaper headlines – *Woman found starved to death after getting stuck in loft*. Gathering her senses, she scratted around in her empty pockets, annoyed at having not brought her mobile. Without it she couldn't call for help. Still, at least death got her out of gym duty, she considered, trying to look on the bright side.

She managed to get to her feet and spotting Nick's leather

tool bag, supposed she could do a bit of organising while she was at it. She might be about to die a slow hunger-fuelled death, but that didn't stop her putting the room in order beforehand.

She decided to place anything ex-husband related to the right, anything pertaining to either herself or Willow to the left, and any joint bags and boxes, such as those containing paperwork, in the middle. Although, getting on with the task at hand felt a lot more emotional than Ronnie had anticipated. She tried to be pragmatic, but long-forgotten memories leapt into focus while she worked, the whole room serving as a reminder of what she and Nick once had and the life he'd thrown away. She had to keep telling herself that it was only stuff and that, apart from Willow's belongings, none of it mattered anymore. Ronnie took a deep intake of breath and slowly exhaled. It didn't feel good to know that, like her, it could all be replaced.

With only one bin liner and one box left, Ronnie had become so engrossed in her trip down memory lane she'd almost forgotten what she was looking for. "You have to be here somewhere," she said, reaching for the last of the big black bags. She tried to pull it towards her, but it caught on something and, giving it a yank, it tore on release, leaving a large hole in the plastic. Ronnie tried to prevent its contents from spilling out, while at the same time scanning the area for the culprit – a loose protruding brick in the wall. She let go of the bag and, wondering if she should be concerned, prodded the brick with her finger. Despite the spattering dust and cement, she told herself there was nothing to worry about, the houses on Holme Lea Avenue had been standing for over a century.

Realising she was looking at the dividing wall between her house and Gaye's, a mischievous smile appeared on Ronnie's lips. She looked over at a screwdriver sticking out of Nick's tool bag, knowing it wouldn't take much to get the brick out altogether. Only to take a peek, of course.

"But why stop there?" a little voice at the back of her mind said. "Why not make a hole big enough to climb through?"

Ronnie felt a frisson of excitement. She'd always wondered what Gaye's house looked like on the inside. Was it full of gilt and chandeliers? Or was it cold and minimalist? Neither would have surprised her. Ronnie readily imagined herself sneaking in and tiptoeing from one room to another to find out. The fun she could have if only she had the guts.

Her smile faded as reality set in. With a harassment warning hanging over her head, no way could she risk a charge of trespassing. Besides, wasn't getting in and out of her own loft a struggle enough?

"You can't," she said, trying to ignore her naughty side.

She looked at the screwdriver again.

"But who'd know?" the little voice asked.

6

Ronnie turned on the cold tap and slushed her face with water. She avoided looking in the bathroom mirror, she didn't need to, she knew the state she was in. Night after night her mind refused to quieten, and the distinct lack of sleep was taking its toll. To say Ronnie was knackered was an understatement and the previous night's brain activity no doubt added to her increasingly crazed appearance. She slammed off the tap and headed downstairs in search of some much-needed caffeine.

Her feet dragged as she made her way to the kitchen, thoughts about her recent trip to the loft still whirring through her mind. According to Nick, even as he made the decision to leave, his affair with Gaye hadn't been going on that long. And as easy as it was for Ronnie to blame his infidelity for their marriage breakdown, things no longer felt so clear-cut. Like it or not, her stroll down memory lane suggested their relationship had begun to unravel well before Gaye came along. Ronnie sighed as she put the kettle on. It was an uncomfortable realisation. "You're still a cheater though," she said, refusing to let him off the hook.

Like most couples with children, her and Nick's life had centred around their offspring, so it came as no surprise to find the loft packed with relics from Willow's childhood. Drawings dating back as far as pre-school; text and exercise books spanning right up to her college years; a box of numerous trophies that Willow had accumulated...

Their daughter was a fantastic chess player and Ronnie and Nick had spent many a weekend on taxi duty, ferrying Willow to this tournament or that championship. Not that Ronnie and Nick begrudged giving up their time, it was what proud parents did. And leaving Willow to get on with the business of competing, the two of them would go for a long walk or find a little café in which to while away the hours.

As she waited for the kettle to boil, Ronnie recollected their conversations during those times. As much as they loved being a little family of three, she and Nick would often discuss their own dreams come the point when Willow left home to travel or go to university. That was when the two of them would jet off as well. They'd go to Australia, New Zealand, America, and maybe on a cruise. Do all the things they would have done together had two not become three quite so early in their relationship.

The kettle finally clicked off and Ronnie made herself a strong cup of coffee, at the same time wondering where those dreams had gone. It seemed the older and more independent Willow became, the less Ronnie and Nick seemed to talk about their future. Until, thanks to Nick, they had no future at all.

Drinking her coffee, Ronnie knew it was useless to dissect the past. What she really needed to do was get back to earning a living. Having continued to pay the bills as normal, Nick might have been generous on the financial front up until then, but Ronnie wanted to make her own money. She wanted a clean break, to be independent. Besides, if Gaye had her way, Ronnie knew it wouldn't be long before Nick's purse strings were knotted once and for all, never to be opened again.

Ronnie stared out of the window and down the garden to her studio, telling herself that instead of standing in the kitchen drinking coffee, she should be out there getting on with it; work was beginning to pile up. She had a collection of seven hand-bags to design and make for an up-and-coming arts fair, for a start. But despite the growing pressure and looming deadline, she still didn't know where to begin. Usually a walk in the countryside or a gaze up at the night's sky would ignite her creative juices. She'd be sketching and fabric dyeing and ordering in all kinds of *passementerie* – textile trimmings like fine cottons, tassels and woven ribbons always did excite her. In recent weeks though, inspiration seemed to be in short supply. The best she'd been able to come up with was the *Marriage Breakdown* collection, a range that probably wouldn't go down well with the bag-buying public.

Ronnie supposed in the meantime she did have her commission to finish – a one-off deep-purple velvet mother-of-the-bride clutch. She frowned; that wasn't exactly screaming out for attention either. While Ronnie usually loved working on such individual pieces, after recent events, she wanted nothing more than to ring the customer concerned and insist the woman tell her daughter to call the whole thing off. It felt like Ronnie's public duty to intervene. How else could the bride be saved from the inevitable pain of divorce further down the line?

A knock at the front door interrupted her reverie and putting down her cup, Ronnie went to answer. Opening the door, she stood still, suddenly surprised. She pulled her dressing gown tight over her chest, before trying and failing to straighten her wild bedhead of hair. Having avoided her for weeks, Nick was the last person she expected to see.

Wondering what he wanted, she took in the new version of

her husband. Instead of the baggy T-shirt and jeans he always wore, he sported a crisp short-sleeved shirt and pair of chinos. His usual mop of dark curls had been tamed with a short back and sides, and a tad too much Brylcreem. An overall image that, after twenty-five years of marriage, Ronnie knew he wouldn't be comfortable with. As for his demeanour, Nick looked sheepish, nervous even, like some naughty schoolboy stood outside the headmaster's office. It wasn't a wholly unpleasant sight. After the way Nick had treated her, Ronnie considered any discomfort on his part a good thing.

"We need to talk," he said.

7

Ronnie stared at Nick, dumbfounded. As far as Ronnie was concerned, he'd left her for the next-door neighbour, and unless he was about to tell her they were moving, there wasn't anything left to say.

"Please?"

Despite his apparent sincerity, Ronnie still thought the man had some cheek. "Talking is what you should have done before you had an affair, Nick. You could have talked instead of packing your bags and leaving." Images of pizza man and PC Shenton flitted through her mind. "And you certainly should have said something before your girlfriend tried to have me arrested."

"Well, yes, I'm sorry about that."

Ronnie wasn't so sure. "Are you?"

"Of course I am. She was just finding your behaviour a bit difficult to cope with."

"My behaviour?" Ronnie couldn't believe what she was hearing. A rising heat suddenly surged through her veins, but he wasn't going to get the better of her, Ronnie was determined to remain calm. "She isn't exactly sainthood material herself, Nick. Or haven't you noticed?"

"I'm not here to argue with you, Ronnie."

It didn't sound that way.

Nick gestured inside. "May I?"

His eyes locked on hers and unable to remember the last time he'd looked at her so intently, Ronnie felt unnerved. "What choice do I have?" she said, masking her unease with a glance up and down the street. "I think the neighbours know enough of our business already, don't you?" Standing aside to let him in, she closed the door before following him down the hall to the kitchen.

She stood in silence, waiting for him to speak. Whatever it was he wanted, she had no intention of making things easy.

"I want to start by saying I'm sorry," Nick said.

If it was forgiveness he was after, he wasn't going to get it.

"I didn't mean for any of this to happen. It just did."

Ronnie scoffed. He sounded exactly like his fancy woman.

"And you were right in what you said, I should have talked, been honest about how I was feeling."

Ronnie wasn't about to disagree.

"I should have confided in *you*, not Gaye."

Ronnie flinched at the sound of that name leaving his lips. She scowled. "Tell me something I don't know."

Nick's shoulders dropped. "You have every right to be angry. And if I could turn back the clock I would."

Nick might claim to regret his actions, but as far as Ronnie was concerned, that didn't make them any less hurtful. She scrutinised his face, wondering why the sudden need to apologise. The way he was talking, anyone would think he was hoping to move back in. All at once, her chest felt light. Was that what he was telling her? That he'd made a huge mistake?

"The last thing I wanted was to hurt you."

Ronnie recalled the aftermath of their wedding anniversary, how the shock of his infidelity had left her numb and dazed. She spent the first few weeks after he'd gone aimlessly wandering from room to room, insisting that Nick was having some ridiculous mid-life crisis and she'd have done anything for life to return to normal. The hours she'd spent praying for Nick to realise he'd been wrong to leave her...

And suddenly there he was, saying the things she'd hoped he'd say, causing her mind to race as she tried to make sense of everything. She took in his sheepishness once more, wondering if she could forgive him his transgression and try again. After all, no matter how many wishes a person made, no-one ever really knew how they'd react to a situation until they were in it.

She knew that in some ways taking him back would be easy. She'd have no money worries, there'd be no more lonely nights in front of the TV, and no starting over with someone else. She might not be ready for that quite yet, but a future without Nick meant rejoining the dating game at some point, the one prospect of singledom that freaked out Ronnie the most. The only man she'd ever known in the bedroom department was the one stood in front of her.

As sorry as Nick might look and sound, Ronnie knew life wasn't quite that simple. After all, could she really ever trust him again? Was the man before her worth that kind of effort? Or, thanks to his adultery, was their marriage forever irreparable?

She took a deep breath, realising she had her answer. "It's too late, Nick."

"Too late?" He looked confused, as if that was the last thing he expected to hear.

Ronnie almost felt sorry for Nick and his misplaced confidence. More than anything though, she felt annoyed. Could he really be so arrogant as to think an apology was all it took? "Look at the state of me, Nick." She held out her arms, highlighting her physical mess. "Even you must see the damage you've done. And that's only on the outside. There's been too much upset for us to have any real chance..."

"What?" Nick's puzzlement continued.

"Well, hasn't there?"

"Oh Jesus," Nick said. Running his hands through his hair, he paced up and down. He stopped. "You think I'm asking you to take me back, don't you?"

Ronnie stared at him. "Aren't you?" she asked, surprised he'd suggest otherwise.

"No."

Ronnie shook her head in bemusement. "But all that stuff about wanting to turn back time? About wishing you'd done things differently?"

"I do wish I'd done things differently," Nick said. "But that doesn't mean I'd change the outcome."

"Excuse me?"

With his words hanging in the air, Ronnie felt sick. How could he be so blunt? This had to be some cruel joke that she wasn't in on.

Realisation began to dawn and with that all-too-familiar numbness enveloping her, Ronnie grabbed a chair from the table and sat down. Not only had Nick yet again made a fool of her, this time she'd helped him do it. How could she have been so stupid? "You're here to ask for a divorce, aren't you?"

"Yes," Nick replied. "I am."

Of course he was. After everything that had happened, how could she have thought anything different? "You need to leave," she said, her voice cold.

"But..."

"Now."

She could sense Nick's unease at the situation, but Ronnie couldn't bring herself to even look at the man. Instead, she remained silent and motionless, leaving him no choice but to eventually make his exit. As he headed out into the hall, Ronnie held her breath, waiting until she heard the front door open and close again, before, at last, exhaling.

A mix of embarrassment, anger and sorrow flooded Ronnie's body and she suddenly jumped to her feet, picked up her cup and threw it in Nick's direction. Remnants of coffee splattered against the walls as she grabbed at anything and everything else to hand, hurling one thing after another. She cursed Nick and Gaye for doing this to her in the first place, the police officer for his harassment notice, and Bea and Willow for their six-step plan. Who did they all think they were?

Finally, Ronnie ran out of steam and the room fell silent as the throwing, clattering and shattering stopped. Surveying the mess, it seemed to reflect the life she'd been left with. A sob escaped from her mouth, followed by another and another until she burst into full-blown tears.

8

Making her way downstairs to the kitchen, Ronnie felt a spring in her step. She'd just had the best night's sleep ever. There'd been no tossing and turning, no weird dreams, and no pointed conversations playing out in her head; only eight wonderful hours of pure comatose bliss.

She might not be ready to thank Nick for it, but Ronnie believed in credit where credit was due. Were it not for his humiliating visit she wouldn't have cried her last tears, never mind come up with the master of plans; one that didn't involve takeaways, social media posts, or anything remotely connected to her previous antics. Unlike her efforts in plan A, plan B was one hundred per cent genius.

Ronnie had no intention of being a bunny boiler or trying to make her neighbours think they were going mad. There'd be no hiding things only for them to suddenly reappear like she'd seen in the movies, and neither would she be planting a horse's head in their bed. Rather, if Nick and Gaye wouldn't move out, she'd make them think a ghost had moved in. Surely even they wouldn't want to share a house with an uninvited lodger like that? Ronnie let out a satisfied sigh, knowing that if everything went accordingly, Nick and his fancy woman would soon be living next door to someone else. Whether they wanted to or not.

Ronnie hummed to herself as she poured a bowl of cereal, dancing to the tune as she got the milk from the fridge and grabbed a spoon from the cutlery drawer. She couldn't wait to get *Operation Poltergeist* underway, starting with part one of phase one, a parcel delivery. Mid note, she stopped, cocking her head at the sound of the front door opening and closing. Surely it was a bit early for visitors?

"I came as soon as I heard," Bea said, bursting into the room. Her jewellery jangled as she plonked her bag down and raced over to give Ronnie a hug. "What's wrong with that son of mine?" She pulled back. "You must be devastated."

"Nope," Ronnie said with a smile.

Bea narrowed her eyes. "I'm confused." Letting go of her daughter-in-law altogether, she took in Ronnie's sunny disposition. "This isn't what I'd expected."

Ronnie thought about the aftermath of Nick's visit, feeling guilty. She'd been wrong to direct as much anger towards Willow and Bea as she had him, especially when her daughter and mother-in-law were only trying to help. However, she couldn't deny their naivety. As far as Ronnie was concerned, their ridiculous six-step plan wasn't the answer to her problems. Getting rid of Nick and Gaye was. "You wouldn't be saying that if you'd seen me when he'd gone." Ronnie recalled her swollen bloodshot eyes and the resulting mountain of tear sodden tissues. "I've never cried so hard in my life."

"So, what's changed?" Bea asked. "I can't remember the last time I saw you this cheerful."

"Did he tell you I agreed to the divorce?"

"Really?"

Ronnie scoffed. That was a no then.

"Why would you do that?"

"I messaged him to say I'd sign any papers he wanted, on condition they moved and left Holme Lea Avenue for good."

"And?"

"And nothing. He said no."

"But why? That's the least they could do."

Ronnie shrugged. "Apparently Gaye is quite happy where she is, thank you very much."

Bea shook her head. "I'm sorry, Ronnie."

"What are you apologising for?" The last thing Ronnie wanted was Bea shouldering any blame.

"Because I raised him."

"Which has nothing to do with anything. Nick's responsible for his own actions, Bea. He's not a child anymore."

"Isn't he? Because he's certainly acting like one." Bea frowned. "I still don't get why you're so happy."

Ronnie felt a quiver of excitement. She was bursting to tell Bea the details of *Operation Poltergeist*. As plans went, this one was inspired and she knew that, were it aimed at anyone else, her mother-in-law would love it. But Nick was Bea's son and, like it or not, Gaye his new partner, and Ronnie wasn't green. She knew there would come a day when Bea accepted that.

"Mum!" Willow's voice suddenly rang out.

Ronnie sighed. Bea must have called her – again. Ronnie gave her mother-in-law a pointed look. "Did you have to?" she asked. Still, at least with the both of them there, she could explain how she wouldn't be taking part in their six-step plan.

Clearly unimpressed, Willow glowered as she appeared in the kitchen doorway. "I know Dad's behaving like an idiot right now, but I thought you'd agreed to stop with your games?"

Ronnie didn't have a clue what her daughter was talking about. "Nice to see you too."

"Mum, you promised."

"I promised what?"

"The delivery van? Outside?" Willow gestured down the hall.

"You mean they're here!" Ignoring her daughter's concern, Ronnie squealed in anticipation, clapping her hands as she exited the room. "I can't believe I almost forgot." She hesitated at the front door, a mischievous smile appearing on her face. If Willow was troubled by the van's presence, the two next door were going to freak; a fact that Ronnie hadn't even considered.

She looked back to Willow and Bea, who hovered in the kitchen doorway and, disregarding their quizzical expressions, put a finger to her lips instructing them to stay quiet. She counted backwards. *Five... four... three... two... one...* Her neighbour was nothing if not predictable and no sooner had Ronnie finished and *bingo!* Gaye was out through her front door, ready to turn the driver away.

More than happy to give Gaye a head start, Ronnie, at last, opened the door and coolly made her way outside. Refusing to let the poor man speak, Gaye was well into her spiel by the time Ronnie reached them. Red-faced and flustered, her neighbour seemed determined not to let the driver get a word in.

"Is everything all right?" Ronnie asked, making sure to put on her best smile.

"It would be," the delivery driver said. "If big mouth here would shut up for a second."

"Excuse me?" Gaye replied. She looked at Ronnie. "And I don't know what you think you're playing at, but–"

"Not again, Gaye, please," Ronnie interrupted. She rolled her eyes and let out an exaggerated sigh as she turned to the delivery chap. "She does this all the time. A pizza man nearly got arrested last week thanks to her." Gaye almost choked, but Ronnie moved swiftly on before her neighbour could give a full and true account of events. "Apparently she's not coping well at the moment." She made a half-hearted attempt at discretion. "At least that's what her *boyfriend* told me."

Gaye's brow furrowed. "What are you talking about? You've spoken to Nick? When?"

Ronnie raised an eyebrow, amazed to hear that Nick had kept his little visit to himself. Then again, knowing him, he'd probably wanted to surprise Gaye with some sort of tacky divorce celebration. Of course, his silence on the matter did play into Ronnie's hands, and she jumped at the opportunity to be even more wicked. "When he popped round yesterday," she said, nice as anything. "I can't believe he didn't mention it." Ignoring Gaye's irritation, she turned her attention back to the delivery man. "Now, how can I help you?"

The delivery man checked his clipboard. "I'm looking for a Mrs Jacobs."

Ronnie gloated, raising her left hand and flashing her wedding ring. "There's only one of those around here, isn't there, Gaye?" Ronnie looked her neighbour directly in the eye, her expression loaded. "And it isn't you." She put on her best innocent smile, rolling her eyes and feigning despair as she got back to the matter at hand. "Honestly, all that fuss for nothing."

The delivery chap took this as his cue and headed to the back of his van, pulling out a parcel, ready to hand over. "If you could sign here, please," he said, offering Ronnie his mobile signature device first. "To confirm receipt."

Using the accompanying stylus, Ronnie sounded out her name as she wrote. "Mrs R. Jacobs," she said, and all for Gaye's benefit. Handing them back in return for her package, Ronnie again pretended to be subtle. "And please don't mind my neighbour. As I explained, she's a bit fragile at the moment."

While the delivery driver nodded and went on his way, Ronnie looked at her increasingly frustrated neighbour. "Gaye," she said, smiling as she turned, happy to leave the woman standing there, open-mouthed.

Such was her excitement for her parcel, it was all Ronnie could do to stop herself running up the garden path. But as she put one foot in front of the other, she could feel Gaye's eyes boring into her back and knew she had to remain calm.

Letting herself into number six, it was only when she closed the door behind her that she finally let out her delight and she raced down the hall to the kitchen. She squealed again as she placed her parcel on the dining table, pausing to relish the moment.

"What is it?" Willow asked. She and Bea stared over Ronnie's shoulders, clearly intrigued.

"You'll see," Ronnie replied. Unable to hold off any longer, she ripped open the packaging to reveal a shoebox. And opening it, she pulled out the most fabulous pair of trainers. "Aren't they gorgeous?" she said, holding them up for the others to see. She smiled. With a little help from those beauties, she'd soon be traversing loft hatches like a gymnast on a trapeze.

"They're very white," Willow said, less than enthusiastic.

"Don't knock them," Bea replied. "I didn't think she'd go for it. Especially after your father's latest stunt."

Their conversation broke into Ronnie's reverie and, putting the trainers back in their box, she looked to her daughter and mother-in-law. "What are you talking about? Go for what?"

"Joining a gym," Bea said.

Ronnie laughed. "But I have to if I want to get fit. I mean, how else am I..." She stopped short before she said too much.

Her gaze went from Willow, to Bea, to the trainers and, realising how everything looked, Ronnie cringed. She watched her daughter and mother-in-law nudge each other, seemingly as proud of themselves as they were of her. It was obviously quite something to know she'd taken their advice and was about to embark on the first step of their plan.

Except she wasn't.

Ronnie suddenly felt guilty and seeing their continued delight, couldn't bring herself to disappoint them. She fixed a desperate smile on her face. "How else am I going to complete my first task?"

9

R onnie drove into the gym car park, eager to start her fitness regime and, determined to enjoy every moment, she pushed any whispers of guilt to the back of her mind.

In her view, feeling bad about misleading Willow and Bea was one thing, forfeiting the opportunity to get rid of Nick and Gaye for good quite another. Ronnie knew if she told her daughter and mother-in-law what she was up to, no way would they let her see it through; especially with a harassment notice hanging over her head. Besides, like Ronnie kept telling herself, they seemed so delighted at the prospect of her following their advice, and it would have been cruel to take that from them.

Pulling up right outside the entrance, she jumped out of the car, standing proud in her leggings, loose fitting T-shirt and brand new trainers. She slipped a bobble from her wrist she'd put there in readiness and, piling her hair on top of her head, secured it in place. About to complete part two of phase one in *Operation Poltergeist*, Ronnie was on a mission.

She smiled as she looked at the building's tired signage, glad to see that Jim's Gym was the kind of no-frills establishment she'd hoped for. If her reckoning was right, unlike in one of the snazzier fitness centres about town, there'd be no make-up clad goddesses swanning around to make her feel insecure, and no posing gods to distract. Inside, she'd simply find a bunch of individuals working hard to keep fit. "Perfect," she said, marching towards the entrance.

Letting herself into the foyer, there was no reception desk or anyone there to meet and greet; simply four white walls, a dirty-brown weaveless carpet and a glass panelled door that Ronnie peeked through. Staring in at what was obviously the workout area, she observed a couple of teenage boys who seemed more interested in taking selfies than getting fit. Frowning, Ronnie wondered what they were even doing there. Shouldn't they have been at school?

Ronnie turned her attention to the more dedicated handful of men and women in the room, cringing at the sight. Battling against various pieces of equipment, their strained facial expressions, muscle-clad physiques and bulging veins suggested there was some truth to the often heard *no pain, no gain* mantra. Theirs wasn't quite the extreme Ronnie wanted to go to, but still, she had to admire the dedication.

She pushed the door, opening it just wide enough to slink through and, hoping not to disturb the bodybuilders, glanced at her surroundings. Two more doors to the right identified the male and female changing rooms and a slightly ajar third, this one to the left, revealed what was evidently an office. Ronnie couldn't see the man inside, presumably a member of staff, but she could hear him chatting to someone on the phone. Listening to the conversation, Ronnie gathered it had something to do with an up-and-coming spinning class and as she again looked around, clocking the line of heavy-duty exercise bikes with their weighted solid flywheels, she couldn't think of taking part in anything worse.

Finally, the office fell silent and the staff member appeared from within. "You must be Ronnie Jacobs," he said, smiling.

Ronnie smiled back and nodded, taking in his size as she excitedly stepped forward. Although not particularly tall, what he lacked in height, the man certainly made up for in width. His biceps looked bigger than her thighs, even his muscles seemed to have muscles.

"I'm Michael, your personal trainer."

Michael thrust out his hand to formally greet Ronnie, and she accepted the gesture. His was a hand that clearly had the power to crush hers in an instant.

"Now if I remember correctly, when you rang you said you're new to this."

"I'm afraid so." Ronnie surveyed her surroundings again. The bodybuilders might be pushing themselves to the limit, but thanks to brute force and serious muscle power, they made operating the gym's equipment appear straightforward. To a novice like her, everything looked seriously complicated thanks to the various rope and pulley systems. She took a deep breath, holding on to her optimism. "And I can't wait to get stuck in."

A chap preparing to tackle a few pull-ups caught Ronnie's eye and as she watched him, he leapt up with a surprising grace. His hands effortlessly caught hold of the metal bar above his head and the rise and fall of his body quickly settled into a rhythm. Ronnie couldn't help but marvel. He had such control. She recalled how she'd struggled to haul herself into the loft, her legs thrashing and floundering like they had a life of their own. "I'd love to be able to do that," she said, keen to get started.

Michael laughed. "You'll be an expert in no time. If you could follow me, we'll get you warmed up."

As she did as she was told, Ronnie clapped her hands, unable to hide her excitement.

"So, what we'll do is go around the room and I'll show you

how to operate the equipment. We can discuss your fitness aims along the way and then I'll draw up a tailored exercise plan for you, based on the session as a whole. How does that sound?"

"Okay, I guess."

"Here we are," Michael said, as they came to a stop.

Ronnie's smile froze. "You want me to get on that?"

"I certainly do."

She grimaced. Out of all the machines he could have picked, why did he have to choose that one? When he'd mentioned a warm-up, Ronnie had envisaged doing a few stretches, not taking part in a marathon. "But it's a treadmill."

Michael laughed, her reluctance clearly amusing him. "Believe me, the last thing you want is muscle cramp. It's for your own good."

As a woman who couldn't run for a bus, Ronnie struggled to believe him.

"When you're ready?"

Ronnie shook her head as she stepped onto the conveyor belt, insisting that *Operation Poltergeist* was worth the risk of embarrassment. "Don't say I didn't warn you," she replied, already imagining her flapping arms and uncooperative legs.

Michael turned his attention to the control panel, but as he pressed a series of beeping buttons, his fingers moved too quickly and Ronnie couldn't follow. Unable to even recognise a *stop* button, she hoped the man wasn't being too zealous on the machine's speed front.

The treadmill sprang to life, forcing Ronnie into a steady jog.

"Is that okay?" Michael asked.

Ronnie assessed the tempo. "So far, so good," she replied, glad to note that, at that pace, her arms and legs still worked in tandem.

"Great. I'll leave you to it and see you in..." Michael checked his watch, "...fifteen."

Watching him go, Ronnie relaxed into her stride, surprised at how comfortable she felt. Not only with the running, but with being surrounded by other people. Aside of any art fairs, her job as a handbag designer meant spending day after day on her own and while she loved what she did, she had to admit that life in her studio could be a bit isolating; to the point that socialising often felt like a chore. Glancing around, Ronnie wondered if that was the reasoning behind Willow and Bea's choice for step one of *their* plan. Maybe they'd put more thought into it than she'd realised. She smiled a happy smile. The gym was like a halfway house. She could be amongst people, without necessarily having to mingle.

After a while, Ronnie began to feel a tad warm and staring at the treadmill's control panel, she wondered if she could slow it down. When it came to the buttons, however, the machine utilised icons instead of words and trying to figure out their different functionalities didn't only prove hard, it was like trying to decipher Egyptian hieroglyphs. Ronnie wiped her brow and with no other choice, focused on the timer instead, soon realising that that was equally as frustrating. The countdown seemed to be taking forever, leaving Ronnie convinced there had to be a fault in the machine's programming. In her view, real time wasn't that slow, no wonder she was starting to feel a bit breathless.

Ronnie scanned the room, hoping to catch Michael's attention. Spotting him, she thrust her arm in the air and waved. However, much to her disappointment, he was too busy chatting to notice any request for assistance, leaving her no choice but to keep on running.

Ronnie squinted as she observed his and the other man's easy interaction, enough to tell her that the unknown male was a regular. Although, unlike the other men present, his build appeared toned rather than beefy. Her eyes narrowed even more, as for some reason he seemed vaguely familiar, not that Ronnie could think why. With his greying blond hair, gorgeous physique, the man wasn't just tall and handsome, he wasn't someone she'd easily forget.

As she watched the stranger shake Michael's hand and then head in her direction, Ronnie immediately tidied herself up, pushing rogue strands of hair behind her ears and pulling down her T-shirt. She ignored the pain developing in her calves, instead making a mental note to purchase extra durable deodorant prior to her next visit. She might not be in the market for a new chap, but that didn't mean she wanted this one seeing her sweat patches.

Smiling his way, her expression suddenly went from demure to demented.

"Hello there," PC Shenton said. "Fancy seeing you here."

"Officer," Ronnie replied, wiping yet more damp hair away from her face. "I didn't recognise you without your uniform."

As if Ronnie's heart wasn't racing enough as she continued to run, it picked up a notch and beat faster. She didn't know what it was about police officers, but even when she wasn't doing anything wrong, they had this ability to make her feel guilty. Except on that occasion she wasn't exactly innocent.

"Please, call me Jack. I'm not at work now."

Too busy trying to get air into her lungs, Ronnie attempted another smile in response.

"Good to see you keeping out of trouble," he carried on. "Getting on with life, after... you know."

Ronnie let out a short sharp laugh. "Oh, I think you'll find I've learnt my lesson," she replied, struggling to both inhale and talk.

"I haven't seen you here before," Jack continued.

"First time," Ronnie said, realising that, for her own sake, she'd have to keep her answers short. She glanced at the treadmill's control panel, trying to deduce which button would bring the machine to a standstill. Forced to guess, the machine beeped as she pressed, but instead of slowing down it sped up. With her feet picking up pace, she stabbed at another icon making the machine tilt. Obliged to run up an incline, it was all Ronnie could do not to whimper.

"I'm impressed," Jack said.

Ronnie pursed her lips. At least someone was.

Usually excellent at multi-tasking, breathing, talking and hill running was proving increasingly difficult and Ronnie wasn't sure how long she could keep going.

"I suppose I should leave you to your warm-up," Jack said.

Warm? Things had gone way beyond that.

Ronnie smiled and nodded. "Okay," she said, all the while doing her utmost to appear in control.

At last, PC Jack Shenton went on his way and she immediately reached for the buttons, pressing each and every one of them over and over in an attempt to stop the treadmill, unfortunately to no avail. Stabbing at them, she suddenly lost what little rhythm she had left in her legs and her feet went from under her. Ronnie heard herself yelp as her face planted onto the conveyor belt. Yelping again, she instantly flew backwards as the belt flung her off and into the wall.

10

"Here, sit down," Jack said. Having taken Ronnie's arm, he gently steered her into the gym office, before easing her down onto a chair at the desk. He took the towel he'd slung over one of his shoulders and placed it over Ronnie's chest, like it was some sort of adult bib.

Ronnie thought it a kind gesture, even if it was pointless. Her clothes were already covered in blood thanks to the impact with which her face had hit the treadmill's running belt; her nose hadn't stopped bleeding since.

"Pinch it, like this," Jack said, lifting his hand and placing a finger and thumb on each of his nostrils to demonstrate. "And put your head down."

Ronnie did as she was told.

"You need to stay like that until the bleeding stops."

Thankfully, the excitement over her fall from grace had died down and under Michael's instruction, everyone else had gone back to their workouts. Ronnie's embarrassment lingered, however, and she wished Jack would leave her to it so she could sneak off home, never to put a foot in that place again. "You don't have to babysit me," she said, straightening up a little.

Jack placed a hand to the rear of her head and lightly manoeuvred it back down. "No, but I do need to make sure you're okay before you leave." The man clearly knew what she was thinking.

Forced to stare at her feet, even her new trainers were spattered red. As she took in the congealing crimson against the brilliant white, a lump formed in her throat and a tear fell onto her lap, quickly followed by another and another. Suddenly overwhelmed, she felt stupid for displaying her emotions like that, but she couldn't seem to help herself. Ronnie didn't know if it was the shock from the fall or Jack's need to look after her, but it was as if everything leading up to that point had finally caught up. Nick's abrupt departure; his affair with Gaye and their refusal to move; the fact that, apart from the odd quip, Ronnie had had to keep her true thoughts and feelings to herself out of respect for Willow and Bea; Nick's divorce request... How had her life gone so awry?

She felt a reassuring hand settle on the middle of her back, followed by a soft repetitive stroke. Although grateful, she wondered why Jack was being so nice to her. It wasn't that long ago he was siding with her ex and giving her a harassment warning. The last thing she wanted was sympathy and his action was enough to bring her self-pity under control. "Look at the state of me," she said mid snivel, trying to make light of the situation. "You must think me a right wuss."

Jack smiled. "Not at all. In fact, I admire your strength."

Ronnie raised an eyebrow. She twisted her head slightly to look at him, surprised to see that he appeared to mean it. However, as kind as his words were, sat there covered in blood and feeling more than a tad sorrowful, *strong* was the last characteristic she'd have bestowed upon herself.

"I mean it. I've been where you are and it wasn't pretty."

"Really?" Sitting there wrapped in a towel after majestically showing herself up on the running machine, Ronnie doubted Jack's story compared. "What happened?"

"What often happens when it comes to the life of a bobby. Husband always at work, wife feeling like the job comes first, you get the gist. Eventually Sally got fed up of hanging around and ended up meeting someone else." He fell quiet for a moment, as if reliving aspects of his past.

"Anyway," he finally continued, "it was just like me to blame myself. I mean, it was my job that caused it. And I suppose at the time, giving her everything she wanted felt like the right thing to do. So, instead of fighting back I let them go..."

"Them?" Ronnie asked.

"I have a son. Ben. He's seventeen." Jack's face lit up. "He's a great lad, you'd like him. From what he says, most ladies do." Jack came over all pensive. "The way things are now, I sometimes wonder if I was wrong. If I should've been more like you and stood my ground."

"Where are they now?"

"They moved to Australia. Five years ago."

Ronnie couldn't imagine a life without her daughter. Not having Willow nearby, not being able to give her a hug, or catch-up over a coffee, would be too much to bear. Her heart went out to Jack. "I'm sorry."

"Don't be. Ultimately, it would have been selfish to make them stay. Ben has a great life over there. Better than he'd have had here with me. And when I think about what some of the kids I come across get up to..."

Ronnie smiled. "I can imagine. You're still in contact though, aren't you?"

"We have the odd video call. You know, birthdays, Christmas, that sort of thing. Of course, I wish things were different, that we could talk more often. But with the opposite time zones, the job I'm in, and the fact that Ben is always off doing something... If it's not cricket, it's football. If it's not football, it's surfing..."

"You must miss him."

Jack nodded. "But that's life, I guess."

Despite his philosophical attitude, Ronnie could see the distance bothered him. "You've never flown over for a visit?"

"Not yet. But I will. One day."

"And what about your ex?"

"If you're asking if I miss *her*, then the answer's no. Would I like someone to come home to at night? Of course. Would I like someone to share the ups and downs of life with? Most definitely. But that woman isn't Sally. We've both moved on."

"I sometimes wonder why some people bother with marriage. Take Nick. Why devote twenty-five years of his life to something, to then bail the way he did?"

"Because people change. As for those of us they leave behind... simply because one relationship breaks down, it doesn't mean they all will."

Ronnie smiled. After everything Jack had been through, she'd have expected a bit more scepticism when it came to matters of the heart. "Willow, my daughter, thinks we're not built for monogamy. She doesn't believe in love at all. As far as she's concerned, one-on-one relationships are too claustrophobic."

"Ah, one of life's cynics. She'll change her mind when she meets someone special."

Ronnie laughed. "Which is exactly what her grandmother and I say, but Willow won't hear a word of it. I dread to think about the number of hearts she's broken."

"Takes after her mum, no doubt."

Ronnie blushed. "You have seen the state of me, haven't you?" she said, indicating to her bloodied appearance.

The sincerity in Jack's words surprised her. As did the earnest expression he wore as he looked at her. Staring back, she found herself wondering what was wrong with Jack's ex. He seemed so understanding, almost selfless. If she were married to a man like that, she'd be hanging on to him for dear life.

Pulling herself together, Ronnie couldn't believe what her brain thought it was playing at. She clearly had concussion, why else would such thoughts be entering her head? "Maybe they'll come back? Sally might realise her mistake?" Ronnie cringed. Not only did she not know where that question came from, five years down the line, even she realised how ridiculous it sounded.

"Will Nick?" Jack asked with a twinkle in his eye.

Ronnie felt affronted. "Even if he did, I wouldn't have him."

Jack laughed in response. "See. There it is again. That fighting spirit."

Ronnie smiled as she held his gaze, a little piece of her heart melting. Considering the events of their first meeting, she never thought she'd end up liking the man, let alone having such a meaningful conversation.

The office door suddenly opened and Michael breezed in with a glass of water. "Thought you might like this," he said, holding it out. He looked from Ronnie to Jack, clearly wondering if he'd interrupted something.

Ronnie blushed once more. As far as she was concerned, at least, he most definitely had.

"Sorry. I'll leave it here, shall I?" Michael said, and placing the water on the table, he left as quickly as he'd arrived.

Back to just Ronnie and Jack, the room fell silent. It seemed their heart-to-heart had come to an end and thanks to the continued quiet, Ronnie began to feel awkward. "So," she said, trying and failing to come up with something to say.

"So," Jack replied.

Without warning, he put a hand up to Ronnie's chin, his expression serious. Her tummy tickled at his touch, her mind racing as she wondered what he would do next. As he looked into her eyes, his face drawing near, her pulse also picked up pace. Maybe their heart-to-heart was gearing up a notch? She felt scared yet excited. Was this gorgeous man really about to kiss her? Taking heed of her body, she blooming well hoped so.

His gaze moved to her nostrils and he tilted her head back for a closer inspection.

Ronnie's heart sank. Of course he wasn't.

"It would seem the bleeding has stopped," Jack said with a smile. He let go of her face and leaned back in his seat. "Looks like you're free to go."

11

Ronnie cautiously drove her car onto Holme Lea Avenue. Bringing it to a standstill outside number six, it stalled before she'd even had time to switch off the engine. Thanks to it having played up throughout the whole of the journey home, Ronnie sighed. On top of everything else, vehicle problems were all she needed.

She looked at her reflection in the rear-view mirror, feeling silly for wearing sunglasses on such a dull cloudy day. Not that she'd had much choice. Because of the gym incident, it was a case of either hiding her face when out in public or give any children she came across nightmares for the foreseeable future. She looked like something from *The Walking Dead*.

Ronnie winced as she lifted the glasses to survey the damage, the sudden arm movement paining her ribcage that still hurt from the force at which her body had hit the wall. Lucky that she hadn't broken her nose, her eyes were bruised and swollen as if she'd gone ten rounds with a heavyweight boxer. She sighed at the state of the face looking back. "Blue and purple are so not your colours."

Securing her sunglasses back in place, Ronnie reached for

her handbag, carefully placing it over her shoulder as she eased herself out of her vehicle. Heading to the back of the car, she recalled the whole episode. Tripping over her own feet, landing face down on the running belt, shooting off the end... and the embarrassment when she came to.

Opening her eyes, numerous concerned faces looked down on her, including PC Jack Shenton's. She wanted to die from the humiliation alone. She thought about their conversation in the office, about how the two of them had opened up to each other. The conversation that Ronnie thought would end with a kiss. She shook her head. The shame of it all. If Ronnie never saw him again, it would be too soon.

Admiring her latest purchase, Ronnie supposed it wasn't all doom and gloom. Her pride might be as dented as her face, but the treadmill mishap had made her come up with another means of carrying out *Operation Poltergeist*. One that didn't involve life-threatening fitness regimes, or rely on upper body strength. She stroked the shiny aluminium rungs that stuck out of the boot. As stepladders went, these were bigger and better than Nick's rickety old pair, and wasn't he going to know it. Undoing the bungees used to clamp the boot lid down and secure them in place, Ronnie couldn't wait to put the ladders to use.

The young man at the DIY store had been very accommodating, even suggesting she could have gotten them cheaper online. But Ronnie had wanted to check their sturdiness before handing over any money, something the young man agreed made sense. He'd opened them out for her so she could give them a good shake down, and climb a couple of treads to make sure they didn't have the slightest of wobbles. Easier said than done with an aching torso, but in Ronnie's view well worth the pain. Seeing her discomfort, it was the young man who'd fortified them in the car for her, something that, thanks to her injuries, she'd never have managed on her own. Ronnie put a hand on her ribcage as she looked from the ladders to the house, wishing he were there to help in this instance.

"Here, let me," a male voice called out.

Ronnie looked over the road to spot Mr Wright heading her way. She smiled as she watched his approach. Her neighbours might be nosey, watching everyone's comings and goings at every opportunity, but they were also kind, one of the reasons she loved Holme Lea Avenue. Unlike in town, where anonymity was key, that little street had a sense of community. Without having to ask, there was always someone at hand in a time of need or conversely of celebration. Of course, under normal circumstances she'd have declined Mr Wright's offer. The man was, after all, an elderly gentleman. On that occasion, however, she'd have accepted assistance from the devil if he'd come to her aid.

"A pretty young thing like you shouldn't have to lift and carry."

Ronnie appreciated the man's generosity, even if his choice of words could have been better. The way her body ached, she could feel every one of her middle-aged years and with what was going on behind the sunglasses, *pretty* most certainly seemed a little too generous. "I suppose we could take one end each," Ronnie said, determined to do her bit.

Mr Wright leaned in and pulled the stepladder out of the boot in one swift movement. "No need," he said, smiling. "Now, where do you want them?"

Ronnie was impressed, his agility enough to ease her guilt at not helping. "In the hallway, please." She made her way to the front door and with Mr Wright directly behind, unlocked it to let them in. "Can I get you a cup of tea or coffee?" she asked, as he placed the ladders down, leaning them side on against the hall skirting board. "To say thank you."

Mr Wright rubbed his hands together. "That would be lovely."

Ronnie led the way into the kitchen, dumping her handbag down and heading straight for the kettle. "Please," she said, indicating her guest take a seat while she waited for it to boil. "So, how is Mrs Wright?"

He pulled a chair out from under the table and sat down. "She's fine. Out with her sister. It's Thursday, you see. The day they meet for lunch, then go to the cinema. Mrs Wright does like her routine."

It came as no surprise to hear his wife liked order. Whenever Ronnie spoke to Mrs Wright, the woman's response was always polite, yet to the point. And as was the case with Mr Wright in his perfectly ironed shirt and tie, she was always impeccably dressed, never having as much as a hair out of place. Even the way she carried herself appeared efficient. Ronnie smiled. Like her and Nick, the two of them had been childhood sweethearts, except in their case, their marriage was still going strong.

"Sounds lovely," Ronnie replied. She thought for a moment. "I've often wondered what it would be like to have siblings. Only child, you see." Her sunglasses suddenly felt heavy, so she took them off and gently rubbed the bridge of her nose.

"Jesus, Mary and Joseph!"

Ronnie took in her neighbour's horrified expression, realising she should have warned him.

"What happened to you?"

"Don't worry, it's not as bad as it looks," she said, trying to lessen the shock. "I had a bit of a fall, that's all."

"A fall? You look like someone's been at you with a baseball bat."

Ronnie would've laughed if it didn't hurt her ribs so much. She watched Mr Wright get up from his seat and move towards her.

"Come on, you sit down. I can make the tea."

As he put his hands on her shoulders and guided her to a chair, Ronnie could see why his marriage had held firm. Mrs Wright was one lucky lady. "Thank you," Ronnie said, doing as she was told.

"You've certainly had it tough recently," Mr Wright said, reaching for the tea caddy. "What with the nonsense next door. And now this." He turned and gestured to Ronnie's face.

Ronnie considered everything that had happened. Nick's adultery, his request for a divorce, her fall from grace at the gym... Wondering what other delights life had in store, she couldn't help but ask if things could get any worse. "That's one way of putting it," she replied.

"He's a foolish man that husband of yours. Leaving a woman like you for a woman like her." He handed Ronnie her cup, before taking the seat opposite.

"That's very kind of you to say, Mr Wright."

"Please, call me Harry."

"Okay." Ronnie took a sip of her tea. "That's very kind of you to say, *Harry*."

"Mum!" a voice interrupted.

"Ronnie!" another called out.

12

Willow and Bea charged into the room.

The two women stopped in the doorway, Willow's face crumpling at the sight of her battered and bruised mother. She raced over to Ronnie, her arms outstretched, ready for an all-encompassing embrace. "You look worse than I thought," she said.

Ronnie winced in response. Under the circumstances, she'd have preferred a much gentler squeeze.

At last, Willow pulled back, taking in Ronnie's wounds in all their purple and blue glory. "I don't think I've ever seen someone look so grotesque."

Ronnie attempted a laugh. "As if I didn't feel bad enough."

"I should go," Harry said, rising to his feet.

"But what about your tea?" Ronnie asked.

"Some other time." He smiled at everyone in the room as he bid his farewell. "Ladies."

Bea's stern gaze followed him as he made his way down the hall and out through the front door. "I wondered how long it would take."

"For what?" asked Ronnie.

"For the vultures to start circling."

Ronnie wondered what the woman was talking about.

"It was the same when Nick's dad passed away. Eric wasn't even cold when they started turning up, one by one." Bea rolled her eyes. "Like they were doing me a favour. What was it they'd say?" She shivered as if trying to dismiss the memory. "A woman like me has needs."

"Grandmother!"

"Their words, not mine."

Ronnie let out a chuckle. "And you're suggesting that's why Mr Wright was here? I don't think so. He's simply a kind old man who helped me carry in a set of ladders from the car."

"Don't say you haven't been warned," Bea said.

"The ladders we nearly tripped over?" Willow asked. "I thought Dad already had some."

"He has. But I needed a sturdier pair."

"Why?" her daughter asked. "It's not like you'll ever use them. You don't like heights."

Ronnie pictured her attempt at getting into the loft, recalling how proud she'd felt when she finally managed it. "Let's say, I'm dealing with my fear." She tried to think of an excuse for her new purchase. "Starting with a spot of decorating."

"You?" Willow asked, as if she'd never heard anything so ridiculous.

"Decorating?"

"Yes, me."

"In your state?" Bea said.

Willow scoffed. "Mum, how are you going to hang wallpaper while standing up on a ladder? You can't even stay upright on a running machine."

"Who says I'm wallpapering. I might simply paint." Ronnie froze, her expression all at once quizzical.

Bea giggled. "I know I shouldn't laugh, but you did go with a bang."

"You saw me?" Ronnie asked, wondering how. "You can't have. You weren't there."

"Us and about a million other people," Bea said.

"What million people? What are you talking about?"

"You mean you don't know?"

Ronnie watched Bea's smile vanish. Her mother-in-law and daughter shared a look, something that seemed to be happening far too regularly of late. "Well?" Ronnie said. "I'm waiting."

Finally, Willow relented. "We saw it on the Internet." She reached into her bag, pulled out her phone and clicked a few buttons, before handing it to Ronnie.

"Saw what on the Internet?" Ronnie's bewilderment continued. She looked at the screen, her eyes widening as she saw herself and her *gymtastic* demise. One minute she was upright and chatting to PC Jack Shenton, then bang! she was face down, before crashing into a heap. "Who would do this?" she asked.

As the recording repeated itself, only this time in slow motion, Ronnie felt the colour drain from her face. She took in her contorted expression, the way she bounced up and down on the rubber conveyor belt, before flying backwards and slamming against the wall and with such force, it was no wonder her ribcage felt sore. She looked up from the footage. "And this is out there, for the whole world to see?"

Willow nodded. "You've gone viral."

"Facebook, Twitter, YouTube..." Bea said. "You're on them all."

"But I can't be."

"In fact, the way the numbers are growing," Bea continued, "you might even end up on one of those TV mishap shows."

"You mean I'm a laughing stock?"

Willow sat down next to Ronnie, giving her mum's hand a reassuring rub. "I wouldn't put it that way, exactly."

"See it more as bringing a smile to people's faces," Bea said, "brightening their day."

Ronnie threw her a look.

"I'm just saying. Silver linings and all that."

As far as Ronnie was concerned, her mother-in-law could be as optimistic as she wanted. Ronnie still wouldn't be able to ever show herself in public again. She thought back to that morning, trying to recall everyone present. Michael, Jack Shenton, the bodybuilders, she couldn't imagine any of them uploading her onto the Internet. She let out a long drawn-out sigh, her heart sinking as she realised who the culprits were.

"Those bloody kids," she said, recollecting the two selfie-taking teenagers. She looked down at the screen again. "Just when I thought life couldn't get any worse."

13

Pausing in her work, Ronnie gently pinched the bridge of her nose. The bruising around her eyes might be less prominent, but they were tired and strained from the delicate hand stitching she'd been doing. "Almost there," she said, looking down at the mother-of-the-bride clutch. She ran her fingers over its purple velvet, before wrapping them in Sellotape and patting the fabric to get rid of any stray pieces of fluff. She smiled. Once she'd filled it with tissue paper to give it its body, the bag was complete and ready to send off to the customer. Stunning, even if she did say so herself.

Ronnie glanced around her studio, taking in her trusty Bernina sewing machine, her rows of colourful textiles and linings, shelves stocked high with fabric dyes, button and zip boxes, and ornate handbag frames and clasps – everything a bag designer could possibly need. Surrounded by such beautiful things, that room had always been Ronnie's happy place, her sanctuary.

Locking herself away after the gym incident had seemed like a good thing to do. Her ribs could heal and her bruises fade, along with the laughter over the video. *She* might forever cringe at the memory, but given time, someone else would become the latest Internet sensation and goodness knew she'd been putting off work for long enough. Escaping the world felt like an opportunity to get on with something productive. Instead of wallowing in self-pity, she could complete her commission piece and hopefully come up with a few ideas for the brand new collection.

Being in her studio at the bottom of the garden also gave her the opportunity to monitor next door's comings and goings in preparation of *Operation Poltergeist*, something Ronnie couldn't wait to get on with. She looked at the notepad and pen by her side, before turning her attention to Gaye's car poking out of number eight's rear garage.

Productivity on two fronts; it was a win-win situation.

Reading her notes, Nick's routine seemed pretty much the same as it had always been; leaving the house at eight in the morning and not returning until after six evening time. Gaye's schedule, however, was less predictable. She came and went at various intervals, which did nothing to help in Ronnie's planning. Ronnie scoffed. Neither did it do much for her self-esteem. Unlike her neighbour, a husband-thieving so-and-so, who had places to go and people to see, Gaye's comings and goings highlighted the fact that Ronnie herself had nothing and no-one. Apart from Willow and Bea, she conceded. But, she supposed, being family, in the bigger scheme of things they probably didn't count.

She checked her watch and realising that Nick would be home from work soon, thought back to the life he once shared with her. She readily pictured him dumping his bag in the hall, moaning about the stresses of his day before he'd even reached the kitchen. Not that Ronnie had minded listening to his complaints. After hours in her workshop, they provided her with a connection to the outside world, albeit vicarious. Since his departure, however, she didn't even have that. It was just her and the telly for company.

Ronnie considered her lack of contact with the outside world, a place she supposed she'd never fully engaged in. She'd had acquaintances over the years, such as the other mums dropping their kids off at the school gates when Willow was young. Then there were her neighbours, but again, she hadn't formed particularly close relationships with any of them. She might say hello and stop to chat for a minute or two, but no-one on Holme Lea Avenue had become what Ronnie could call a firm friend.

Looking back, it was as if Ronnie and Nick had lived in their own little bubble, even more so since their daughter had flown the nest. She wondered if that was why Nick had strayed. Was life with her too boring? Were they too insular? Not that that excused his behaviour. Ronnie had craved a bit of excitement herself at times. She sneered. Just not enough to commit adultery.

Having insisted that Willow and Bea give her some space to recover, the only person Ronnie had conversed with in what felt like weeks was the supermarket delivery guy and even then, only because her Hobnobs had been substituted for Digestives. She frowned as she contemplated her situation. "You could be dead and no-one would know it." She thought about how easy it would be to fall into a completely solitary life. Everything a person needed to survive could be ordered over the Internet and dropped at the door, it was no wonder people found themselves cut off.

Ronnie shrugged herself out of it. Having never been one for pity parties, she saw no reason to hold one now. Besides, didn't she like her own company? Didn't her job as a handbag designer call for a quiet existence? And since the gym incident, she had placed herself in solitary confinement, so it shouldn't really have come as a surprise to find herself feeling starved of human contact. If anything, her miserable state of mind was a good omen; a sign that she was ready to rejoin the outside world. Even if that world did only consist of her daughter and mother-in-law.

Turning her attention back to the handbag, Ronnie rubbed her eyes again. Sewing could be difficult at the best of times, let alone when the daylight faded. She opted to call it a day and getting up from her seat, unravelled the Sellotape from her hand before placing the mother-of-the-bride clutch on her worktable – a huge wooden construction that Nick had purpose made when she decided to take her designing dreams seriously. Running her hand along its surface, she couldn't help but admire the table's well-worn patina. It had served her well and would, no doubt, last for years to come. She thought it a shame how a piece of furniture could turn out to be more reliable than the man who built it.

A squeal from next door interrupted Ronnie's thoughts and, checking her watch, she frowned. Obviously lover boy was home, but going off her own experience, Ronnie couldn't think why the excitement; especially when during the latter years of Ronnie's marriage, Nick always came in from work rather glum. With her curiosity getting the better of her, she tiptoed over to her workshop door and, glad to see their kitchen window open, prepared to eavesdrop.

As she listened to the two of them, Ronnie watched on as Gaye jumped up and down and threw her arms around Nick.

"Oh, darling," her neighbour said. "What have I done to deserve this?"

Ronnie sneered. She could only imagine.

"I wanted to treat you," Nick replied.

"Treat her!" Ronnie found the smile on her ex's face nauseating. She waited for him to hand over a bouquet of garage flowers. Probably carnations, they were always carnations; an afterthought when he stopped off to put petrol in the car. Ronnie's eyes narrowed when she saw nothing of the sort, instead finding herself watching Gaye rip open an A4 envelope.

"A mini break." Gaye threw herself at Nick again. "When do we go?"

Ronnie stood there lost for words.

"This weekend."

She couldn't believe what she was hearing.

"But it doesn't say where?"

Ronnie rolled her eyes in disdain.

"That's because it's a surprise."

Ronnie shook her head, furious as Gaye hugged Nick again. "You've got to be kidding me," Ronnie said. She recalled the last time she'd tried to embrace her husband like that, on their wedding anniversary to beat all wedding anniversaries. She could still feel her husband's cold response, followed by the heartbreaking realisation that she couldn't have gotten it so wrong, she wasn't heading for anywhere except the divorce court. "How could you?" she asked, and as she continued to take in the scene before her, she yet again felt like she'd been kicked in the stomach.

"After everything we've been through," Nick carried on.

Ronnie narrowed her eyes. What were they talking about? After everything *they'd* been through? Ronnie felt her blood pressure begin to rise. She was the one who'd been tossed aside like a piece of garbage, not them. She was the one forced into watching her husband begin a new life with another woman, simply because that same said woman was too selfish to move.

"I thought some time away would do us good. Give us a chance to relax, away from you know who."

Ronnie almost spluttered, knowing full well that Nick was talking about her. How dare he mock her like that.

"It hasn't exactly been fun, has it?" Gaye replied.

Fun! Fun! What did they expect? Was Ronnie supposed to simply let them get on with it? Should she have faded into the background? As if life had been all rainbows and sunbeams for her of late.

"Not in her dictionary, I'm afraid," Nick said, much to Gaye's amusement.

Ronnie felt sick. Is that what the two of them did? Laugh at her?

She opened her mouth to say something, to tell them what she thought about their much-needed few days away from it all, but the words stuck in her throat. Suddenly unable to catch her breath, Ronnie tried and failed to fill her lungs. She forced herself to take short sharp gasps, at the same time grabbing the door frame to steady herself. She began to feel dizzy, her body becoming increasingly overwhelmed by a need to pass out. But Ronnie refused to give in, and she struggled back to her seat and plonked herself down.

It took a few moments of concentration for Ronnie to finally regulate her breathing. *In, out. In, out*, she insisted, over and again, until she regained control. Why were Nick and Gaye doing this to her?

Sitting there, she dropped her head in her hands, wondering how they could be so cruel. It wasn't enough that they'd ruined her life, they seemed to have painted themselves as the victims. And to laugh at her like that. In all the time she'd been married to Nick, she'd never witnessed that side of him. It was as if, since getting together with Gaye, he'd had a personality transplant as well as a new wardrobe. Unless he had always been like that and Ronnie hadn't paid attention?

She turned her head to glance at their adjoining houses, knowing she wasn't asking for much. All she ever wanted was for them to do the decent thing and move, something Ronnie felt sure anyone else in their position would have done from the off. She scoffed, as she looked their way. *Decent.* They didn't know the meaning of the word.

Straightening herself up again, Ronnie pushed her hair from her face, at the same time clocking her notebook and pen. A steeliness came over her as she realised Nick and Gaye had provided her with the perfect opportunity for *Operation Poltergeist* to begin in earnest. "You want fun," she asked of Nick and Gaye, deadly serious. "Then you can have it."

Determined never to let either of them get the better of her again, Ronnie rose to her feet and smoothed down her clothes. "Let the games commence."

14

Ronnie stood in her lounge bay window, her determination tinged with excitement as she observed Nick and Gaye loading up their car. "Come on, come on," Ronnie said, as they manhandled bag after bag. She shook her head. With that number of suitcases to squeeze in, anyone would think they were going away for a month, not on some two-night break.

The masses of luggage might be frustrating, but it didn't come as any real surprise. Having kept an eye on next door's movements all week, Ronnie knew that Gaye had spent many an afternoon hitting the shops. With no clue as to where she would be spending her weekend, the woman clearly wanted to cover a range of eventualities. Day after day, off Ronnie's neighbour went, a big smile on her face and handbag in hand; only to return a few hours later, laden with designer carriers. Ronnie smiled. Gaye's shopping sprees had certainly played into her hands. Waiting until the coast was clear, they gave Ronnie the chance to get the next stage of *Operation Poltergeist* underway – making a hole in the adjoining loft wall.

She pictured herself creating her entry point, how she'd

painstakingly used Nick's screwdrivers and chisels to carve out a hole, brick by brick, big enough to comfortably crawl through. Going from bottom to top, she'd individually numbered them with chalk, ensuring she knew where each one sat when it came to blocking the void back up. And thanks to her grit, Ronnie had become quite adept when using her newly acquired stepladder.

She chuckled as she looked back on the previous few days. It was surprising what a scorned woman could achieve if pushed hard enough. After much practice, she seemed to have tackled her fear of heights. She'd gotten to the point where she could whip the ladders open, nimbly hotfoot up the rungs and into the loft, then reach down to snap them shut. All before hoisting them up through the hatch, ready to reverse the procedure once she was through to the other side. Not that she'd gotten that far. She'd been saving her first trip into number eight until she could wander through the house at leisure.

Half nervous, half keen to get on with it, Ronnie giggled. That day was the day.

She watched Nick and Gaye put the last of their bags into the car, before getting in themselves. "At last," Ronnie said as the engine started up and the vehicle pulled away. "Have fun," she called after them. "Because I know I will." She kept her eyes on the car until it disappeared from view, telling herself that the next time that scene played out it would involve boxes instead of suitcases, a couple of removal men, and a great big truck. Waiting a few minutes until she felt sure they weren't coming back, she clapped her hands. "Let's do this," she said, spinning and leaving the room.

Stopping at the front door, Ronnie tried its handle to make sure it was locked; the last thing she wanted was anyone letting themselves in and discovering what she was up to. Satisfied everything was well, she headed upstairs and made her way into her bedroom, smiling at the outfit she'd laid out in readiness.

She laughed. Gaye wasn't the only one to do a spot of shopping this week, except unlike her neighbour, Ronnie hadn't had to leave the house. The only thing she'd had do to was delete her Internet browsing history.

Determined not to leave a single identifying clue inside number eight, Ronnie began by securing her hair in the net she'd purchased, before stepping into her newly acquired paper forensic suit. Covering her feet with a pair of new socks, she focused on the final item of her outfit – a pair of rubber gloves. She felt quite the expert, putting them to her lips, filling them with air and then snapping them on.

Ronnie turned to the full-length mirror in the corner of the room. Taking in the whole ensemble, Ronnie could see she looked a treat. "Very fetching," she said and, twisting her body round from left to right and back again, she recalled the number of times Nick had ridiculed her love of crime dramas. "Who's laughing now, eh?"

She smiled at the carrier bag containing a couple of extra goodies, picking it up as she made her way out to the landing and up into the loft, hauling up the ladders once she was safe inside. Her heart raced in anticipation as she began dismantling the wall. She let out a nervous laugh, a part of her not quite able to believe she was doing this.

With the relevant bricks set to one side, Ronnie turned her attention to the stepladder. Lifting the top plate, she closed them up, pausing to take a deep breath before continuing. She slowly exhaled and with thoughts of her harassment warning hovering at the back of her mind, she asked herself if she really wanted to go through with *Operation Poltergeist*. She scoffed, shaking any doubts away. Of course she did. Nick and Gaye deserved everything they had coming to them.

She pushed the ladders through the hole before picking up the carrier bag, dropping to her knees and shimmying into next door. Rising to her feet, she glanced around. Ronnie couldn't see anything of interest, just a few boxes, typical of any storage area. It was all a bit normal and somewhat disappointing. She grimaced. Whatever it was she'd expected, *ordinary* wasn't it.

Her frown turned into a smile as she spotted Gaye's loft hatch, and she was unsurprised to find it identical to her own. The two houses did, after all, mirror each other. Ronnie manoeuvred the board to one side in preparation for her descent. "Ready?" she asked, hesitant. She grabbed her ladders before she could change her mind and fed them down the hole, using the top plate to flip them open. She took a deep breath and ignoring her galloping pulse, climbed down onto Gaye's landing. "There's no going back now."

Taking in her surroundings, Ronnie instantly found her bearings. She knew from her own property which door led to the box room, the bathroom, the guest room and the master, and she knew full well which one she wanted to open first. She stepped forward and reached for the chosen door handle, but paused. She couldn't bring herself to turn it. Her curiosity replaced with anxiety; that was where Nick and Gaye slept – together. And, no doubt, where they had consummated their affair. Insisting she was there to carry out *Operation Poltergeist*, nothing more, nothing less, she let her hand drop. "Maybe later."

Getting back to the task at hand, Ronnie headed for the bathroom instead. *Very nice*, she thought as she let herself in. From the glossy tiles, to the towels, to the surfaces and cupboards, the whole space wasn't only spotless, everything was brilliant white. Apart from the ornate guilt framed mirror, Ronnie noted, and the painted gold feet of the bath. Ronnie had always wanted an authentic roll-top, but Nick favoured bathing in something more modern. Apparently, water didn't stay as hot for as long in cast iron, and according to him plastic was far more practical. Quite an opinion, she considered, for a man who preferred showers. She ran her gloved hand along a shelf, home to various potions and lotions, bath bombs and salts, all of them expensive looking. Turning up prepared, Ronnie had guessed the woman enjoyed pampering herself. She chuckled at the thought of what she was about to do. "Not for much longer."

She reached into her carrier bag and pulled out a bottle of anti-freeze. Unscrewing its lid, she delved into the bag again to retrieve a single cotton bud. She dipped it into the liquid, smiling as she gently shook off any excess fluid and, holding it like a pen, turned her attention to the bathroom mirror. "I'm Watching You," she said, as she spelled the words out onto the glass. Job done, Ronnie stepped back to admire her invisible handiwork. She didn't have a clue if her prank would triumph, but having seen it succeed enough times in films and on TV, thought it worth giving a go. "Onwards and upwards," she said, and securing the bottle's lid back in place, stuffed both the anti-freeze and the cotton bud away again.

Exiting the room, she left the carrier bag on the ladder and made her way downstairs, pausing at the various pictures that lined the fresh white walls as she went. Pictures of Gaye and whom Ronnie assumed to be family and friends. She observed the numerous happy faces staring back, sneering as she tilted each and every image, ensuring each hung at the same strange angle. Ronnie laughed. Who'd have thought that trespassing could be such fun.

Ronnie's next stop was the kitchen, another room so white and shiny that she had to wonder what her neighbour had against colour. And the cleanliness, there wasn't a speck of dust or a crumb of food to be seen, thank goodness for her rubber gloves. She checked out the clear-glass dining table, amazed to find not a single smudge. Scanning the room, Ronnie sniffed. She much preferred her own home and its lived-in look.

Taking in the kitchen units, she approached the stack of five drawers. Opening the first, she couldn't believe how ordered its contents were. Knives, forks and spoons sat perfect in their respective sections; even the larger utensils that lay next to the cutlery tray were precision lined. Ignoring the second drawer, Ronnie opened the third. "Blimey," she said, staring down at rows of impeccably rolled tea towels. She knew there was a fad for decluttering and cleaning sweeping the nation, but Gaye appeared to be taking organisation to a whole new level. With drawers one and three still open, Ronnie couldn't bring herself to look inside drawer five. Instead, she simply pulled at its handle until its front sat level with the others.

Turning her attention to the cupboards, there was no getting away from the fact that they were equally as ordered. Again, opening every alternate door, she couldn't avoid the flawlessly lined jars, tins and containers. Cup handles pointed in the same direction, plates and bowls were stacked according to shape and size. Such tidiness was enough to make her twitch. She stood back to survey the room as a whole and, telling herself that that would do for now, she had a skip in her step as she headed off to the lounge.

Ronnie stopped as she reached the living room door, popping her head in first as she slowly opened it. Her gaze went straight to the window and only when she felt confident that no-one could see in from the street did she finally slip inside. She rolled her eyes at the pristine décor, again various shades of colourless. In her view, for someone so loud and in your face, Gaye had no personality on the home front. Ronnie took in the pale cream stain-free sofa, with its neatly positioned scatter cushions. How on earth did the woman keep the place so clean? Not that it mattered. Ronnie wasn't there to critique her neighbour's interior design choices. Then again... thinking ahead,

Ronnie began to feel excited. House buyers loved a blank canvas and you couldn't get blanker than white.

Spurred on, she commenced her second round of picture tilting, sniggering as she imagined the further mischief she planned on carrying out. Not that day though. In order to be successful, *Operation Poltergeist* couldn't be rushed, it had to unfold in stages. She paused as she reached the mantelpiece, home to a photo that caught Ronnie's eye. A picture of Nick and Gaye. She felt a stab of annoyance as she leaned in for a closer look. Taken in what looked like some fancy restaurant, their smiles looked smug and self-satisfied. Ronnie let out a scornful laugh, knowing she was going to wipe those grins clean off.

Ronnie's ears pricked at the sound of a car pulling up outside, her heart skipping a beat as she wondered who it could be. Her eyes went from the photo to the street. Surely they hadn't forgotten something? She hurried over to the window and peeped out from behind the curtain. "Willow? Bea?" she said. "What are you two doing here?"

While her mother-in-law appeared to root for something in her handbag, Ronnie's daughter glanced her way, forcing Ronnie to jump back, praying to God she hadn't been seen. "Bugger!" she said, and trying to keep her wits together, she raced out of the room, quickly closing the door behind her.

As she charged up the stairs, she tripped and stubbed her toe mid-clamber. "Ouch!" she said, hobbling forward. Checking all the doors on the landing, she was relieved to find them already shut and grabbing her carrier bag, scrambled up the stepladder.

Once in Gaye's loft, Ronnie hauled them up behind her and hastily replaced the hatch. Without thinking, she threw both the ladders and herself through the hole that led back into number six, her panic rising with every passing second.

The doorbell rang.

Attempting to put the bricks back where they belonged, Ronnie's hands shook, making the job harder than it should have been. "Thank goodness," she said, the task finally complete.

The doorbell rang once more.

Ronnie momentarily froze before quickly pulling herself together. Using the ladders to get down onto her own landing, she shut up her own loft before hiding the steps in her bedroom. Ronnie ripped off her paper suit, hairnet and, hopping about, swapped her new socks for a pair of slippers.

"Mum! Are you in there?" Willow shouted through the letterbox.

Ronnie shoved everything under the bed before taking a second to calm herself. Wiping her brow, she took a deep breath. "Coming!" she called back and, putting a smile on her face, headed downstairs to greet her guests.

15

Ronnie smoothed down her clothes before opening the door to Willow and Bea. "This is a surprise," she said, fixing a smile on the two women. Still a little out of breath thanks to the obstacle course she'd moments ago run, she hoped her voice didn't sound as shaky as it felt.

"You took your time," Willow said. "And since when did you take to locking yourself in?"

"I was about to run a bath. You know, enjoy a bit of pampering."

Willow raised an eyebrow. "A bath?"

Her questions did nothing to calm Ronnie's heart rate.

"In the middle of the day?" Willow continued.

Not only was Ronnie telling a lie, she couldn't believe how easily it came. She could, however, understand her daughter's surprise. Ronnie had always thought long soaks great in theory, but in practice, lying in cold soapy water held little appeal, a fact she'd often made clear when Willow still lived at home. She thought about the number of hours her daughter had spent marinating in bubble bath. "And is there something wrong with that?"

"Not at all," her daughter replied. "You know me. I'm all for a bit of decadence."

Ronnie pictured the numerous lotions and potions she'd seen in Gaye's bathroom and suddenly felt lacking. When it came to *me time*, Ronnie much preferred a walk in the fresh air or to lose herself in a good book or TV show. She'd never think to spoil herself with products like every other woman she knew. And she hated to think that Willow had more in common with Gaye than her on that score.

"Me too," Bea said. "We each deserve a bit of self-love."

Ronnie stood aside to let her daughter and mother-in-law through, then followed them down the hall to the kitchen. "So, what can I do for you?" she asked while her guests sat down at the table.

"Firstly, we've come to make sure you're all right," Bea replied. "You were in a bit of a state the last time we were here."

"And as we hadn't heard from you..." Willow said.

Ronnie immediately felt guilty. She'd had every intention of asking the two of them round for dinner, but after overhearing about Nick and Gaye's weekend away Ronnie had gotten so engrossed in preparing for *Operation Poltergeist*, everything else went clean from her mind. Not that she could admit that – her daughter and mother-in-law would be horrified if they knew what she'd been up to. "I was going to call you both," she said, lying to them for a second time. "Later today, in fact."

Willow and Bea exchanged a look, causing Ronnie to narrow her eyes, suspicious. "And the second reason for being here?"

Bea grinned, reaching into her handbag.

Ronnie's shoulders slumped. The last time she'd been in this position, they'd given her an envelope.

"Step two," her mother-in-law said, sitting proud as she held out another one.

Recalling the gym incident, Ronnie stared at the offering. How could they do this to her?

"Don't worry, Mum," Willow said. "There'll be no need to hibernate after this one. Quite the opposite, if anything."

The two women smiled as they looked at each other. Despite Ronnie's concerns, they were obviously pleased with themselves, making it nigh on impossible for her to refuse. Holding her hand out, she reluctantly accepted, dreading to think what was inside.

"Go on then," Bea said, gesturing to the envelope. "Open it."

Ronnie did as she was told and took out what appeared to be a gift card. Staring at it, she couldn't believe what she was reading; that six-step plan of theirs had clearly been designed for someone else. She attempted a smile. After all, what else could she do but feign delight after the lie she'd just told? "Oh, wow. Thank you."

"Perfect timing, wouldn't you say?" Willow asked. "Considering you're in the mood to spoil yourself."

"That's one way of putting it," Ronnie replied.

"Great minds think alike, eh?" Bea said.

16

F orced to cadge a lift because of her vehicle issues, by the time Willow and Bea had dropped her off, Ronnie had come around to their way of thinking. After all, they'd put up a good argument. Like they said, having been battered and bruised both emotionally and physically, it was time she showed herself some love. She deserved it. Besides, wasn't it customary for women to change their image when embarking on a new chapter in life? Ronnie might have been unawares, but according to them, it was. And what better way to start her transformation than with a new hairdo.

Approaching the salon, Ronnie couldn't remember the last time she'd visited the hairdressers. Tending to keep her tresses scrunched into a pile on the top of her head, she hadn't paid her hair any attention for years. If ever it needed a trim, she simply lobbed some off with the kitchen scissors and then tied it up again, and catching her reflection in the window, there was no denying it needed professional help.

The receptionist was busy dealing with a paying customer when Ronnie entered, both of whom wore perfect make-up and beautiful smiles. In fact, glancing around, it appeared they weren't the only striking people in the room, and standing there, Ronnie began to feel a tad self-conscious. She'd never frequented an establishment so modern and stylish, and compared to her, everyone in the room looked young and edgy.

A sweet-smelling mix of hairspray, sculpting waxes and shine serums permeated the air. The place was a hive of activity and clutching the gift card from her daughter and mother-in-law, Ronnie had to wonder how they'd managed to get her an appointment. Glamorous stylists chatted to their clients as they worked their magic, forced to raise their voices over the white noise of their hair dryers. Juniors ferried drinks to customers and swept the floors around the various work sections that lined the walls. And at the back of the salon, patrons rested their heads against backwashes, enjoying a shampoo or a conditioning head massage. All to the beat of the latest chart-topping hits. Ronnie found the atmosphere both daunting and thrilling at the same time.

"Can I help you?" the receptionist finally asked.

Ronnie stepped forward. "I'm here for my appointment."

The receptionist checked her computer. "Ms Ronnie Jacobs?"

Having been referred to as *Mrs* for the last twenty-five years, Ronnie was momentarily taken aback. Her left thumb automatically searched for her wedding ring, something she knew she should take off, but being honest, she didn't know who she was without it. She felt herself redden, more out of awkwardness than anything else. Her new title felt strange, but she supposed that was the identity she'd been left with. "Yes. *Ms* Jacobs."

A young girl appeared as if from nowhere to swap Ronnie's coat for a gown. "If you could come this way," she said, gesturing to the sink area.

Ronnie followed her over and sat down in the chair indicated, before leaning back as instructed. Once the young girl had gotten the water to the correct temperature, she began washing Ronnie's hair – two rounds of expert scrubbing with shampoo, followed by one head massage with conditioner. Ronnie almost fell asleep when it came to the latter, she found it so soothing. Clearly she'd underestimated this pampering malarkey.

After the final rinse, the young girl wrapped a towel around Ronnie's head and led her over to a seat at one of the sections.

A stylist approached from behind. "Ronnie?"

She put on her best smile.

"I'm Pete."

The man was gorgeous.

"And I'll be doing your hair today." He began by combing it through. "I believe you're here for a restyle."

Ronnie nodded.

"And did you have anything specific in mind?"

Ronnie shook her head. "No, sorry. I didn't even know I had an appointment until an hour ago." He lifted swathes of her hair, immediately letting it fall back down, only to repeat the action over and again. Ronnie shifted in her seat, suddenly feeling a tad warm. She'd never had such a handsome young man's sole attention before.

"I hope it's not too much of a lost cause," she said.

"Let's say you've come to the right place."

Ronnie blushed as she looked into Pete's twinkly blue eyes. He had the cheekiest of smiles and the most perfect teeth.

"I think we should start by trimming the length a little, maybe add in some layers, and if you're really in the mood, a few highlights. I'd love to get rid of this bulk at the front and put in a fringe, nothing blunt, of course, something soft to frame your face." He paused, resting his hands on her shoulders. "What do you think? Shall we do it?"

The changes Pete suggested seemed radical, but glancing

around, thankfully nowhere near as extreme as some of the other styles about the place. She smiled as she returned her gaze to Pete, daring herself to go for it. "You're the expert. Why not?"

"Great. I'll go and mix some colour and then we'll get started."

Pete was back before Ronnie knew it, segmenting her hair, brushing in the dye, and wrapping each division in pre-prepared foils. He was as amiable as he was good-looking, conversing while he worked, asking about Ronnie, as well as sharing snippets about himself. Ronnie enjoyed their small talk. Nattering about the weather, sharing tastes in music, and discussing favourite TV shows made her feel lighter somehow, normal for a change. It enabled her to forget her woes.

Once her highlights had developed, Pete sent Ronnie off for another shampoo, and upon her return, was ready and waiting to begin the next stage in her transformation – the cut. "Now the real work begins," he said. Smothering her hair in this product and that product, he secured it into sections, before his hands and comb danced to the sound of the snip-snipping of his scissors. He made tackling her wild tresses look effortless.

The more he worked, however, the more Ronnie began to feel nervous, her eyes widening as lengths of hair fell on her lap. Pete had clearly been a bit loose in his definition of the word *trim.*

"Don't worry," he said, obviously clocking her fears. "It's going to look great."

Ronnie blushed again. She hadn't meant for him to see her reaction, but what did the man think he was doing?

Pete worked fast and before Ronnie knew it, he had a dryer in one hand, a brush in the other, and a look of concentration reminiscent of Willow's all those years ago during a chess match. Pete clearly took his job seriously, but as he styled her hair, root to tip, and in every direction, rather than feel reassured by his work ethic, Ronnie found herself wanting to cry. She swallowed hard, holding back the tears as he created a volume in her locks that defied gravity. She looked ridiculous.

Finally, he switched off the dryer, finishing Ronnie's transformation with yet another product. He smiled, evidently pleased with his creation. "So," he said, "what do you think?"

Ronnie knew she should say something, ask him what the hell he'd done. But staring at her reflection, words failed her.

"It's probably going to take a bit of getting used to," he added.

That was one way of putting it. Ronnie no longer recognised herself.

Her smile bordered on manic as she finally found her voice, muttering phrases like *It's certainly different, What a transformation*, and *I don't know what to say...* All of which Pete took as complimentary. The man might be good looking but he was clearly an idiot.

Holding her head up high as she got up from her seat, Ronnie could sense everyone's eyes on her as she crossed the salon floor, but she didn't return anyone's gaze. "Thank you," she simply said to the young girl already waiting with her coat.

Desperate to get out of there, Ronnie spotted Willow and Bea parked up on the other side of the street, waiting to drive her home. However, as she hastily made her exit, she failed to watch where she was going as she stepped out onto the footpath. "Ouch!" she said, as she walked smack bang into a passer-by. Her handbag flew from her hands, its contents spilling out as it hit the floor. "Bugger!" she said, immediately crouching down in a desperate bid to retrieve her belongings. Of course that wouldn't have happened if she'd been using one of her own bags, giving her yet another reason to be upset. It was just like her to treat everyone else and never create something for herself.

"Sorry," a male voice said, its owner joining her at floor level to help.

Ronnie paused for a second, before lifting her gaze. "PC Shenton," she said. As if the day couldn't get any worse. "Fancy seeing you here."

"Ronnie?" he asked, as if not quite sure.

As he continued to look at her, Ronnie flushed red, momentarily mesmerised by his eyes. They were the palest shade of blue and he had the kind of long dark lashes most women would die for. Realising she was staring, Ronnie suddenly remembered her dodgy haircut and, diverting her attention, swept everything back into her bag at double speed. "Sorry, I have to go," she said and straightening back up, hurried across the road.

"Ronnie!" he called out, but she pretended not to hear as she threw herself into the back of Willow's vehicle.

She waited for her daughter to start the engine and drive away, but as they turned to look at her, both Willow and Bea froze.

"Please, take me home," Ronnie said, staring directly out of the front window.

"What have they done to you?" Willow asked.

"Jesus, take the reins." Bea stifled a giggle. "It's Rod bloody Stewart."

17

Having retreated to her studio for the foreseeable future, Ronnie stared down at the sketchpad resting on her knee. She chewed on her pencil, assessing the potential handbag design she'd come up with. Hating it, she sighed, and unable to think about anything but the state of her head, added a face and spikes of unruly hair to the drawing. "It's like looking in a mirror," she said, scribbling over the whole image. She scoffed, supposing that thanks to Pete, she at least had plenty of time to come up with a collection she'd be happy with; about six months, the rate her mop grew.

Ronnie hadn't been able to concentrate at all since that man had gotten his hands on it. Goodness knew what he'd done, because in the forty-eight hours since, she'd tried styling and restyling and still ended up looking like an ageing rock star. She wondered if there was a call for Rod Stewart lookalikes of late. After all, if her creativity didn't show itself, she'd have to earn money somehow. Ronnie let out a mocking laugh as she pictured herself prancing around on some stage or other. As long as they didn't need her to sing, considering she was tone deaf.

Deciding to give up for the day, she slung her pad and pencil to one side and, letting herself out into the garden, locked up behind her. Making her way towards the house, she stopped at the sound of number eight's back door opening.

"I'm telling you," Gaye said, charging out into the open air. "It's a ghost!"

Ronnie put a hand up to her mouth, surprised by her neighbour's voice. *Operation Poltergeist*. How could she have forgotten? She reached up to touch her hair and for the first time since getting it done, Ronnie smiled, wondering if she should be grateful for the debacle at the hair salon. Having thought about nothing but next door for months, thanks to Pete, her ex and his new woman had been the last thing on her mind.

She ducked down, hoping no-one would spot her as she listened in.

"Come on, Gaye," Nick replied.

He sounded dismissive, but Ronnie had always known that *he'd* need hard evidence before falling for her stunt. Nick had always been a sceptic when it came to talk of the spirit world; one of the reasons that made *Operation Poltergeist* such fun. Ronnie, however, recognised a believer when she saw one and, from the beginning, would have put money on Gaye being like her, a fan of all the TV ghost hunting shows; shows that Nick readily dismissed as hocus-pocus trickery.

"You can't possibly think that," he continued.

Determined to enjoy every second of this, Ronnie tried her best not to laugh.

"What else can it be?" Gaye asked.

"I don't know," Nick replied, clearly getting frustrated. "An earthquake, maybe?"

"An earthquake?" Gaye was having none of it. "Now who's being ridiculous?" The woman's voice crumpled. "Oh, Nick, you saw those pictures. They're hanging at the exact same angle. And the kitchen drawers..."

Ronnie couldn't deny Gaye's nervousness, but as far as Ronnie was concerned, the woman had brought everything on herself. All Gaye had to do was move, which according to Nick's prior text message, she refused to do.

"Sweetheart, I'm sure there's a reasonable explanation."

"Well, I can't think of one."

Ronnie rolled her eyes; she didn't have to see the pout, she could hear it.

"Why don't you go and run yourself a nice hot bath," Nick carried on. "And I'll do a bit of research."

Ronnie imagined Nick putting his arms around Gaye in an attempt at reassurance. Ronnie stuck a finger in her mouth, pretending to make herself sick.

"I'll bet you anything there'll be reports about local tremors all over the Internet."

"You think?"

"Yes, I do."

I don't, Ronnie thought.

Ronnie continued to listen as footsteps headed back into number eight. She congratulated herself on her cunning and, not yet a hundred per cent sure a *For Sale* would go up, looked forward to the next stage in *Operation Poltergeist.* Clapping her hands in excitement, she headed indoors herself, eager to start preparing.

Once inside, Ronnie's tummy began to rumble and realising she hadn't eaten that day, she headed for the fridge. Pulling out a block of cheese, some fresh tomatoes and a bag of pre-prepared salad leaves, she decided to make herself a sandwich. Surfing the net for more ghostly goings on to imitate wouldn't be half as much fun on an empty stomach. As she moved to get a loaf out of the bread bin, a sudden hammering on her front door stopped her. "What the...?" she said, wondering why the commotion when she had a perfectly good doorbell.

Ronnie headed down the hall ready to give her caller the what for, but before she could answer, the door flung open and Nick thundered in. Ronnie was forced to jump out of the way as Nick barged passed and headed to the kitchen. *Someone's not a happy bunny*, she said, ready for the onslaught.

"You've gone too far this time, Ronnie," he said.

She tittered in delight as she followed in his footsteps. He and Gaye had to be on the move now, Ronnie had never seen Nick so angry.

"It's one thing playing childish games with food orders but to break into someone's house."

While Nick paced up and down, clearly doing his best to control himself, Ronnie did her best not to laugh.

"What are you saying?" she asked, feigning surprise. "You've been burgled?"

Nick stopped to look at Ronnie square on. "Oh for God's sake. You know exactly what I'm talking about."

"What? You think I'm responsible?" She let out a burst of fake laughter.

"I don't think, I know."

Ronnie returned his gaze, calm and collected. "And why, pray tell, would I do that?"

He glared at her in response, but Ronnie refused to be intimidated. The man could stomp around as much as he wanted. Without evidence, his accusations couldn't be substantiated, and Ronnie felt safe in the knowledge that she'd covered her tracks well.

"Because you're off your bloody rocker, that's why!"

Ronnie smiled as she continued to look at him. "Goodness me, that's no way to talk to your wife, Nick."

Throughout the time they had been a couple and no matter

his level of frustration, she'd never noticed a tic on his right temple before. Then again, Ronnie supposed that hardly surprising; she hadn't even clocked the fact that he was having an affair. As the tic continued to throb, she couldn't understand how he couldn't feel it. It was like some pulsating Belisha Beacon which once seen, refused to be unseen.

"And you'd do anything to get rid of us."

Not quite anything, Ronnie considered. As much as she'd thought about it, she wouldn't go as far as murder.

Nick started pacing again. "I mean, to try to make us think next door is suddenly haunted. It's exactly the kind of stunt you'd pull."

"Ha! And you think I'm the one who's losing it?" She crossed her arms tight over her chest. "So, how am I supposed to have done this? Climbed in through a window? On this street? With these neighbours? Or have I somehow managed to get hold of a key and simply wandered in through the front door?"

Nick stopped again to look at her. "You think I care about *how* you got in? I'm just here to warn you. You step another foot inside next door and you won't only have me to contend with..."

"So, you're threatening me now? Over something I didn't do?"

As the glare on Nick's face intensified, the tic on his temple sped up. He took a deep breath, as if trying to calm himself before speaking again. "As I was saying, you won't only have me to contend with, I'll have the police back round."

Ronnie laughed. Nick could bring in who he wanted. Thanks to a paper suit, a pair of socks and a hairnet, it's not like they'd find any evidence. "Why wait?" she said. "If you're so convinced the goings on in *your* house are somehow *my* fault, call them. I don't care."

Nick's expression turned scornful. "Obviously."

"What do you mean by that?"

He raised an eyebrow. "Looked in the mirror lately?"

In all the excitement, Ronnie had forgotten about her hair. "Excuse me?" Trying to keep up her bravado, she willed herself not to blush. But she could tell by Nick's sneer that he knew he'd struck a nerve. Anger began to well inside of her but, unlike him and his tic, no way was she going to show it. Ronnie flicked her head. "It's called trying something new." She looked her ex-husband up and down. Taking in his beige slacks and cricket sweater, he reminded her of a cheesy home catalogue model. "Something you know a lot about, I see."

A long spine-chilling scream sounded from next door.

"Gaye!" Nick said. His eyes widened in horror as he raced out of the room and down the hall, leaving Ronnie standing there.

Remembering the secret message she'd written on Gaye's bathroom mirror, Ronnie knew she should have been smiling a satisfied smile. She should have imagined Gaye turning on the hot tap and steam billowing as the woman added one of her fancy lotions and potions to the water. Ronnie should have pictured her neighbour breathing in the scent as she stepped into her brilliant white tub in her brilliant white room, enjoying the fact that instead of a nice calming bath, Gaye was freaking thanks to a so-called *message from the dead*. Gaye deserved the upset, of course. Ronnie's ex-husband did too. But instead of relishing in the moment, Ronnie's sole focus on was the way Nick had looked at her only seconds before.

His expression had been contemptuous and mocking, while his ridicule felt both hurtful and gratuitous. Had she become that much of a fool to him? Did he and Gaye really think they had all the rights and she had all the responsibilities? Ronnie scoffed. Yes, it seemed they did. It was her job to be the adult, after they'd sneaked around like a pair of desperate teenagers. It was her job to suck it up after being dumped on her wedding anniversary. It was her job to appreciate that twenty-five years of marriage, of trust, of compromise, didn't compare to the sordid, squalid and downright selfish ardour that Nick and Gaye had found. Ronnie felt herself becoming increasingly incensed. It was her job to shut the fuck up and get over it.

Well, she'd show them.

Overwhelmed by a sudden sense of purpose, Ronnie took off her wedding ring and placed it in the centre of the dining table. She turned and headed for the kitchen drawers. Opening the first, she pulled out a large pair of kitchen scissors, their metal blades feeling cool to touch as she laid them on her palm and wrapped her fingers tight around them. She headed out of the kitchen and facing straight ahead, calmly made her way upstairs to the bathroom.

Ronnie gave herself a long hard stare in the mirror, unwavering as she grabbed a fistful of hair. Opening the blades out to their fullest, she used the scissors to bite the shock off at the root. Letting every last strand drop into the sink below, her eyes didn't move from her reflection as she repeated the action over and again, until finally there was nothing left to cut.

18

Ronnie stood at the kitchen counter flicking through various Internet pictures on her laptop. She paused to look at one photo in more detail – chairs stacked on a table in the weirdest of configurations. She picked up a pen and made a note on the pad lying to one side. Poltergeists, it seemed, could be creative when they wanted to be, and Ronnie chuckled, looking forward to imitating some of their more intricate activities.

Planning on going bigger and better on her next visit into number eight, Ronnie checked her watch, pleased to see she still had plenty of time to continue her research before Willow and Bea landed. Feeling nervous yet excited about their arrival, they still didn't know about her new hair-free look. Ronnie smiled as she raised her hand to rub the stubble on her head, unable to quite believe she'd taken a pair of scissors and then a razor to her own scalp. She anticipated their response. No doubt something along the lines of her having had a nervous breakdown; whereas in truth, it had been the most liberating act Ronnie had ever carried out.

She frowned as the doorbell rang, wondering who'd come a

calling. She knew it wouldn't be her daughter or mother-in-law; they always let themselves in. Heading down the hall to find out, Ronnie took a deep breath before answering. She herself might love her new image, but she'd yet to see how anyone else would respond.

Opening the door, she froze.

"Ronnie?" PC Jack Shenton asked.

Ronnie stared at her visitor. Despite his threat to ring the police if she dared step inside next door in the future, it seemed Nick had decided to get them involved anyway. She knew she shouldn't be surprised; her ex-husband's words and actions hadn't been the same thing for quite some time. She took in PC Shenton's uniform; bringing in the boys in blue was a useless exercise. Ronnie had, after all, covered her tracks well. She smiled, as confident as any untouchable. "Please, come in."

As she led the way into the kitchen, Ronnie felt a slight panic as she clocked the photo still visible on her laptop screen. Remembering the pizza menu from Jack's previous home visit, she hastily shut the screen down in what could only be described as a case of *déjà vu*. She turned to Jack who, too busy looking at her, thankfully hadn't seemed to notice. "So..." she said as she waited for him to speak. "What can I do for you?"

He continued to stand there wide-eyed and silent.

"Jack?" she said. "PC Shenton?"

He appeared to shake himself out of it. "I've got one word," he finally said. "Wow!"

Ronnie felt herself redden. More concerned about Nick's threat and the computer image, she'd forgotten about her lack of hair for a moment. She took in his expression and, putting a hand up to her head, wondered if that was wow in a good way? Or wow as in bad? It was the first bit of feedback she'd had since shaving her head.

"You look incredible," he added, his face lighting up.

Ronnie felt relieved, pleased to know she hadn't swapped one rock star image for another. She didn't think she'd appreciate being accused of doing a Britney. She waited for him to say something else, but he seemed transfixed and the more he stared at her, the more she found herself getting lost in his gaze. Jeez, the man was gorgeous. She recalled their conversation at the gym and thinking she'd have liked to have gotten to know him more, deemed it a shame he was there in the line of duty.

Unable to hold his regard any longer, Ronnie diverted her eyes. Embarrassed, she wasn't used to receiving that degree of attention from a member of the opposite sex, let alone from someone as handsome as Jack. Not even from Nick, she realised, and he'd been her husband. She wondered why she hadn't thought of going bald sooner. If she was reading Jack's response correctly, it might have saved her marriage.

An awkward silence descended as Ronnie waited for him to start questioning her. When it came to next door, she'd deny any accusations, of course, but doubted she'd be believed. After all, during his last visit, Jack had issued her with a harassment notice. "So..." she said, deciding she should get everything over and done with. "How can I help?"

"Sorry?" As if remembering himself, Jack cleared his throat. "Oh, yes."

Ronnie watched him reach into his inside jacket pocket, steeling herself for the imminent lecture about how she'd left him no choice. *Here we go*, she reasoned, recalling how things had gone the last time. *Him and his blooming notebook.*

"I brought you this," he said.

Ronnie looked at the item in his outstretched hand. It was a notebook all right, only not the one she expected. She took in its pale pink outer and gold lettered cover quote: *Live, Laugh, Shine.* She was sure she had one of those already. "I don't understand."

"You left it on the pavement," Jack said. "On the High Street."

He let out a laugh, back to fixating on her new image. "I can't believe how different you look."

Ronnie cringed as she recalled bumping into Jack outside the hair salon. Picturing the contents of her handbag strewn all over the place, she'd obviously missed seeing it lying there. Not sure she'd ever forget the absolute horror written on Jack's face that day, she felt embarrassed that he'd seen her in such a bouffant state. Although, on a positive note, at least Nick hadn't tried to get her into trouble again.

"Thank you," she said, reaching out to retrieve the notebook. "It's kind of you to return it." As her hand inadvertently touched his, she quickly pulled back, sure something electric passed between them. *Static*, she silently insisted as she rubbed her palm. On account of her bristly head.

"No worries. I was in the area and had a spare five minutes, so I thought why not drop it in."

"I hadn't even noticed it had gone," Ronnie said. "I mean I would have done. Eventually. Like when I needed it for work." Realising she was waffling, she flicked through its pages, glancing at sketch after sketch of handbag design ideas as a means of shutting herself up.

"They're very good," Jack said, taking a step forward. "I hope you don't mind but I had a quick browse. You're really talented."

Ronnie smiled. Personally, she didn't find any of them worth developing further. But two compliments in one day, *incredible* and *talented*, she could handle that. She placed the notebook down on the dining table. "Can I get you a drink? A tea? Or coffee?" Under the circumstances, it was the least she could do. "To say thanks."

"I would if I could." He indicated to his uniform. "But I should get back to work."

"Of course." Her degree of disappointment surprised her. "Sorry." Ronnie indicated to the door. "I'll see you out, shall I?"

She began following Jack down the hall, realising the man's physique was equally as impressive from the back. Her eyes lit up at the sight of his rather firm-looking rear. However, she found herself forced into a standstill, almost bumping into him again when he suddenly turned to face her. She flushed red as she quickly lifted her gaze and, hoping he hadn't noticed, told herself to focus.

"I was just wondering..." Jack suddenly appeared nervous.

"Yes?"

"If you'd consider maybe going..."

Ronnie's heart rate quickened. Was this man really about to ask her out? Remembering how she'd misread the nosebleed situation at the gym, she tried and failed in her insistence not to get too excited. Staring at him in anticipation, he stared back.

Ronnie jumped as the front door flew open, interrupting the moment; Bea's bangles and bracelets jangling as she and Willow rushed in from the street.

19

Looking from Jack to her daughter and then her mother-in-law, Ronnie couldn't believe it. Talk about bad timing.

Bea came to a sudden standstill, her eyes narrowing as she looked up at Jack. "What's going on? Why are you here?" She turned to Ronnie. "Please don't tell me you've been up to more mischief."

"Mum?" Willow said, Ronnie's lack of hair clearly coming as a bit of a shock.

"Oh my word," Bea said, suddenly clocking it too.

Jack smiled at the sight of them, both standing there open-mouthed and trance-like. Obviously amused by Ronnie's new guests, he had to squeeze passed them to get to the door. "Ladies," he said to the unresponsive women, pausing to give Ronnie one final look and a wink before making his exit.

While Willow and Bea continued to gawp, Ronnie almost swooned. She couldn't believe Jack might have been on the verge of asking her out on a date. What would she have said if he had? Her shoulders slumped as he disappeared from view. She supposed she'd never know.

She growled at her daughter and mother-in-law for their interruption, an act that brought them out of their reverie. Turning, Ronnie stomped back to the kitchen, leaving them no choice but to follow her.

She sat down at the table, waiting for the onslaught of questions about to ensue. *What was she thinking? Why would she do that to herself? Was she having a mid-life crisis? A nervous breakdown even?*

Ronnie had known shaving her head would invite comments. Instead of appearing confident to the wider world, most people would see her as aggressive and confrontational. Or at the other end of the scale, worthy of pity, because she must have some sort of condition or god-awful disease. The fact of the matter was, getting rid of her hair had been liberating, each cut of the scissors and swipe of the razor making her feel that bit lighter and freer. It felt like an emboldening, a means of taking control. Moreover, it forced people to look her in the eye, to really see her. She smiled to herself. If she'd read the situation right, PC Jack Shenton had *definitely* taken notice.

Her daughter and mother-in-law took the seats opposite, spellbound once again.

"I know we suggested a restyle, but this is something else," Bea said.

"It's certainly different," Willow replied.

"And I have to say, it's not exactly a look many people can pull off."

"Not many people would want to."

Bea put a hand up to her chest. "I can't believe how much younger she looks."

"I can't believe she actually suits it. Or how much she looks like me."

"Oh, that's nothing to do with the bald head. You two have always been the image of each other."

Ronnie rolled her eyes. "I can't believe you're both talking about me as if I'm not sitting here." Still, at least their words told her they liked it, even if their expressions weren't so sure.

"Oh, you're here all right," Bea said.

"Yep. There's no denying that," Willow added. "To think, I have a mother with a buzzcut."

"Not quite. I wet shaved."

"What made you do it?" Bea asked.

Ronnie didn't one hundred per cent know; it wasn't as if she'd planned on getting rid of her hair. If anything, thanks to Pete and his blooming hair salon, she'd accepted the fact that she'd be living like a hermit for the foreseeable future. Then Nick turned up, shouting the odds and mocking her, not that Ronnie could tell Willow and Bea he'd been round, because if she did, she'd have to explain why. She must have snapped and ended up on automatic pilot. At the time, it simply felt like the right thing to do. "You called me Rod Stewart," Ronnie replied. "After a compliment like that, I didn't have much choice."

"Don't remind me," Bea said, her face breaking into a smile. "I haven't stopped giggling since."

Willow chuckled too. "Sorry, Mum. But you did give us a good laugh."

"Glad to be of service," Ronnie replied. She got up from her seat, just pleased they hadn't accused her of losing the plot. "Anyway, enough about my hair."

"What hair?" Willow said.

Ronnie raised an eyebrow. "Fancy a cuppa?"

"I don't know about anyone else," Bea said, "but I think I need something stronger."

"Me too," Willow said. "For the shock."

Ronnie checked her watch; it was still early afternoon. "I suppose it's five o'clock somewhere." She headed for the fridge and pulled out a bottle of wine, before grabbing three glasses from the cupboard. She began to pour.

"Cheers!" Bea said, raising her glass.

Ronnie and Willow followed suit. "Cheers!"

"Now we've gotten that excitement out of the way," Bea said. "Maybe you'd like to tell us what that police officer was doing here."

20

Ronnie glanced around her spotless kitchen. She'd scrubbed it to within an inch of its life. In fact, the whole of number six had had a good going over; the smell of bleach, polish and floor cleaner creating a heady mix that permeated the air. It flowed from room to room in an invisible chemical cloud, pervading Ronnie's nostrils and sticking to the back of her throat. She looked down at her dry tingling fingers, hoping the house appreciated her efforts. Even if her hands didn't.

As a rule, baking was Ronnie's go-to activity when she felt frustrated. On that occasion though, arming herself with a wooden spoon and electric whisk held little appeal. It was as if something inside of her had shifted. She didn't want the disarray of her cake making activities, she wanted order; *tidy house, tidy mind* seemingly her new mantra. Telling herself that one out of two wasn't bad, she looked down the hall to the front door, something she'd found herself doing often of late.

Picturing Jack, Ronnie wondered if she'd imagined the whole attraction thing. As a woman who'd been royally dumped by her husband, who was to say she wasn't desperate for some male attention and had read more into the situation than was there? It would've been easy to confuse *you look incredible* as in 'gorgeous', with *you look incredible* as in 'Oh my word, what have you done to yourself'. Especially when, as a police officer, Jack was no doubt trained in the art of communication.

Ronnie sighed. As for thinking the man was about to ask her out... Looking back, he could have been about to suggest anything. If she'd considered going to see a psychiatrist, for example, on account of having shaved her head. Recalling their time at the gym, it wouldn't be the first time that she'd gotten her signals mixed up. All of which would certainly explain why she hadn't heard from him since.

With no choice but to continue working through her uncertainty, Ronnie wondered what other jobs she could conjure up. Turning her attention to the window and the bottom of the garden beyond, she supposed she could always reorganise her studio, a task that would keep her busy for a couple of days. "Or you could simply go down there and get on with work," she told herself, neither option sparking joy.

Ronnie picked up the pink sketchpad she'd set to one side, ready to take to her workspace. She smiled as she recalled Jack's comment about her designs being good, and flicking through its pages, she wondered what it was about them that he liked? With a bit more consideration, maybe they could be reworked?

Butterflies fluttered in her tummy as, unable to help herself, she again dared to think he might like her. She pictured Jack's soft expression, heard the unsure manner with which he spoke. Both not only endearing, but in stark contrast to the man's stature and uniform which exuded authority. *Kind, yet manly.* Ronnie liked that. She let out a wistful sigh as the words *what if* ran through her mind once more.

Ronnie couldn't deny the fact that she fancied him, although if he had gotten to the point of suggesting a date, she knew she'd have had to decline. Thanks to *Operation Poltergeist*, she was an active criminal and she could imagine the stick he'd get back at the station if word ever got out. Comments about his girlfriend also being the enemy would be abound... Ronnie froze. "Oh, no." Horrified by her use of the word *girlfriend*, she frowned as she glanced around her spotless gleaming kitchen. "You're turning into Gaye!" Ronnie shuddered at the prospect and, dismissing the idea, returned her thoughts to the delectable Jack.

A vehicle door slamming hard shut sounded from the street and Ronnie stopped, her heart skipping in anticipation of it being a police vehicle. She felt like a giddy teenager as she left the room and headed into the lounge to investigate. Having spent the days since his visit telling herself that he'd be back one minute, only to dismiss the idea in the next, she crossed her fingers in the hope that, finally, the former would be proven right. Positioning herself in the bay window, however, instead of a police car, Ronnie took in an Interflora van. She scowled. Obviously another grand gesture from Nick to Gaye.

She watched the driver make her way to the vehicle's rear, before pulling out the most colourful bouquet of flowers Ronnie had ever seen. Ronnie felt a stab of jealousy. In the whole time she'd been married to Nick, she only ever got crappy garage sprays and even then only on her birthday. "Creep!"

The delivery lady looked in Ronnie's direction with a smile and a wave, enough to make Ronnie want to run out and slap the woman. Although Ronnie's annoyance fast turned to confusion when the delivery lady began walking up Ronnie's garden path. "For me?" she mouthed. Ronnie giggled as she clapped her hands and hopped from one foot to the other, doing her best not to believe that the flowers had to have come from Jack.

Ronnie rushed out into the hall, beaming as she went to collect them.

"Ronnie Jacobs?" the lady asked.

Ronnie nodded at double speed.

"Then, yes, these are for you."

Ronnie's eyes widened as she accepted the offering. The bouquet was even more beautiful up close. Orange gerbera daisies, orange spray roses, pink gillyflowers and lavender mini carnations were accented with fronds of Queen Anne's lace and lush green foliage. She put her nose to the ensemble, breathing in its soft sweet fragrance. "Thank you," Ronnie said, feeling a tad overcome. She'd never been gifted anything so beautiful.

Ronnie stood smiling for a moment, watching the delivery lady go on her way, before heading back inside. Once in the kitchen, she laid the bouquet down on the counter, marvelling at what had to be Jack's gesture. She checked the wrapping to see if there was a card and, rummaging through the layers, found a little white envelope stapled to the sheer plastic, hidden under copious amounts of pink ribbon. She pulled the envelope free, before holding it up and tapping it against her chin. Feeling nervous, she giggled, deciding to save the card for later when she could properly savour his words.

Laying the envelope to one side, Ronnie reached into a cupboard for a glass vase and filled it with water, before grabbing the scissors from the drawer. Careful not to damage the flowers, she cut through the pretty packaging and, opening it out, placed a firm hand over the bouquet's gathering of dark green stems. Ronnie hated what she was about to do but recalled reading somewhere that it enabled bunches of flowers to live a longer healthier life. "Sorry about this," she said, not sure if it worked or whether it was an old wife's tale. Ronnie took a deep breath as she held the closed scissor blades tight in her hand and bashed the stalks with the handles, crushing each and every one of them until they flattened and split.

The flora and fauna might not have appreciated her actions,

but Ronnie had to admit she found it therapeutic and, job done, she wiped her forehead as she stood back to regard her efforts. Taking in the green mulch, she wondered if she'd battered them a bit too much. Still, admirers would be too enamoured with the orange, pink and lavender on display above the water line to notice the mess below. She lifted the whole ensemble and placed it in the vase, titivating each individual bloom until they stood to perfection. "Beautiful," she said and glancing around for the best place to sit them, she positioned the whole thing in the centre of the dining table.

Hearing another vehicle door slam shut, Ronnie cocked her head, her tummy once again fizzing in anticipation. Surely Jack hadn't come to make sure his gift had been delivered? She straightened her clothing, quickly retracing her footsteps back into the lounge in the hope of spotting him.

But her shoulders slumped when, much to her disappointment, he was nowhere to be seen. Instead, she found herself looking at a rather serious chap. Dressed in a shirt and tie and carrying a clipboard, he stood staring up at number eight, his eyes narrowed in concentration. Ronnie's heart lifted as she wondered if this was the day that she'd been praying for? Was the chap before her an estate agent? She looked from him to his vehicle, reading the signage on his car. *Graham Sharpe, Chartered Surveyor*, it said. "Do chartered surveyors sell houses?" Ronnie asked.

Her attention was diverted when Gaye appeared at her front door.

"Mr Sharpe?"

Ronnie noted that Gaye's appearance seemed less together than usual. Her hair wasn't as perfect, her outfit not quite effortless and she looked tired. Ronnie smiled, imagining the woman forced to sleep with one eye open. Even her voice sounded different; equally as loud, but less self-assured.

"Thank you for coming." Gaye wrung her hands as she waited for her guest to approach.

"No problem," Mr Sharpe replied. "Although I'm not sure why I'm here." Making his way up number eight's garden path, he took another glance at the house. "From what I can see, everything looks okay, on this side at least. Obviously I'll need to do a detailed assessment, but there are no trees and therefore no roots undermining your property. There doesn't seem to be any cracks. Unless they're internal? Or round the back?"

"Oh no, we don't have anything like that."

"So, what makes you think the house is subsiding?"

Subsiding! Ronnie hoped not. That could spell disaster for her own property.

"To be honest, I don't. There's been some funny goings on lately and..."

Ronnie's eyes widened. She put a hand up to her mouth, realising the chap's visit was a result of *Operation Poltergeist.* He might not be the estate agent she'd hoped for, but in her view the man's presence was still good news. "First flowers and then this. Can the day get any better?" she said.

"My boyfriend..."

Ronnie winced. Did she have to keep calling him that?

"At first he thought there'd been an earthquake. But when there were no reports, let's say he came up with the idea of it being the house that's moving."

Ronnie smirked as she thought about her trip into next door. "And that would explain the secret message in the bathroom mirror, how?" A question that Gaye had, no doubt, posed too.

Remembering Nick's last visit, Ronnie knew her ex didn't really think number eight was moving. He'd guessed she was behind everything from the start, the poor man simply couldn't prove it. Ronnie's smile widened. It felt good to know her efforts were paying off. Gaye clearly believed her house was haunted, and Nick was doing everything he could to ease the woman's ghostly worries. Ronnie planned on keeping the pressure up, of course; Nick had to run out of potential excuses for the unexplained activity at some point. Maybe then he'd turn into a believer himself?

Ronnie watched them head indoors and, deciding to celebrate *Operation Poltergeist's* initial success with a well-earned cup of coffee, made her way back to the kitchen. Ronnie paused at the dining table to look at the vase of flowers. Reaching out to stroke one of the daisies, she knew Jack had sidetracked her enough already; that instead of acting like a lovesick schoolgirl, she should have focused on the task at hand – getting rid of Nick and Gaye. She sighed. Ready to capitalise on her progress so far, thoughts of Jack and any potential date would have to wait.

Determined, she put the kettle on. However, at the same time, the little envelope that came with the flower delivery caught her eye. Picking it up, she again insisted she'd wasted enough time on such silliness and maintaining her resolve, tossed it into the bin. Grabbing a cup from the cupboard, a part of her wavered, that little voice of hers insisting there was no harm in reading Jack's note. After everything Ronnie had been through, a little confidence boost might even spur her on.

She put down the cup and, opening the bin lid, retrieved the envelope, her childish giddiness returning as she ripped it open. As she read though, her smile vanished and her heart sank. That was not what Ronnie had expected.

21

Ronnie glanced around the kitchen as she sipped on her coffee, wishing she'd arranged to meet Willow and Bea in town rather than keep having them round. It would do her good to get out and about, instead of wandering from room to room in an empty house, talking to herself. Admittedly, thanks to her disappointment over the flowers, her one-sided conversations were again about PC Jack Shenton's visit, and as his handsome face popped into her head once more, she again had to dismiss it. Like she kept insisting, she was far too old to be dreaming about *what ifs*.

Ronnie sighed, fed up. Sick of looking at her four walls, she imagined herself sitting in a café, waiting for Willow and Bea, chit-chat coming at her from every angle. Twenty-something colleagues, scathing in their complaints about their overbearing boss; a younger twosome, brows creased as they struggled to decide what to have for lunch; an elderly couple looking forward to an up-and-coming holiday, their first in years. All very mundane, but at least such parlays would drown out the conversations turning over in her own head. Ronnie exhaled again. *A holiday.* She could do with one of those herself.

Ronnie put her cup in the sink. She checked the time before exiting the room and making her way into the lounge, and paused to straighten an already straight cushion as she moved to the window. Looking out, she wondered where her daughter and mother-in-law had gotten to. Not that their lack of punctuality mattered, she supposed. It wasn't as if she had anything better to do. Besides, they were only delivering another blooming envelope and if the last couple were anything to go by, that could only spell trouble.

She clocked Mr and Mrs Wright exiting their house. They were such a cute elderly couple that Ronnie couldn't help but smile as she observed them. Being the perfect gentleman, Mr Wright made a point of opening the car's passenger door for his wife, waiting until she got comfortable in her seat before closing it again. It was such a heartwarming sight, yet saddening at the same time. A reminder of what she and Nick should've been looking forward to when it came to their retirement.

As the elderly couple set off down the avenue, Mr Wright tooted his horn at Mrs Smethurst, who raised a hand in acknowledgement. Getting on with her weeding, the woman cut a formidable figure. Ronnie didn't know how she did it. Watching her, she had to admire Mrs Smethurst's seventy-odd-year agility as she reached down and, in one fell swoop, pulled out a couple of rogue dandelions. In fact, Ronnie admired the woman full stop. Her neighbour kept such a beautiful house and garden, and every inch of both down to her own hands. Ronnie often wondered why there'd never been a Mr Smethurst to share them with, or another Mrs for that matter. Ronnie didn't know if it was in relation to herself or her single neighbour, but she couldn't help but think that no-one should have to spend their twilight years alone.

A vehicle pulling onto Holme Lea Avenue caught Ronnie's eye and glad to see it belonged to Willow, she smiled. At last, a real-life person to talk to. She waved as the car came to a stand-still, but it appeared her daughter was too busy rooting in her handbag to notice. Ronnie shook her head. It was no wonder Willow couldn't find what she was looking for; she always seemed to carry around everything but the kitchen sink. Ronnie smiled again thinking about the clutter in her own handbag. *Like mother, like daughter.*

Finally, Willow climbed out, but instead of heading for her childhood home, much to Ronnie's dismay, she headed straight for number eight. Ronnie's heart sank. It wasn't enough that her daughter was late, she had to pop in and see *him* first. "And what's that?" Ronnie frowned, focusing on the piece of metal in her daughter's hand. It was clearly a key. "Since when did you get one of those?"

Ronnie dragged herself away from the window. She told herself it was wrong to sulk, but as she made her way back to the kitchen, she couldn't seem to help it. As much as she accepted the need for Willow and Nick to maintain their relationship, their continued contact still made her feel uncomfortable. Ronnie knew she was being daft, selfish even, and despite her pout, she didn't really want her daughter to take sides. But after everything Nick had done, whenever Willow and he got together, a part of Ronnie felt betrayed. "All the more reason to get on with *Operation Poltergeist*," she said, disappointed that like everything else in her life, her plans for next door had stalled.

When it came to *Operation Poltergeist*, Ronnie might have conceived its next step, but much to her annoyance she hadn't been able to see it through. Aside of greeting the chartered surveyor, Gaye hadn't put one step over number eight's threshold to go anywhere since. Ronnie stuck her bottom lip out further. Unsurprisingly, the woman was being her usual incon-siderate self.

. . .

"Sorry I'm late," Willow called out.

Ronnie clicked the kettle on as her daughter entered the kitchen. Determined to at least appear neutral in front of Willow, Ronnie grabbed three mugs from the cupboard, guessing Bea wouldn't be far behind.

"Ooh, these are nice." Willow stopped as she entered the room, indicating to the vase of flowers sat on the dining table. She reached out to stroke one of the gerbera daisies.

"They're from a customer," Ronnie said.

Her daughter leaned in to smell their fragrance. "I can't believe you say that like it's nothing. If someone sent me a gorgeous gift simply for doing my job, I'd be on cloud nine."

"A mother-of-the-bride had them delivered. She couldn't find a bag to match her outfit. I think I was her last resort and they're her way of saying thank you."

"Nothing to do with the fact that you're brilliant at what you do then?"

"Oh, I don't know about that." Ronnie could feel her daughter's eyes on her.

"Is everything okay, Mum?" Willow asked, her brow furrowed.

"Of course. Why wouldn't it be?" Ronnie approached the table with two mugs of tea.

"You seem a bit quiet."

"Do I?" Still feeling a bit sorry for herself, Ronnie fixed a smile on her face. "I don't mean to be." She watched her daughter's expression soften.

"I know you don't want to hear it, but you need to stop letting Dad and Gaye get to you. You're going to have to pick yourself up at some point."

Willow was right, of course. Ronnie only wished she knew how. Of late, her life seemed to be dictated according to everyone else's actions. She considered next door's refusal to move. Or rather *lack of* action, she acknowledged. She handed her daughter her drink. "I know," she said.

Willow hung her coat over the back of a chair and took a seat. "I have just the thing to cheer you up." She reached into her bag and after a rummage around, produced an envelope. She smiled as she placed it on the table in front of her mum. "Ta da!"

Ronnie looked down at the offering. Considering what those things had put her through already, if she never saw an envelope again it would be too soon. "Shouldn't we wait for your grandmother to arrive," she said, delaying the inevitable.

"She's not coming. Something about her not feeling well."

"Really?" Ronnie frowned, and forgetting her own woes for a moment, wondered if she should be concerned. Bea had hardly had a day's sickness in all the time Ronnie had known her.

"It's nothing to worry about. She's a bit run down, tired, that kind of thing. She'll be back to her usual self tomorrow. Probably age related. I keep suggesting she might want to slow down a little, but will she listen?"

Ronnie chuckled, unable to ever imagine her mother-in-law taking things easy. She was a doer, too busy having fun and making the most out of life to let her advancing years get in the way. "Tell me about it."

"As for my lateness, you can blame Dad for holding me up."

Ronnie's back stiffened, her irritation on the matter returning.

"I don't know what's going on next door, but there's definitely something up." Willow drank a mouthful of tea. "I'm not meant to tell anyone, but they've gone away for the night."

Ronnie's ears pricked at the news. "Really?" She hadn't seen them leave.

"Yep. They left first thing."

Keen to know more, Ronnie put her cup to her mouth, doing her utmost to appear disinterested. "And have they gone anywhere nice?"

"To see Gaye's mother, who's not well either, by all accounts. Goodness knows why Dad wants it kept quiet, but anyway, he asked me to check on the house while they're gone. I wouldn't care, but they'll be back first thing tomorrow. It's a bit strange, if you ask me."

Under the circumstances, Ronnie knew Nick's request wasn't strange at all. Not that she could tell Willow that. He, no doubt, wanted to make sure there were no surprises to greet them upon their return. Ronnie smiled a secret smile. It felt good to know that he and Gaye had gotten so worried they'd only go out if someone kept an eye on their property. Worries that were about to get worse. Ronnie's brain went into overdrive at the prospect of getting *Operation Poltergeist* restarted. "It would seem that way," she replied.

"At least when Dad rings, I can tell him everything's in order." Willow appeared pensive for a moment. "I don't know. Maybe age is getting to him too?" She nodded to the envelope. "Aren't you going to open it?"

"Sorry?" With her mind still elsewhere, Ronnie forced herself into the present. "Oh, yes." She reluctantly tore at the seal and pulled out yet another piece of paper. Opening it out, she read the words: *Monday, 10am, sharp.* "What's happening on Monday?" she asked, not sure if she really wanted to know.

"It's a surprise."

"A surprise?"

"Yep."

Ronnie's face crumpled. How many times did she have to tell them she hated such things?

"And no matter what you're thinking right now, you're gonna love it."

Ronnie frowned as she considered what they'd already put her through. "That's what you always say."

22

Ronnie's spirits had lifted since her daughter's visit. Instead of feeling betrayed by her offspring, she finally appreciated the fact that Willow's contact with Nick did, after all, have its benefits. She chuckled. Without their continued relationship, she wouldn't be standing there for a second time, wearing a paper forensic suit, rubber gloves and a great big smile, while dropping her ladders down onto Gaye's landing. Rather, she'd be moping about in her own house, still not moving forward with *Operation Poltergeist.*

With only two items on the agenda and no intention of loitering, Ronnie headed straight down to her neighbour's kitchen, ready to complete her next task. She let out a nervous giggle as she took in the room's clear glass dining table and six large white high-back chairs. "Here goes," she said, knowing her ex and his floosy were soon to get the shock of their lives. "Let's do this."

Ronnie took a deep breath to calm herself; whether Gaye's furniture was expensive or not, the last thing Ronnie wanted was to cause any criminal damage. Deciding it was better to be safe than sorry, she began by checking the underside of every chair leg, pleased to note each had a rubber scratch-proofing pad attached. "Wonderful," she said, knowing that without them she'd have had to abort. Although, she knew she shouldn't be surprised. If she'd learnt anything during her visits into number eight, it was that Gaye was a perfectionist.

Making sure she was careful, Ronnie lifted three of the chairs, one by one, and placed them in a neat line on top of the table. Picking up a further two, she created a second tier, before putting the final chair on top again. Ronnie stood back, smiling as she admired her handiwork. It was like a six-chair pyramid.

Turning to exit the room, her heart thumped. As she made her way upstairs, it wasn't the next task in itself that bothered her; Ronnie thought it was inspired. Coming to a standstill outside the master bedroom, there lay the issue. Entering was like venturing into uncharted territory and as her hand hovered over the door handle, she had to steel herself in readiness of letting herself in. She wondered what she'd find on the other side. After all, Gaye was a scarlet woman, and through there was where the action happened. Ronnie inhaled and exhaled a few times, imagining handcuffs chained to the bed frame, a mountain of sex toys and a mirrored ceiling, before finally plucking up the courage to open the door.

"Wow!" she said. The sight before her was not what she expected. The room was even more special than the rest of the house.

Glancing around, the only aspect that didn't surprise Ronnie were the four white walls and pale cream carpet. As for everything else, she didn't know what to look at first. From the art deco dressing table, made solely from mirrored glass, to the matching bedside cabinets; from the king-size bed with its crisp white sheets, to the giant pastel grey headboard made up of padded vertical columns. Ronnie would've put money on there not being another bedroom on Holme Lea Avenue like it. Even she had to admit it was fabulous. Anyone would think she'd stepped into a luxury hotel.

She felt tempted to peek inside a couple of drawers and have a snoop in the white lacquered wardrobe. But keeping herself in check, as much as Ronnie wasn't there to cause any physical damage, neither was she there to be nosey.

Getting to work, Ronnie pulled the black and white geometric throw off the bottom of the bed and placed it to one side, along with the pillows. She flipped the duvet round so the fastenings at the bottom lay hidden at the top. Ensuring the duvet was as crease free as when she found it, she reinstated the throw, except this time at the head of the bed. All before precision lining the pillows, which she repositioned at the foot.

She stood back to assess the result, approving of her efforts. "If an unwanted visitor in your boudoir doesn't freak you into moving," Ronnie said of Nick and Gaye, "then nothing will."

Job done, Ronnie didn't want to loiter, but as she prepared to leave, she realised she'd stepped a little too near the window. She quickly looked out to make sure she hadn't been seen, her eyes widening in horror and her pulse quickening as she spotted Mrs Wright looking straight at her. "Shit!"

She froze, her mind racing as she wondered what to do next. With no choice but to stand there, Ronnie knew making a run for it would create more suspicion. "Fuck!" Too scared to move, she hoped she hadn't been identified.

While her neighbour squinted her eyes, clearly trying to decipher who or what she was looking at, Ronnie tried to think about what a real ghost might do under the circumstances. "Think! Think!" she told herself, before realising the answer was obvious, they'd disappear. Not that that helped. It wasn't as if a living breathing human being like her could just vanish. She began to sweat.

Remembering something she'd seen lots of times on TV,

Ronnie pictured many a cinematic ghost either floating towards or away from the camera. Of course, her only option was to try to replicate that, but without an actor's platform and track, Ronnie wasn't sure she could pull it off.

She swallowed hard as she stood, dressed head-to-toe in her white paper suit. Staring back at her neighbour and maintaining her gaze, she inhaled and exhaled in an attempt at calming herself down. Making sure to keep every other part of her body perfectly still, Ronnie discreetly repositioned her feet, thanking God she only wore socks and not shoes as well. She told herself to concentrate as she counted down in her head. *Three... two... one...* Attempting not only her first moonwalk, but her first backwards moonwalk, she glided in her retreat until she was safely out of the room.

Having been up since dawn, Ronnie yawned, feeling knackered. Sleep had come in fits and starts thanks to the previous day's excitement with Mrs Wright. When Ronnie did manage to snooze, images of being arrested by PC Jack Shenton in full view of the street only woke her up again, until in the end she'd given up trying to get anywhere near her eight hours.

Standing there with a strong cup of coffee, Ronnie felt like the retreating dead she'd tried to imitate. She sighed, not even sure she'd gotten away with it. She supposed time would tell.

On a positive note, should any fingers point in Ronnie's direction, she knew there was no physical evidence to prove she was responsible; it would be Mrs Wright's word against hers. And better still, being up at such an ungodly hour meant Ronnie had arisen in plenty of time to hear number eight's initial reaction to *Operation Poltergeist*. Ronnie cocked her head, her attention suddenly diverted. "Speaking of which..."

Excitement swelled in Ronnie's chest as she caught sight of Gaye's car pulling up in front of next door's rear garage. Watching her and Nick disembark, Ronnie pushed her concerns about Mrs Wright to the back of her mind. Observing her neighbour pause to look up at the house, Ronnie delighted in Gaye's wariness. The woman clearly dreaded going inside. "Serves you right," Ronnie said.

Nick did his utmost to reassure Gaye, Ronnie noted. A kiss on the forehead here, a reassuring smile there, and a comforting hand at the small of the woman's back to guide her forward... Actions that Ronnie found both amusing and futile considering what they were about to be met with. She watched them disappear as they headed round to their front entrance, giving Ronnie enough time to open her kitchen window as she waited for the fallout. *Any minute now...*

Suddenly a loud shriek pierced the silence. Number eight's back door flew open and a frantic Gaye bolted into the garden. Ronnie almost spat out her coffee; her neighbour's response was more than she could have hoped for.

"We're being punished," Gaye said, her voice loaded with panic. "Paying for what we've done."

Nick appeared in the doorway. "Sweetheart, it's nothing of the sort."

Oh yes, it is, Ronnie thought.

"I'm telling you, we're being haunted," Gaye continued. "We need to get someone in. An expert. To cleanse the place."

Good luck with that. Because what you really need to do is move. Ronnie watched her ex-husband step forward to console Gaye, but the woman put her hands up, refusing to have any of it.

"Please don't try to tell me there's another simple explanation. Earthquakes, moving houses, whatever excuse you're about to offer... None of them result in fancy seating arrangements atop of tables, Nick." The woman was getting hysterical.

"I was going to suggest I ring Willow," Ronnie's ex replied. He was clearly trying to remain calm. "To see if she put them there."

"And why would she?"

"I don't know." Nick put a hand to his head, as if it somehow helped him think. "Maybe she spilled something and had to mop the floor?"

Gaye appeared less than impressed. "And if she didn't? If she's not responsible?"

She's not.

"Then will you believe me? Then will you accept there's a ghost in this house? Because even if Willow does admit she had something to do with this..."

She won't.

"That doesn't explain what happened the last time we were away."

Ronnie clamped her mouth shut to stop herself from laughing. Even she heard Nick's exasperated sigh.

"Just let me give her a call."

"Not until we've checked the rest of the house," Gaye said. "I'm telling you, this is the work of something far more sinister than your daughter."

Ronnie chuckled. *You got that right.*

She counted backwards again, except this time from ten, telling herself that that should give them enough time to get up to the bedroom. Ronnie smiled as she got to number one, ready for the anticipated scream that rang out from next door. "Try to explain that one away, Nicky boy."

23

R onnie stood at her front garden gate awaiting Willow and Bea's 10am arrival as instructed. She had no idea what the two of them had organised. She simply hoped that step number three in their plan was better than steps one and two. She could have kicked herself for not getting her own vehicle sorted. If she had she could have met them there and would know exactly what she had in store. *Oh well*, she thought. *There's nothing you can do about it now.*

She looked at her watch and as she wondered where they had gotten to, a car pulling up outside next door caught her eye. Ronnie glanced up – Nick's car. *Strange*, she thought. *Shouldn't he be at work?*

She knew from experience that the man would have a few choice words to impart, especially after her weekend endeavours in *Operation Poltergeist*. This time though, she was more than ready for him and she straightened her back and held her head high in anticipation of his onslaught. She giggled. That's if he could get past the sight of her shaven head. Ronnie smiled a satisfied smile while she waited for him to disembark. Not only could he say what he wanted about number eight's ghostly goings on because no-one could prove anything, Nick was in for one hell of a shock.

She watched him get out of his vehicle and as predicted, open his mouth to give her the what for. However, also as expected, nothing came out of it. "Nick," Ronnie said, greeting him with her biggest smile. She stood a little taller, unable to help but feel powerful as he gawped back in stunned silence. "How are you this fine morning?" She recalled the numerous occasions of late, when Nick had been more than capable of getting his words out. In those instances, insults and jibes had readily tripped off his tongue. Not that day though. For the first time since he left, he didn't know what to say. For once, it seemed Ronnie had the upper hand.

Nick continued to stare, as if his brain refused to believe what his eyes were seeing.

Ronnie had an idea he was questioning her sanity. In all the years she'd known him, it wasn't as if she'd made a habit of shaving off her hair. He probably thought she was having a nervous breakdown, she presumed, an assumption that could very well be of benefit. Ronnie was no expert in the mental health field, but she guessed taking the scissors and then a razor to her head suggested an element of unpredictability on her part. Enough for Nick to question what she might do next and, therefore, get the estate agents in? Ronnie certainly hoped so.

"Not at work today?" she asked, her politeness only freaking him out more.

Nick muttered something unintelligible in response, his disconcerted expression remaining as he reached into the back of his car and pulled out a box.

It's all right for some, Ronnie thought, taking in the fancy electrical equipment displayed on the cardboard. She couldn't even afford to get her car looked at.

Nick took another long hard stare at Ronnie before turning

and hastening towards Gaye's front door. Letting himself in, he slammed it shut behind him.

Amused by his actions, Ronnie laughed. Her bald head had certainly made an impact and her grin continued well after he disappeared from view. She laughed again. In twenty-five years, she didn't think she'd ever seen the man move so fast.

Returning her attention to the street, Ronnie at last spotted Willow's car approaching, her self-satisfaction continuing as it came to a standstill and she jumped in the back. Sensing an atmosphere, her smile faded and her eyes narrowed. "Everything okay?"

"Don't mind us," Willow replied, putting the car into gear and setting off again. "We're having a moan about Dad. I had the weirdest phone call from him, you wouldn't believe."

"Really?" Ronnie knew what it was regarding, of course, but did her best not to sound too interested.

"I didn't have a clue what he was saying. He just kept banging on about chairs on top of tables and beds that weren't made properly."

"I got the same when I spoke to him," Bea said. "I don't know what's going on in that house, but it's certainly making things a bit fraught."

"He seemed to think I had something to do with it," Willow said.

"Apparently Gaye's convinced the house is haunted," Bea continued. "Not that your dad's having any of it. He's probably blaming you, Willow, to shut her up."

Sitting there listening to them, Ronnie's naughty side relished the fact that her actions were making an impact and coupling that with Nick's face only moments before, she had to bite down on her lip to stop such delight from showing.

"I wish he'd never given me that damn key."

Ronnie was glad he had.

Naturally, a part of Ronnie felt bad that her daughter and mother-in-law were bearing the brunt of her antics. But, in truth, that was on Nick. He knew full well who was behind *Operation Poltergeist* so had no right to drag Willow and Bea into it. In fact, all he had to do was persuade Gaye into moving.

"What do you think, Mum?" Willow looked at Ronnie through her rear-view mirror. "Have you noticed any strange happenings next door?"

"Me? Nothing at all."

Bea turned to face Ronnie, her brow creased. "I must say, you do seem quiet on the subject. I thought you'd be loving the fact that all's not well between those two love birds." She let out a chuckle. "Call me terrible, but I know I am."

Ronnie smiled, wanting nothing more than to join in, to dissect every detail of Nick and Gaye's anguish. But one slip of her tongue would be enough to raise suspicion and the last thing Ronnie wanted was to drop herself in it. "I'm more concerned about where it is we're going," she replied, in a quick change of subject. "I don't know why you can't tell me."

Bea raised her hand and pretended to zip her lips shut, before returning her attention to the road ahead.

"Because it's a surprise," Willow said.

Unwanted images of the night Nick left flooded Ronnie's mind, her good mood diminishing as a result. "But you know I don't like surprises."

"You will this one," Bea replied. "I assure you."

Positive they'd said that last time, Ronnie wasn't convinced.

24

Ronnie stared out of the car window, hoping the journey would give her some sort of clue, but street after street, none was forthcoming. Ronnie sighed. If she'd thought knowing exactly what Willow and Bea had in store for her was bad enough, not knowing felt worse. After step one's gym incident and step two's hair salon debacle, Ronnie couldn't help but worry about what they had planned. As things stood, she could be walking into anything.

Willow drove out of town and into the countryside and, gazing out at green field after green field, Ronnie's concerns went into overdrive. She prayed they hadn't wasted their money and booked her onto one of those outward-bound events. In her view, not only were her confidence levels fine, thank you very much, she had no team upon which to build. Treetop obstacle courses and scaling rock faces were nothing like climbing a stepladder and would do zilch for her acrophobia. And as far as canoeing, windsurfing, or indeed *any* kind of water sport was concerned, they could offer her all the chocolate in Willy Wonka's factory and she still wouldn't take part.

As the car slowed and Willow took a left, Ronnie began to

feel a tad warm. Her nerves coming to the fore, she crossed her fingers in the hope that her fears weren't about to be realised. Making their way down a narrow lane, however, she spotted a sign that read *Woodhaven Dog Rescue Centre.* "What are we doing here?" she asked, as the car pulled into its car park.

Willow unclipped her seat belt before turning to face Ronnie with a smile. "Why do people normally come to these places?"

"Come on," Bea said. Coming over a tad excited, she was obviously keen to get going. "Let's go and give a dog a home."

As the other two headed off, Ronnie realised she couldn't simply sit there. "But I don't want a dog," she said, climbing out of the vehicle.

"Yes, you do," her daughter called back. "You just haven't realised it yet."

Staring at the building before her, Ronnie imagined the amount of poop scooping and all-weather walking that came with owning a dog. She whimpered. Suddenly the outward-bound course seemed a goer.

Ronnie sighed, dragging her feet like a reluctant teenager as she followed her daughter and mother-in-law into the centre's reception area. Willow had already explained who they were and why they were there by the time Ronnie joined them.

While professional, the volunteer, Carla, according to her name badge, responded with a mix of gratitude and enthusiasm. "If you'd like to come this way," she said, heading for a door off to one side. She held it open for Ronnie, Willow and Bea to step through, the sound of incessant barking suddenly assaulting their ears. "I'll be here for a chat when you've made your decision." Clearly used to the noise, Carla didn't flinch.

Ronnie entered the dog kennelling area, almost too nervous to step forward for fear of what she was about to see – abandoned dog after dog, desperate for attention. She took in two lines of kennels, one down the left of the room and one down the right, each fronted by floor-to-ceiling metal bars. To Ronnie they resembled rows of prison cells and thanks to the concrete floor and grimy plastered walls, the whole room looked grey and dismal. It didn't only look depressing, it felt it. The sound of yapping and woofing bounced off the walls, but Ronnie couldn't blame the dogs for the echoing clamour. She'd be desperate to get out of there too.

"Come on, Mum," Willow said, guiding Ronnie forward. "And take as much time as you like."

Ronnie felt a sadness come over her as she made her way up one side of the room to go back down the other. Faced with dogs of most breeds, mixes and sizes, there were so many of them it was almost too much for Ronnie to bear. Of course she wanted to give one of them a home, she told herself. How could she not? Some scratted at the metal bars, yowling and yapping, desperate for her attention; some didn't see her at all as they chased their tails or jumped up at their kennel walls over and over, thanks to either madness or boredom; while others sat huddled in piles of old blankets, too scared or too used to rejection to move.

Each enclosure had a write-up attached. Some of the animals could be rehomed in families with cats and children, some most definitely couldn't. Wondering what each had been through, Ronnie found the whole place distressing and, soaking up their desperation, wished she could give every dog in there a new place to live. She identified with them. She knew what it was like to be tossed aside, to be no longer loved or wanted.

With Willow and Bea close behind, Ronnie at last reached the final kennel. Standing there staring at the dog within, a tear rolled down her cheek. "This is the one," she said to her daughter and mother-in-law.

"This one?" Willow said, as if needing to clarify.

"Are you sure?" Bea said, sounding doubtful.

Ronnie smiled at the dog looking back, a gesture that appeared to be reciprocated.

She crouched to its level, calmly observing the yellow Labrador. Sat a few feet in, it took a couple of steps forward, before sitting back down again. Ronnie waited patiently as the dog repeated its action. It was as if the dog needed to approach Ronnie in stages rather than wholeheartedly commit.

Ronnie didn't mind. Plonking her bum down on the concrete, she thought it safe to say the dog had probably been at Woodhaven for quite some time. She took in its warm friendly eyes that sat unnaturally close together, the thick vertical fold of skin protruding from its forehead, and the tongue lolloping out of the side of its mouth.

"It says here his name's Charlie," Willow said, reading the dog's information sheet. "He looks the way he does because of a receding skull."

"You're beautiful," Ronnie said.

Finally, the dog came close enough to touch.

Poking her fingers through the bars, Ronnie laughed as Charlie leaned in, all the while encouraging Ronnie to rub the side of his face.

"Would you like to come and live with me?" Ronnie asked.

She looked up at her daughter and mother-in-law. "So, what happens now?"

25

R onnie stood in the lounge bay window waiting for Willow and Bea to arrive. A part of her wished she was going on her own, but Willow seemed keen for them all to attend. Ronnie knew it would have been mean to say no, especially when getting Charlie had been the result of her daughter and mother-in-law's plan. Ronnie struggled to contain her excitement. That day was the day they could bring Charlie home.

She and Charlie had forged quite a friendship. Since their first meeting, Ronnie had risked driving her car to visit him almost daily, spoiling him with meaty treats both before and after their long bonding walks. Ronnie had even gotten used to the less-attractive aspects of dog ownership; she had poo bags in every pocket and had even purchased a full set of waterproofs.

Looking forward to picking him up, Ronnie glanced around the living room, wondering what Charlie would make of his accommodation. She took in the new dog bed and collection of dog-friendly toys awaiting him. She smiled. Like Carla had said on her home visit, Charlie was going to love it.

Ready far too early, Ronnie looked out onto the street, something she had to admit she'd done a lot of in recent months; staring out, watching the world go by instead of joining in with everything it had to offer. The trouble was, when it came to forging a new life for herself and herself alone, she didn't know where to start.

She wondered how different things might have been had she had an inkling that all wasn't well between her and Nick. The outcome may have been the same, but at least she would have had the opportunity to consider a future without him. She could have imagined herself as an individual in her own right, instead of merely one half of a couple. As things were, Ronnie and Nick had been together so long, his departure seemed to leave her not only without a husband, but without an identity.

She considered the support she'd received from her daughter and mother-in-law. Feeling guilty, she realised she'd been wrong to mock their six-step plan, that she should have trusted them. Steps one and two might have been complete failures, but at least they'd tried. As for step three, Ronnie had to admit it was the best thing that had happened to her in quite some time.

She knew some would think her strange for relying so heavily on Willow and Bea, that most women her age had a solid group of friends around them. But aside from her daughter and mother-in-law, there'd never been anyone else. And when it came to her and Nick, it never seemed to matter that it was just the two of them.

Looking back, it was as if her life hadn't started until she met her husband. Indeed, she often joked that she'd been married since she was a foetus. Everyone laughed in response of course but deep down, Ronnie knew that that was her way of keeping the past where it belonged. Life with an abusive and attention-seeking mother wasn't exactly something to brag about. It was something Ronnie did her utmost to forget.

Ronnie found herself questioning if deep down that was why she had married Nick? If falling pregnant had given her the excuse she needed to get away from a dysfunctional household. It had clearly crossed Nick's mind on occasion, because he'd asked her about it once; a question that had offended her at the time. As far as she'd been concerned, she loved Nick from the moment she met him. Subconsciously, however, who knew what the truth was? Perhaps he had been her saviour and she'd simply never wanted to admit it.

Fed up with her own thoughts, Ronnie told herself to stop dissecting the past and enjoy the present. Shaking herself out of it, she thought the last thing Charlie needed was to end up living in an atmosphere as miserable as the one he was leaving. From that point on, she told herself, it was onwards and upwards, for the yellow Lab's sake as well as her own.

She looked out onto Holme Lea Avenue, wondering what her neighbours would think of the new addition to her family. She couldn't wait for them to meet Charlie, and easily imagined herself introducing him to each and every resident. She smiled. When it came to building a new and positive future, maybe that yellow Labrador was her saviour too.

Unable to stand there any longer, Ronnie headed out of the room, grabbing her coat, bag and Charlie's lead from the hall as she made her way outside. She had a spring in her step as she walked along the path to her gate, eager to get going. She and her dog were going to have so much fun together.

Putting on her coat in readiness, a car horn beeped, signalling Willow and Bea's arrival. Ronnie jumped up and down in excitement. "Not long now, Charlie. I'm coming to get you."

26

"We're so pleased he's finally found a home," Carla said, escorting Ronnie and Charlie out to the car park. She crouched down to give the dog a fuss. "He's been here for so long and deserves a new start, don't you, boy?" She rose to her feet again. "If you wouldn't mind letting us know how he's getting on. Once in a while. We're all so fond of him, it'll be strange not having him around."

"Of course," Ronnie replied. "I wouldn't dream of not keeping you up to date. And I promise, from now on, he'll have the best life ever." She took in Charlie's adorable misshapen face, his lolloping tongue and wagging tail. Letting out a bark and pulling on his lead, he seemed as eager to get to his new home as Ronnie was to take him there. "And thank you," she added. "For everything."

"No, thank you."

While Carla headed back inside, Ronnie led Charlie towards their awaiting vehicle.

"Here he is," Willow said, adopting the kind of voice usually reserved for babies. She hunkered down to give the dog an all-embracing cuddle. "Who's a good boy?"

Shaking her head, Bea opened the car door in readiness of their departure, letting out a laugh when Charlie suddenly abandoned his hug in favour of jumping straight onto the back seat. "Someone's ready to go."

"And who can blame him," Ronnie said, thinking about his life up to that point. "What the...?" As she was about to climb in alongside the dog, a car raced into the car park. Coming to a sudden halt right next to Willow's vehicle, Ronnie, her daughter and mother-in-law had to leap back out of harm's way. Ronnie glowered, wondering what on earth the lunatic behind the wheel was playing at?

The driver jumped out. "I haven't missed him, have I? I meant to get here sooner but got held up at work."

"Jack?" Ronnie said, her annoyance quickly replaced by confusion.

"Ronnie?" Jack said, appearing equally as bemused. "You mean...?" His gaze went from her, and as he ducked his head, to the inside of Willow's car, and spotting the yellow Lab his face immediately lit up. "You're Charlie's new owner? That's fantastic."

"But I..."

"Sorry about the grand entrance, I didn't want him to leave without me saying goodbye. When it comes to special dogs like Charlie, I tend to get a bit attached."

Ronnie's confusion continued.

"You mean you don't know? Of course, you don't. Why would you? They held an adoption day here a while back. It was a big community event and me being the local bobby, the powers that be insisted I got involved. Anyway, after that I started volunteering. You know, cleaning out kennels, spending time with the dogs to help with socialising, that kind of thing."

"What? At Woodhaven?"

"Yep. A man's got to have something to do in his downtime,"

Jack said. "And this one..." He reached into the back seat and rubbed Charlie's head. "I know you shouldn't have favourites, but well, you know."

Ronnie smiled. Watching Charlie relish the attention, the dog obviously adored Jack in return.

"I'm really going to miss you, boy," Jack said.

"How could anyone not fall in love with him?" Ronnie replied.

Jack suddenly shifted on his feet. Stuffing his hands into his pockets, it was as if he felt a tad awkward all of a sudden. "If it's not overstepping the mark, do you think I could come and visit him sometime? Take him for a walk, if you're busy with work? We could even walk him together. If you're up for that?"

Observing Jack's sincerity, Ronnie couldn't help but smile. *A gentle giant who happens to love animals*, she thought. Surely Jack Shenton was too good to be true? A romantic image of the three of them, out in the fresh air, enjoying the wild outdoors, appeared in her mind's eye and in that moment, she'd have liked nothing more. "That would be lovely."

Jack grinned. "Great. It's a date."

Ronnie blushed. However, not only had *she* picked up on his choice of wording, so had Willow and Bea. Ronnie could feel their eyes boring into the back of her head and hear their giggling. The two of them were, no doubt, reading more into the situation than Jack intended.

"Hang on a second," he said. "I'll be back in a tick."

While Jack ran towards Woodhaven's reception, disappearing inside, Ronnie took the opportunity to throw her daughter and mother-in-law a look. "You two are so embarrassing," she said, willing them to stop sniggering.

.   .   .

"Take this," Jack said on his return, holding out a scrap of paper. "It's my number."

"Oh," Ronnie replied, not quite sure what else to say.

"Give me a call when you're ready to organise that dog walk." He began heading back towards the building, turning to face Ronnie again as he got to the door. "Or anything else you might fancy," he called back, with a wink.

As Jack disappeared, Ronnie's cheeks reddened again. This time it wasn't only what he'd said, it was also the way he'd said it. And in front of her daughter and mother-in-law too. Ronnie cringed, closing her eyes for a second before turning to face them. As expected, she could tell by their grins they weren't going to let her live the man's remark down.

"Wow," Willow said. "How much does that man fancy you?"

"Rubbish," Ronnie replied, ignoring the butterflies fluttering around in her tummy. Doing her best to dismiss the idea, she climbed onto the seat next to Charlie.

"I think you'll find he does," Willow added.

Willow and Bea got in the front, before putting on their seat belts ready for the drive back to Holme Lea Avenue.

"There's no *think* about it," Bea said. "All that talk about joint dog walks." She reached into the back, giving Charlie a pat on the head. "You're just his ruse, aren't you, sweetie? He's using you to get to Mummy."

Embarrassed enough already, Ronnie shook her head.

"And that wink at the end," Willow said. "There was no denying what that meant."

"No wonder he hand-delivered your sketchbook that time. Talk about any excuse. Although I must say, he's a bit of all right," Bea said. "You could do worse."

Ronnie knew it was wishful thinking, but she wanted the conversation to end.

"I agree." Willow looked at Ronnie through her rear-view mirror. "Make sure you keep hold of that number, Mum."

Ronnie sighed, resigned to the fact that neither of them was going to leave it. "I knew as soon as Jack opened his mouth, the two of you would be like this. And don't think I couldn't hear your childish sniggering."

"I'm not sure how I feel about having a police officer for a stepdad though," Willow continued.

"What are you talking about now?" Ronnie couldn't believe what she was hearing.

Bea cocked her head. "What relation would he be to me when they get married?"

"He's not going to be anything to either of you," Ronnie said, but she was clearly talking to herself.

"Yeah, right," Willow said as she started up the engine.

Charlie let out a bark.

"See, even he agrees with me."

"Charlie wants to go home," Ronnie replied, giving him a fuss.

Willow put the car into gear and drove away from Woodhaven. "Anyone would think we didn't see the way you two looked at each other."

"All coy and innocent," Bea said, backing her granddaughter up. "Batting your eyelids at the bloke like there was no tomorrow."

Ronnie almost spluttered. "I did nothing of the sort. Besides, you couldn't have seen that. I had my back to you the whole time."

"I think the lady protesteth too much," Bea said, staring out at the road ahead.

"So do I," Willow said, doing the same.

27

Ronnie pulled up outside number six after enjoying a long energising walk with Charlie. A couple of hours rambling in open countryside was perfect for blowing away the cobwebs.

Since Charlie's adoption, the two of them had explored all the locality had to offer. They'd toured the local parks, pavement pounded through the streets and headed out into the country to roam free over hill and dale. Ronnie hadn't quite appreciated how much natural beauty she had on her doorstep before. A mere five-minute drive, albeit in a dodgy car, and they were wandering through green field after green field.

Ronnie's favourite spot was up at the old gigantic viaduct. No longer in use, its long-neglected rail track had become popular amongst walkers and she could understand why. It was like a pathway into the skies. The views it provided went on for miles and Ronnie especially enjoyed taking a couple of minutes to just stand and stare; she felt in awe of the vista, it created a real sense of time and distance.

Sometimes, if she and Charlie went early enough, the fields below would be covered in a blanket of mist and Ronnie would pretend she was standing above the clouds. Because no-one else was daft enough to be out and about at that time of the morning, she'd shout into the void, getting rid of her frustrations. She'd even encourage Charlie to join in, but he simply looked up at her with his adorable smile. He probably thought she was going mad and much preferred to sniff the ground around him, never wandering more than a few feet from Ronnie. He'd become her extra shadow.

Ronnie climbed out of the car then opened the rear door so Charlie could make his exit. "Come on, boy," she said, as he hopped out, his tail wagging as usual. Ronnie smiled. He'd settled into his new life better than she could have anticipated. He seemed to have a permanent grin on his face, one that Ronnie refused to believe had anything to do with his disfigurement. A belief that was backed up by all who Charlie encountered, his big wide smile touched everybody.

As Ronnie headed up the garden path, Mr Wright appeared at his front door. "I'm glad I've caught you," he called out, heading straight for number six. "I have something for Charlie." He held out a gift that had been wrapped in newspaper. "Just a little something Mrs Wright picked up from the butchers. I must say he's made quite an impression on that wife of mine."

Ronnie smiled in appreciation. "Thank you." Accepting the package, she could see she wasn't the only one to guess it was a rather large bone. Charlie flitted around Ronnie's legs, desperate to get his paws on the juicy marrow. "I'm sure he's going to love getting his teeth into this."

"Would you like a cup of tea?" Ronnie asked. Being a Thursday, she knew from their previous chat that Mrs Wright would be out for lunch with her sister, and Ronnie didn't see the point in him sitting over the way on his own.

"Don't mind if I do. If you're not too busy, that is?"

"Not at all. Come on in."

Opening the front door, Ronnie dropped Charlie's lead by the stairs and led the way down the hall to the kitchen. "Which would you prefer? Tea or coffee?"

"A tea would do nicely."

Ronnie put on the kettle, took out a couple of mugs from the cupboard and popped a teabag in each. "Please," she said, indicating to the table and chairs. "Sit down." She unwrapped the bone. "Look at this, Charlie."

Charlie wagged his tail, excited at the offering.

"Especially for you from our kind neighbour here."

As soon as Ronnie placed it on the floor, Charlie whipped it away. He headed to a corner of the room, ready to tuck in. Ronnie stood for a second, watching the dog's lip-smacking, gentle gnawing.

Leaving Charlie to it, Ronnie finished making the tea, handing her neighbour his mug as she joined him at the table. "So how are things with you, Mr Wright?"

"Harry. Please. Anything else seems far too formal."

Ronnie smiled, remembering the fact that he'd corrected her for that the last time he visited. "Apologies. Harry it is."

"You know me. Fit as a fiddle." He took a sip of his tea, as if needing a moment to consider his next words. "Mrs Wright though, I'm afraid that's a different story."

"Really?" Having spoken to her only a few days prior, Ronnie was surprised to hear Harry's wife was unwell. They'd talked about the weather, the new supermarket opening in town, and Mrs Wright had given Charlie a right old fuss. The woman wasn't only chattier than normal, she'd seemed perfectly fine. "How so?"

"Oh, physically she's all right. Strong as an ox, that one. I'm more concerned about what's going on up here." He lifted a hand, using his index finger to tap the side of his head.

Again, Ronnie considered her conversation with Mrs Wright.

Ronnie frowned. As well as appearing in good bodily health, her neighbour seemed mentally on the ball too. "I'm sorry to hear that," Ronnie replied. "I haven't noticed anything untoward."

Mr Wright lowered his voice. "She thinks she's seeing things."

Ronnie's heart skipped a beat. She drank a big mouthful of tea, hiding her face behind her mug as she recalled her last visit into number eight. She pictured her poor neighbour looking straight into Gaye's bedroom window, as Ronnie looked back in her paper suit. "What kind of things?" Ronnie asked, hoping Mrs Wright's failing mental health was unrelated.

"Spirits. Ghosts. Whatever it is they're called these days."

Ronnie almost whimpered.

"Of course, I told her she was talking rubbish."

"Of course," Ronnie repeated.

"I said I've never heard anything so daft in my life." He took another sip of tea. "I've never believed in any of that stuff. In my view, once we're gone, we're gone."

"Quite."

"The woman was adamant she'd seen something though. Of course, we just had to figure out what that something was. I mean, there had to be some plausible explanation."

Ronnie crossed her fingers in the hope that any conclusion didn't involve her. "And was there?" she asked, not really sure she wanted Mr Wright to continue.

"That's the thing. She said the more she thought about it, the more she realised she wasn't looking at a vision in white at all." He drank some more tea. "She was looking at you."

Ronnie froze. "Me?" Mrs Wright hadn't said a word to her about any of this.

"Yes. In next door's front bedroom of all places."

28

W illing herself not to appear guilty, Ronnie let out a pretend laugh. Her neighbour, however, remained deadly serious. Ronnie swallowed hard, reminding herself that Mrs Wright could make as many claims as she wanted, there was no physical evidence to put Ronnie inside next door. "I don't know why she'd think that," Ronnie said.

Mr Wright suddenly smiled her way, but any joy he tried to portray failed to show in his eyes; they seemed to say something different altogether. Ronnie's discomfort increased as she wondered where he was taking their little chat. She put down her cup and, resting her forearms on the table, breathed a little deeper.

"I suggested she might be imagining things, but Mrs Wright does know her own mind."

Ronnie scoffed to herself. Only a moment before, he was suggesting the woman didn't. Ronnie recalled her mother-in-law's prior conversation about the vultures that circled following the death of Nick's dad. Bea had cautioned her about Mr Wright, and it was beginning to sound like Ronnie should have listened.

"And she was having none of it."

Wherever their talk was headed, Ronnie knew from his expression that he thought he had the upper hand. However, she was done with men thinking they could get the better of her. Mr Wright clearly expected a reaction, a sign of panic or desperation from Ronnie, but she refused to give him the satisfaction. Instead, she sat silently staring back at him, remaining outwardly calm as she listened to what he had to say on the matter. She thought it strange how she'd never noticed the droplets of spittle in the corners of his mouth before. Or clocked the creepy tone of the voice coming out of it. Every word sounded unnecessarily drawn out. He was obviously getting something out of Ronnie's unease, even if she was trying to hide it.

"And then when I heard about the funny stuff going on next door, it was easy to put two and two together. You, the spurned wife. Gaye the other woman..."

Again, Ronnie refused to react.

"Mrs Wright was all for going over and telling number eight what she saw. Naturally, I persuaded her not to. Well, you don't, do you? Interfere in other people's business?" He reached over and placed a hand over Ronnie's.

Staring at the palm wrapped around her fingers, Ronnie felt sick. Her skin crawled under the man's touch.

"Of course, I could convince her I was wrong. Tell her that I think differently now, that she should be honest, having had the chance to think about it. I mean, why keep a secret if there's no reward?"

Continuing to stare at Mr Wright's hand, Ronnie let their conversation sink in. Bile rose in her throat as she considered what Mr Wright was suggesting. Sex for his and Mrs Wright's silence. Anger welled inside of her, while pictures of the ever-so-respectable Mr Wright flitted through her mind. The way he opened car doors for his wife, held her hand in the street and chatted amiably with his neighbours like any good fellow would. When all along he was a predator. A predator wearing a mask.

The room fell silent apart from Charlie's bone chomping; a bone that Ronnie wanted to snatch from the yellow Lab and ram down Mr Wright's throat. She looked from the man's hand, to his face. Taking in his smug expression, he still seemed to think he had the upper hand.

She slid her palm from underneath Mr Wright's. "Do this often?" Ronnie asked. "Blackmail women for sex?"

Mr Wright licked his lips. "What you see as blackmail, I see as *coming to an arrangement.*"

Ronnie scoffed. "Phrase it how you want, Mr Wright, but you're still a dirty old man. Someone who resorts to extortion to get your leg over." Ronnie knew she sounded vulgar, but that's exactly what the situation she found herself in was. "I'm guessing it isn't the first time you've done this? Watching and waiting, until the time is ripe. But I'm not the vulnerable little woman you had me down for, Mr Wright. I think your wife's alleged visions should have told you that."

Mr Wright opened his mouth to say something, but Ronnie had long heard enough from him.

"Excuse me, you've had your say. Now I'm talking."

She watched the man squirm. He clearly wasn't used to being silenced.

"I mean on the one hand, I'm vindictive. I'm somehow sneaking into next door's house with the sole intent of causing mayhem. Yet on the other, I'm a walkover. An easy target." She let out a laugh. "That's not only a contradiction, Mr Wright, that's sheer stupidity."

Ronnie watched the colour drain from his face. "So, feel free to tell next door what you think I've been up to. March Mrs Wright over there right now, if you must. Because I defy anyone to try to prove it. And besides, proof or no proof, I think you'll find I'm the one who'll get the sympathy. You said it yourself, jilted wife and all that. Of course, that's when I'll add my little story into the mix. The one about the kindly old neighbour who, beneath that gentlemanly façade, turns out to be anything but. A man who preys on susceptible women for a bit of you know what." Her tone turned mocking. "Naturally, a man like that *would* invent tales and spread malicious lies if he doesn't get what he wants, wouldn't he?"

She watched Mr Wright turn grey, but Ronnie wasn't done with him yet. "And we both know how the neighbours on this street operate. They love a good gossip. But tittle-tattle is one thing, living next door to a pervert... well, we both know that could lead to a lot more than talk." Ronnie drank a mouthful of tea, enjoying the sense of satisfaction she suddenly felt. "Of course, it's Mrs Wright I feel sorry for. I mean, the shame if it ever got out."

Ronnie put a false smile on her face and rose to her feet. "Now, I think it's time you left. Don't you?"

29

Ronnie leant against the kitchen counter, with Mr Wright's visit still heavy on her mind. He might have heeded her warning and kept shtum over her visits into number eight, but that didn't make Ronnie feel any less angry. She shuddered, her skin continuing to crawl at the thought of his intentions. She couldn't report him to the police and she didn't have anyone to talk to about it, a problem halved being a problem shared and all that. Confiding would mean divulging what she'd been up to, leaving her in a no-win situation. Ronnie sighed. It seemed Mr Wright's secret was as safe as her own.

Realising things in the garden had gone a little too quiet, Ronnie cocked her head. Her eyes narrowed; she didn't have to guess what that dog of hers was up to. "Not again, Charlie," she said, stepping out through the back door. As he bounded towards her, Ronnie looked down at the dog's muddy nose and dirt sodden feet. "Carry on like this and you'll end up in Australia."

She turned her gaze to the Limelight Hydrangea in the far corner. One of the reasons she'd planted it was because it was robust and called for little by way of care. With its soil kept moist, it had done a good job of looking after itself over the years. Although thanks to Charlie, that robustness was being sorely tested. Having grown to about eight feet tall and goodness knew how wide, whatever was living in there, it seemed the yellow Lab was determined to evict it. Every time Ronnie let Charlie into the garden, he'd disappear inside the hydrangea's thick green foliage, digging and scratting like his life depended on it. She took a deep breath and slowly exhaled, forced to acknowledge the inevitable. As much as Ronnie loved its white bulbous flowers, the time had come to cut it back.

Glancing around the whole of her outdoor space, Ronnie had to admit that with everything going on of late, the flora and fauna had been utterly neglected. The bit of lawn she had needed a good mowing, the containers needed planting up, and the pathways could have done with a top up of gravel. "And you're certainly not helping matters," she said, once again taking in Charlie's dirty feet. She ruffled the top of his head. "Come on. You know the drill."

Ronnie grabbed the hosepipe that lay slung beneath the outdoor tap sticking out of the kitchen's exterior wall. Cleaning Charlie's paws had become such a regular occurrence, she'd given up on painstakingly coiling the metres and metres of green tubing around its stand.

"There you are," Willow said, suddenly appearing at the door.

About to start washing Charlie's feet, Ronnie looked up, surprised.

Willow immediately gave the dog a fuss. "I wondered where you'd both got to."

"To what do I owe the pleasure?" Ronnie said, putting the pipe back down to give her daughter a hug.

"I haven't come to see you," Willow replied. "I'm here for Charlie. I thought he might like to go for a walk."

Tempted to ask if her daughter was feeling okay, Ronnie narrowed her eyes, suspicious. There had to be an ulterior motive. After all, Willow hadn't only inherited Ronnie's looks, she'd inherited her dislike for all things exercise. "You? Walking?"

"Yes, me," her daughter said, her face serious.

Ronnie still wasn't buying it. "You, the woman who drives everywhere? The woman who thinks having no car is the same as having no legs?"

Willow laughed. "I'd have said the same about you until Charlie came along. Let's just say that I, too, have re-evaluated."

Ronnie raised an eyebrow. Whatever her daughter was up to, it had nothing to do with getting fit or spending time with their new family member.

"Oh, all right," Willow said, crumpling under her mother's gaze. "There's this gorgeous guy who walks his dog in the local park. And we know how everyone loves this handsome chap?" Again, she rubbed Charlie's head. "So I thought..."

"What? My dog can sidle up to Penny the poodle, so you can do the same with Mr Whateverhisnameis?" Ronnie laughed, half amused and half affronted. "Since when did Charlie turn into your wingman?"

"When you put it like that."

"How else am I supposed to put it?"

Willow sat down on the doorstep, her expression all at once teasing. "I suppose I could always stay here and keep you company. We can talk about PC Whateverhisnameis instead, if you prefer?"

Ronnie preferred nothing of the sort.

"Which reminds me, have you rung him yet? Although I

can't say I'm pleased that he's allowed to walk your dog when I'm not."

Ronnie ignored her daughter's wittering in favour of getting on with washing Charlie's paws. She picked up the hosepipe again, ready to get started.

"Mum, I know what you're doing."

"What do you mean?"

Willow took the green hose from her mother's hand. "You're doing exactly what you just accused me of. Using Charlie, except in your case it's to avoid answering my question."

Ronnie sighed. "No," she said, with no choice but to answer. "I haven't rung him yet."

"Why not?"

"Because if he really wants to take Charlie out like he said, he knows where to find him."

"Oh, please tell me you're not that naive? Him giving you his number wasn't only about a dog walk. He's as interested in you as he is in man's best friend."

Ronnie took the hosepipe back, turned on the tap and began washing the yellow Lab's feet. She didn't want to think about Jack or any other member of the opposite sex for that matter. When it came to men, Mr Wright had tipped her over the edge. She'd had her fill of them all.

"Anyone would think you didn't deserve some fun," Willow carried on regardless. "And you can't deny Jack seems a nice bloke."

Ronnie thought about how nice Mr Wright had seemed and look how wrong that turned out to be. She'd been living opposite a sexual predator for years and hadn't had one iota. "Don't they all," she said.

"If you're referring to Dad."

She wasn't.

"No-one's talking about a full-on relationship. I'm not trying to marry you off here, Mum."

"I should hope not."

"Then give him a call."

Ronnie knew her daughter meant well, but things didn't feel as simple as Willow made them sound. Ronnie had always considered herself a good judge of character, but thanks to Mr Wright, she'd seen first-hand how far people could go to hide their true personalities. She didn't want to think Jack was wearing a guise of any kind, pretending to be someone he wasn't. She wanted to believe he was genuine, and that Willow was right when she said Jack liked Ronnie. But because of her elderly neighbour, it was as if Ronnie couldn't trust her own judgement anymore, let alone anyone else's.

"You know what your problem is, Mum? You're too all or nothing. When what you need is a bit of excitement. You need to dip your toe in the water, to take a risk every once in a while."

Ronnie and Willow's conversation was abruptly interrupted when the sound of number eight's back door opening caught their attention.

"I still don't see why we have to go out for lunch," Gaye said, from over the fence. "I can just as easily rustle up something here."

"Because it will do you good to get out and about," Nick said.

Ronnie's back stiffened at the sound of her ex's voice. *Another man who knows how to wear a mask*, she thought. She shook her head as she listened to the cheek of him. During their marriage, Ronnie had spent hour after hour in her studio, hardly seeing the light of day, and never once had he shown her such understanding.

"You've been cooped up for long enough."

Ronnie rolled her eyes.

"But what if...?"

"There aren't any *ifs*. Nothing's going to happen."

"How do you know?"

"I simply do, that's all."

Ronnie recalled her ex's threat to ring the police if she ever stepped foot inside number eight again, the way he'd spat his words out and that never-before-seen pulsating tic. The man clearly had a lot of confidence in his bully-boy tactics. However, if he thought Ronnie would ignore an opportunity when she saw one, he had another thing coming.

"We could even do a spot of shopping afterwards?" he suggested. "Maybe check out that new boutique in town?"

Please say yes, please say yes, Ronnie thought.

"I suppose I am starting to feel a bit stir crazy," Gaye replied.

Willow shook her head. "Typical," she mouthed.

"Well then. Let me get rid of that..." Nick said.

Ronnie could almost hear the man's smile.

"While you grab your coat."

Footsteps sounded down next door's garden path, followed by a swishing of plastic as Nick threw something into their wheelie bin. As the bin lid dropped shut, he made his way back inside, before number eight's door closed shut again.

"Sounds like someone still thinks the house is haunted," Willow said.

"It does, indeed," Ronnie replied, pensive.

Ronnie had put all thoughts of *Operation Poltergeist* to the back of her mind of late; continuing seemed too risky. But having just heard Nick and Gaye's little *tête-à-tête*, she suddenly found herself excited to get it going again. Ronnie smiled at her daughter. "About that dog walk?"

30

"Make sure you look after him," Ronnie called out to Willow.

"I will," her daughter replied. "And don't forget, I'm bringing Grandmother back too."

With an envelope on the cards, how could Ronnie forget?

Ronnie watched Willow drive off, with Charlie safely ensconced on the back seat. Observing them until they disappeared from view, Ronnie stepped back inside the house, closed the front door and locked it. A steeliness came over her as she headed straight upstairs. If she'd meant business before, that was nothing to how she felt in that moment.

Thanks to Mrs Wright, Ronnie had been in two minds as to whether she should carry on with *Operation Poltergeist*, an indecision made worse following Mr Wright's visit. From that point on it felt too chancy, what with a harassment warning hanging over Ronnie's head. Hearing Nick and Gaye's conversation though, made Ronnie more determined than ever to see it through. Nick was her ex-husband, for goodness sake, she shouldn't have to listen to him sucking up to his new woman. She shouldn't have to listen to them at all.

Ronnie frowned as she recalled Nick's tone. The concern he'd shown for Gaye. The man hadn't even considered the possibility that his wife and daughter might be on the other side of the fence. Then again, Ronnie supposed, *considerate* wasn't exactly in an adulterer's nature. She scoffed. She'd show not only him, but everyone.

It was as if *Operation Poltergeist* had taken on a whole new meaning. As far as Ronnie was concerned, her antics were no longer solely about getting Nick and Gaye to move. They represented payback not only for herself, but for spurned wives, husbands and partners everywhere. They were retribution for the Mrs Wrights on the planet and all the victims who fell prey to the likes of that poor woman's husband. In the world of adultery, Ronnie was a superhero.

Entering her bedroom, she donned her paper forensic suit, new socks and hairnet, before grabbing the stepladder from under her bed. Making her way into the loft, she felt remarkably relaxed as she took out the bricks in the dividing wall. As she crawled into next door, she knew not to take any unnecessary risks and, therefore, limited her plans to the back of the house where she could work unseen. She smiled before climbing down onto Gaye's landing, heading straight for the kitchen.

Unlike on previous occasions when Ronnie had ventured into number eight, her heart wasn't racing. As she opened the cupboard doors, there was no breaking into a sweat or any sense of panic, just a cool, calm and collected knowledge that she had a lot to do and had to work quickly.

She took in the shelves of neatly stored crockery and, beginning with the cups, with each handle pointing to the right, Ronnie set about redirecting them, so everything pointed to the left. Next came the plates, side plates and bowls, stacked in that exact order. Ronnie happily swapped them around, so the plates sat to the top of the ensemble and the bowls changed to the bottom. Pan handles were also repositioned from right to left and tins of food were flipped upside down. And turning her attention to the kitchen drawers, knives, forks and spoons became spoons, forks and knives, and rolled up tea towels were refolded into neat, flat squares. Ronnie chuckled. For someone like Gaye, with her need for precision, Ronnie's handiwork was going to be a nightmare.

Ensuring all cupboard doors and drawer fronts were closed, exactly as she had found them, Ronnie wondered if Nick and Gaye were enjoying their lunch. *Probably not*, she thought, feeling smug. Gaye would be too busy worrying about what she might get home to, leaving Nick no choice but to keep reassuring her. Ronnie imagined Gaye pushing a leafy salad or piece of salmon around her plate, her stomach in too much turmoil to let her eat anything, while Nick, a man who loved his food, picked at his fare, in a resentful show of solidarity.

Ronnie smiled as she left the room, her work for the day over. Making her way upstairs and back into number six, she couldn't wait for Nick and Gaye to get home so she could enjoy the spoils of her labour. Ronnie sniggered as she pictured the scene. Their response was going to be fantastic.

31

Ronnie checked the shepherd's pie in the oven. She hoped Willow and Bea were hungry as she'd made enough to feed an army. Something Charlie would, no doubt, be pleased about; that meant more leftovers for him.

Staring in at the crispy mashed potato topping, Ronnie was surprised she'd managed to put a meal together at all. After her trip into next door, she'd had to reply to a couple of surprising e-mails; potential customers requesting bespoke handbags for various upmarket events. It seemed the mother-of-the-bride was so pleased with her velvet clutch she'd been recommending Ronnie's services to friends in the market for a new bag. Ronnie smiled. For the first time in a while, life seemed to be on the up.

The front door opened and Charlie bounded in and down the hall. Ronnie welcomed his attention; he might only have been gone a couple of hours or so, but it was safe to say she'd missed him. "Did you have a good time, boy?" Crouching down to welcome him home, she found herself forced to dodge his wet sloppy kisses.

"Did he?" Willow replied, dropping Charlie's lead on the stairs. "That dog does have some energy."

She and Bea made their way into the kitchen, where Ronnie greeted them with a hug.

"Something smells good," Bea said, hanging her coat on the back of a chair.

Ronnie pulled a bottle of wine from the fridge while Charlie headed for his water bowl. Willow and Bea took a seat at the table.

"It's nothing exciting," Ronnie said of their dinner. "But it'll certainly fill the gap."

"Good, because after all that exercise, I'm starving," Willow said. "No wonder you're losing weight."

"Am I?" Ronnie asked, looking down at her figure. If she was, she hadn't noticed. "How did you get on with Mr Whatever-hisnameis?"

Her daughter grinned. "Very well actually." She reached into her bag and pulled out a slip of paper. "I only managed to get his phone number."

"I wouldn't get too excited," Bea said to Ronnie. "In a few weeks' time that'll be in the bin with the others."

"Not necessarily," Willow replied.

Ronnie gave her daughter a knowing look, as did Bea.

"Oh, all right. Probably." Willow raised an eyebrow. "What about you, Mum? Did you make any calls while we were out?"

Bea straightened herself up in her seat, as if preparing for any ensuing gossip. "Oh, please say you did."

"Sorry to disappoint, ladies, but no. Apart from sorting out a few e-mails, I haven't even looked at my phone."

"How very boring," Bea said, slumping again. "Why ever not?"

Ronnie plonked the bottle of wine down on the table before fetching three glasses. Like them, she thought Jack a lovely guy too. But the fact of the matter was she no longer trusted her own judgement. She'd been oblivious to the fact that her own husband was having an affair, when there had to have been signs. A slight change in appearance, criticism of things that hadn't previously bothered him, a distancing of himself from her and their marriage... The truth was, Ronnie hadn't clocked anything of the sort. Nick's affair had blindsided her.

Then there was Mr Wright and his despicable behaviour; something else Ronnie hadn't seen coming. Of course, she now appreciated why Mrs Wright seemed uptight. The stress that woman was living under, being married to a man like that. In Ronnie's view, he had to have taken advantage of women before and his wife had to know. Then again, Ronnie considered, was it really a case of eyes wide shut? Or was the woman like her? So invested in her marriage, she couldn't see what went on under her own nose?

As she took in Willow and Bea's disappointment, Ronnie wanted to explain that she no longer believed in her own intuition, that she'd had her fill of men letting her down. But she couldn't. That would mean dragging them into her shenanigans next door, and she couldn't put them in a position whereby they had to take sides.

"Go on then, enlighten us," Willow said. "Tell us why you haven't called Jack."

Ronnie sighed, knowing her hesitation wasn't solely about a lack of self-trust. She had to acknowledge yet another, more embarrassing, reason as to why she hadn't contacted him. "Look at me," she said. "Not only am I approaching too many years to mention, I have a grown-up daughter and spend my working life sitting on my arse for a living. And believe me, I have the wrinkles, stretch marks, lumps and bumps to prove all that."

Bea scoffed. "Tosh! Just wait until you're approaching my *too many years*. Then you'll have cause for concern."

"Come on, you've both seen the man," Ronnie said, which told her they had to understand where she was coming from.

"Oh, yes," Bea said with a smile.

"Yep, we've seen him all right," Willow added.

"Then you know what I'm talking about."

"Some men like the lived-in look," Willow said.

"You're not helping," Ronnie replied.

"I think you're being too hard on yourself," Bea said. "You're gorgeous on the inside and out. And if you don't believe me, I suggest you go and look in a mirror."

Ronnie appreciated the compliment, but it was fair to say her mother-in-law was biased. "It's not only that," Ronnie continued. "Going on a dog walk, or on a date to the cinema, they're both well and good. But what happens when things get, you know, serious?" Ronnie felt herself blush. "When the time comes to..."

"Progress things?" Bea asked.

"Yes."

Willow laughed. "I think I'm living proof that you know exactly what happens, Mum."

"That's not what I mean."

Willow continued to chuckle.

"I'm not that experienced when it comes to the bedroom department." Ronnie couldn't believe she was conversing about her sex life with her daughter and mother-in-law. "What I'm saying is, Nick, your dad, well it's only ever been him."

"All the more reason to get in touch with Jack," Willow said. "Honestly, Mum, you don't know what you've been missing."

If only Ronnie had her daughter's confidence. *And figure*, she thought.

The crashing of the front door bursting open made Ronnie and her guests jump. "What on earth...?" Ronnie looked from her daughter to her mother-in-law.

Rising from her seat, she felt Charlie brush against her ankles as he hid himself under the dining table.

32

Footsteps stomped down the hall. "I've got you now!"

"Nick?" Bea said, clearly surprised by her son's actions.

He stormed into the room, his face oozing smugness and superiority. Momentarily caught off guard, he paused, surprised to see Willow and Bea sat there. The man was clearly too wrapped up in himself to have noticed his daughter's car. "I didn't realise you had visitors."

"If you'd knocked and waited, instead of barging in uninvited, I could have told you," Ronnie said.

"I must say, Nick, I did bring you up with more manners than that," Bea said. "As for coming in here shouting... It's not as if you even live here anymore."

Nick looked at his mother. "Didn't she tell you? When it comes to number six and number eight, there's an open-house policy." He trained his eyes on Ronnie. "Isn't there?"

Ronnie suddenly felt nervous. She'd worked so hard at keeping *Operation Poltergeist* to herself. She'd done her best to stop Willow and Bea getting involved in her and Nick's dispute, full stop. "I don't know what you're talking about," she said.

"Oh, don't be coy. I'm sure Mum and Willow would love to hear about what you've been up to lately." He turned to his family members. "Wouldn't you?" He smiled as he then focused his attention back on Ronnie. "I mean I still haven't worked out how you got in, but I have to say I underestimated your creativity. And I certainly didn't realise how vindictive you can be."

"Nick!" Bea said. "Stop this."

Vindictive, thought Ronnie. Nick was describing the wrong person there. The only ones to fit that mould were him and his new woman. If they'd done the decent thing from the start and moved somewhere else, Ronnie wouldn't have had to resort to trespassing on their property. Everyone would be free to live as they pleased, them as well as her.

"Clever too," Nick carried on. "I mean *I* couldn't have come up with a plan like that."

Ronnie felt herself redden. She willed him to shut up.

"What are you talking about?" Bea said. "What's Ronnie meant to have done?"

"I'm sure if asked, she'll happily explain."

Ronnie swallowed as everyone turned to look at her. "I don't think now's the time, Nick."

"I thought you might struggle to admit anything," he replied. "Which is why I brought this." He reached into his pocket and pulled out a mobile, one of those all-singing all-dancing smartphones that must have been new because Ronnie had never seen it before. "You didn't really think you'd get away with it, did you?"

"Get away with what?" Bea asked, her frustrations coming to the fore.

Willow patted her grandmother's hand in an attempt at reassurance. She looked at her father, her voice suddenly stern. "Dad, you're beginning to sound like a bully. Whatever's going on, let's get it over with."

Watching him, Ronnie couldn't believe Nick's delight despite everyone else's concern. The man seemed to be having way too much fun to listen to his own daughter.

"At least I'm not a criminal," he replied. "Unlike your mother here."

Ronnie took in her daughter and mother-in-law's confused expressions.

Nick swiped his phone screen a couple of times, before handing it to Ronnie. "Ring any bells?"

Ronnie looked down at the video Nick had obviously recorded. It might not have been the best quality, but she knew she was looking at herself. She felt the colour drain from her face as she watched her own image empty Gaye's kitchen cupboards, repositioning and restacking crockery, pans, and anything else she could get her hands on.

Nick laughed. "Not looking quite so clever now, are you?" Without warning, he took the phone from Ronnie's hand, gloating as he passed it to Bea.

Ronnie watched her mother-in-law silently absorb every single still, her face expressionless, before she, in turn, gave the phone to Willow. With no reaction from her daughter either, Ronnie knew how disappointed in her they must be. Why did Nick have to drag them into this? His issue was with her not them.

"I think the police will be very interested in what I have there, don't you?" Nick said to Ronnie. "I mean, you were told to leave us alone, as I remember."

Ronnie's stomach felt like lead as she considered the harassment warning she already had. If Nick carried out his threat and showed the authorities his video footage, goodness knew how much trouble she'd be in. She took in Nick's continued enjoyment, feeling powerless to challenge him. Despite her planning and plotting, the evidence was there in front of everyone's eyes.

"You're no doubt looking at an arrest. Facing a criminal record, I'd say."

Ronnie took her seat at the table. Defeated, she didn't see the point in arguing.

"That's not Mum," Willow said, continuing to look at Nick's phone.

Nick scoffed. "Rubbish. Of course it is."

"It's not. It's me."

"What?" Nick clearly doubted that.

"Willow, please. Don't." Ronnie shook her head, emphasising her request. The last thing she wanted was her daughter taking the wrap for her crime. The last thing she'd wanted was her daughter involved at all.

"Mum, I can't have you taking the blame for something I've done," Willow carried on regardless.

"If you expect me to believe you," Nick said. "Then you're as deluded as your mother."

"You've seen the video, Dad. Can you really say it's not me?"

"Wow, I knew you two were close but, jeez, taking the blame for your mother's actions, that's ridiculous."

"He's right, Willow," Ronnie said. "It's clearly me on that screen."

"Well, I say it's me. Which is exactly what I'll tell the police if you call them, Dad."

Nick's confidence faltered.

"No, you won't," Ronnie said to her daughter.

"Yes, I will," Willow replied, the woman's determination there for all to see.

"Nick, ignore her. I did it."

"I know you did."

"No, Dad. It was me."

Bea suddenly rose to her feet, her head held high. "I'm Spartacus," she said, loud and proud.

Ronnie froze, her eyes wide at the interruption, while Willow put a hand to her mouth, clearly hiding her sudden amusement.

Nick, on the other hand, was less than happy and struggling to contain his irritation at Bea's announcement, spluttered. "Trust you to take their side. As for you two…"

"Remember, Dad. It's me who'll be getting locked up if you do call the police."

Nick looked from his daughter, to his mother, the triumphant nature of his arrival replaced with confusion and frustration. Turning his gaze on Ronnie, she couldn't just see the disgust Nick had for her, she felt it too. A sadness came over her. No-one would ever believe they'd once been husband and wife.

Lost for words, he huffed and puffed as he snatched his phone up and stormed back out of the room, making sure to slam the front door shut behind him.

33

Ronnie sat at the table with a cup of coffee, Charlie's head resting against her thighs. He hadn't left her side since Nick's outburst over his video surveillance, unlike Willow and Bea, who she hadn't heard from since. She couldn't blame them for staying away. They might have stuck up for her during Nick's theatrics, but once he'd left, their disappointment at the situation had shown itself.

Ronnie stroked the top of Charlie's head, feeling sad at how things had turned out. She'd fully expected her daughter and mother-in-law to be furious over *Operation Poltergeist*, which they were. They kept telling her how much trouble she could have been in if Willow hadn't stepped in to save the day, something Ronnie continued to feel guilty for. But it wasn't only her forays into next door that bothered them. In their view, Ronnie hadn't taken their six-step plan seriously; she'd secretly been laughing at their efforts. Although, they seemed equally as upset with themselves. Or more to the point, with their apparent failure.

Up until that evening, as far as Willow and Bea were concerned, their strategy had been working. Thanks to their ingenuity, Ronnie was moving on, in spite of the hiccups along the way. Nick's video footage, however, contradicted that belief. As far as they were concerned, it proved that Ronnie was still fixated with the goings on at number eight. Their plan had failed, which meant they had too.

As she listened to their concerns, Ronnie confessed to her lack of commitment in the beginning. She even admitted her ulterior motive for joining the gym. Nevertheless, she was at pains to explain that her opinion on the whole thing began to change at step two. Yes, her visit to the hair salon had gone wrong. Yes, she'd ended up looking like Rod Stewart. But like she tried to tell them, shaving her head had been like a rebirth. A getting rid of the old Ronnie, ready for the new.

Ronnie couldn't help but smile as she thought about step three. Getting Charlie was a real turning point. Charlie had gotten her out of the house, and the attention he received from strangers forced her into chatting with anyone and everyone, which had to be a miracle for a home bird like her. Thanks to him, she enjoyed getting up in the morning, getting out into the open air. That dog's presence on Holme Lea Avenue was far more a focus to her than Nick and Gaye's. And like Ronnie said, she wouldn't have him were it not for Willow and Bea's six-step plan.

Ronnie looked down at her bare wedding finger, aware that the six steps weren't only about coping with next door; they were an opportunity to discover her identity outside of her marriage. Stripping back the layers she'd wrapped herself in for twenty-five years took time, however, and Ronnie knew she had a long way to go. She sighed, forced to admit that *Operation Poltergeist* hadn't exactly helped. Instead of concentrating solely on herself, she'd wasted precious energy on Nick and Gaye. "Not anymore," she said. "From now, it's all about you, Ronnie Jacobs."

Unfortunately, her daughter and mother-in-law had yet to be convinced, which was why Ronnie was determined to forget about next door's living arrangements and throw herself whole-heartedly into step number four. It was, no doubt, going to get her into more trouble with her ex and his new woman, but Ronnie could stomach that; her daughter and mother-in-law were worth it. What Ronnie couldn't cope with was Willow and Bea's disappointment.

Ronnie picked up the envelope her daughter and mother-in-law had despondently left behind, pulling out the piece of paper within. *Learn a musical instrument*, it said, which admittedly for someone as tone deaf as Ronnie, was quite a challenge. Ronnie was up for it though. She had to be if she wanted to prove Willow and Bea wrong about her dedication to their plan. She took a deep breath to gather herself. With a bit of commitment on her part, Ronnie would make them see their efforts as a success. She smiled as she looked down at Charlie. "Let's do this."

Rising to her feet, Ronnie moved towards the kitchen counter and picked up a large cardboard box of step-four good-ies. Goodies that wouldn't just enable her to complete her next task, but to surpass expectations. She headed out into the garden and down the path to her studio, excited yet nervous. With Charlie at her heels, the two of them piled inside, the dog seemingly as keen to get on with it as she.

Placing the box down on her huge worktable, Ronnie couldn't believe the effort she was going to and she giggled, telling herself that neither would Willow and Bea. She reached in and pulled out a fancy new pen and expensive notepad and, having never had to put together a formal invitation before, considered how best to phrase things.

Music Recital, she finally began. *One night only*. Ronnie chewed on the end of her pen, wondering what to put next, before returning it to the paper. *In this one-off special event, you are cordially invited to enjoy the music of Ronnie Jacobs*, she wrote, chuckling as she added the venue, date and time. *Formal attire*, she added, and then finished off with a swishy *RSVP*. "There," she said, trying to imagine her daughter and mother-in-law's delight when their invites landed on the doormat. "If this doesn't bring a smile back to their faces, then nothing will."

Ronnie had the evening mapped out. It would take place in the garden, weather permitting of course. There would be canapés – asparagus wraps with lemon mayo, sweet potato and ginger parcels, and mini salmon and dill puffs. For a sweeter tooth, she'd serve mini cheesecakes, bite-size apple and marzipan tarts, and a plate of lemon fancies. And, naturally, she'd make sure the wine flowed which, fingers crossed, would make the music almost as palatable as the food. Ronnie still couldn't believe that she was going to play to an audience. "The things I do for my family."

She looked at her watch and seeing it was already noon, shook her arms out and rolled her shoulders to loosen them up. She stretched her neck out, first left and then right. "Now to learn a couple of tunes," she said to Charlie.

Having spoken to her local authority about noise control, Ronnie knew she was good to go between the hours of 11am to 7pm. Outside of that time, she could be subject to a noise abatement order and potentially a fine, although Ronnie had a pretty good idea there was no *could* or anything *potential* about it. Since their video footage altercation, Nick and Gaye would, without doubt, be looking for the slightest wrongdoing on Ronnie's part, and when it came to dishing out her punishment, they'd insist she get the max.

She took a deep breath. "You ready?" she asked Charlie as she reached into the box.

The dog sat staring up at her, smiling as usual.

"You might not look so happy once I get started." Ronnie thought back to her childhood when she was kicked out of the school choir, the music teacher heralding Ronnie's inability to hold even the simplest of tunes as extraordinary. "I'm not exactly renowned for my musical talent."

She pulled out a new recorder, along with the *Teach Yourself* guide that came with it. Turning to page one of the book, she scanned its contents. "Don't say I didn't warn you," she said, putting the instrument to her lips.

34

R onnie bent double, clutching at her midriff. Her stomach hurt, she was belly laughing so hard. She wiped tears from her eyes, unable to remember the last time she'd had so much fun. Learning to play the recorder was better than she'd imagined and she panted, trying to get a grip of herself. However, giggles continued to escape from her lips. "Come on, be serious," she told herself. "You've got a concert to prepare for."

She put the recorder to her mouth and, forcing herself to concentrate, looked at her instruction guide. "From the top."

Beginning with A, she sounded each note and, blowing her way down the scale until she got to G, her fingertips moved up and down as they concealed one instrument hole after another. She knew the sound coming out shouldn't be anything like the screeching and screaming that she produced, but to be fair, she was only a beginner.

As she automatically reversed the scale, going back up from G to A, Ronnie found her giggles erupting once more. She tried to control them, a difficult task when she knew what was coming.

She looked at Charlie while she played and saw his jowl quiver. A whimper escaped his mouth, followed by a whine and then a yelp. Ronnie did her best to keep playing, even when the dog threw his head back and let out a long undulating howl. It reverberated around the room. Like her, the dog couldn't sing for toffee, but he seemed to enjoy trying.

Unable to continue any longer, Ronnie fell to the floor laughing again. She pulled Charlie close and hugged him through her snorting and sniggering. "You, my boy, are an absolute star."

A figure emerged at the window, causing Ronnie to jump. "Jesus!" she said, her heart skipping a beat. What was *he* doing there?

"You two look like you're having fun," Jack said.

Ronnie gathered her wits while Charlie leapt from her arms. His tale wagged at double speed as he scratted at the door, desperate to get at their visitor.

"Traitor," Ronnie said to the dog as she scrambled to her feet and opened the door.

Jack immediately dropped to Charlie's level, reciprocating the fuss being shown. "Have you missed me?" he asked, the dog's answer more than obvious to everyone present.

Finally, Jack stood straight again, turning his attention to Ronnie. "I hope you don't mind me turning up like this. I knocked at the front door and waited. Then I heard the musical fracas and couldn't resist coming for a look." He gave Charlie a pat on the head. "You both sounded great, by the way."

Ronnie couldn't believe he said that with such a straight face. "You thought someone was being murdered, more like." She paused to look at Jack. He seemed to make a habit of disappearing for a while, then suddenly turning up without warning. "So, you're finally here to take Charlie for a walk?"

"And his owner if she'll let me."

Ronnie felt herself blush, not quite sure what to say. She stood there silent, half of her wanting to say yes, of course she'd go with them. The other, telling her to say no, getting to know *any* man beyond polite pleasantries wasn't worth the risk.

"I wanted to give Charlie some time to settle in, plus I was waiting for your call."

Jack also seemed to be waiting for an explanation, but Ronnie didn't offer one. She didn't want to lie and say her phone was broken, but neither could she tell him about her fears and self-doubt. Instead, she stood there continuing to say nothing.

"Fab studio," Jack eventually said, clearly trying to overcome the awkwardness. He glanced inside, clocking the recorder and *Teach Yourself* booklet. "Or should I say music room."

His comment broke the ice and Ronnie let out a laugh. "Studio's fine, you've heard my playing." She lowered her voice. "I'm just keeping out of the way so as not to annoy the neighbours too much." *Speaking of whom*, thought Ronnie as number eight's back door opened.

"About time," Nick said. "If that racket had gone on any longer, I'd have been calling the police."

Ronnie rolled her eyes and shook her head; she knew something like that would happen. Then again, she supposed it was her own fault. She had pushed everyone to their limits of late. She felt grateful when Jack reached out to rub her arm in reassurance, before watching him approach the dividing garden fence, his smile beaming as he looked over into next door's garden.

"No need," he said. "They're already here."

Ronnie put a hand up to her mouth. She couldn't believe Jack had done that, an action that she would without doubt pay for later. She listened to Nick's undignified muttering, wishing she could see his face; the man wouldn't have expected anyone other than Ronnie to respond, let alone find himself face-to-face with an off-duty police officer.

She finally allowed herself to relax in Jack's presence. "Coffee?" she asked. "I mean, you're not on duty, right?"

"I thought you'd never ask."

Ronnie led the way back into number six. As she put the kettle on, Jack leant against the kitchen counter. Sensing him watching her every move, it felt strange having a man in the house; at least a man who wasn't shouting the odds or blackmailing her for sex.

"So, why learn to play the recorder?" he asked.

"It's part of a six-step plan my daughter and mother-in-law drew up. To stop me getting into trouble because of you-know-who next door."

Jack laughed. "And is it working?"

Ronnie paused before answering, her actions in *Operation Poltergeist* running through her head. "They don't think so," she said, deciding the less said about that the better. Jack was, after all, a policeman. "Which is why I'm trying to prove them wrong by not only learning the recorder, but by holding a recital."

"Really?" Jack's eyes widened. "Now that I'd love to see."

"You're more than welcome to come along," Ronnie said, laughing. Her smile froze, as she realised what she'd just said. As soon as the words were out, she could have kicked herself. "I mean it's nothing fancy," she added. "And you'll probably be bored stiff. And you have heard the standard of music…" Ronnie took in the man's expression, realising her U-turn attempts to dissuade him from attending were to no avail.

Jack continued to grin. "It's a date."

35

As Ronnie stood there in her finery, she looked down at the black figure-hugging wrap dress she wore, unable to remember the last time it had seen the light of day. It was probably a work do of Nick's, she considered, or some long-ago neighbourhood party she hadn't wanted to attend. Social gatherings had never really been her thing. She smiled. Neither could she remember the last time it fitted her.

She had to admit it felt good being dressed up for a change. It was surprising how much a nice outfit and a bit of make-up lifted one's spirits. For once, Ronnie felt self-assured and a boost in confidence was exactly what she needed if she and her recorder were to take centre stage. *Along with Charlie, of course*, she acknowledged. After his enthusiastic accompaniments during practice, how could he not perform on the night?

She looked out onto the garden to see her specially purchased music stand taking pride of place in front of the three chairs awaiting her audience. It was clear Ronnie had had a busy couple of weeks. As well as learning to play the recorder, she'd almost finished the first of her handbag commissions, and that was on top of getting the garden ready for that night's recital. The lawn areas had been mowed, the path had been weeded and regravelled, and the neglected containers had been potted up with brightly coloured bedding plants, including African daisies, geraniums and touch-me-nots.

Ronnie turned her attention to the Limelight Hydrangea with a sigh. Having fully intended to prune it back when she'd stood in front of it with her shears, she found she couldn't bring herself to do it. "Which reminds me..." Scanning the whole garden, she realised she hadn't seen or heard that dog of hers in quite some time. "Charlie!" she called out. "Where are you?"

The hydrangea leaves rustled, its branches and blooms dancing thanks to the sudden movement from within. "Oh, Charlie," Ronnie said, as he bounded out and towards her. "What do you look like?" It wasn't only his muddy nose and paws that made him a sight to behold, but the bespoke collar and tie Ronnie had made him for the recital sat wonky and appeared equally as filthy. She unclipped his attire. "It's a good job I put together a spare just in case. Isn't it?" The dog smiled up at her like some canine version of *Orphan Annie.* Ronnie couldn't help but laugh. "What are we going to do with you?"

She picked up the end of the hosepipe and, careful to control the flow of water to avoid any muddy splashback, began rinsing Charlie's feet. It was a routine they'd both become accustomed to and he was happy to lift one foot after the other to be then dried off. "In you go," Ronnie said to him, job done. "At least if you're in the house I can see what you're up to."

As the dog did as he was told, Ronnie took in her efforts again, insisting that the evening ahead would be as much fun as she anticipated. Willow and Bea might have seemed under-whelmed when she'd phoned to check on their RSVPs, but that was because they still felt burned. She was sure that once they saw the time and energy she'd put into step four, they'd be back to their usual happy and smiling selves.

Ronnie understood the reasons behind her daughter and mother-in-law's lack of enthusiasm. She had, after all, let the two of them down. And while she still wanted nothing more than for Nick and Gaye to move on to pastures new, Ronnie recognised she should have found a different means with which to deal with her frustrations.

She sighed, blaming Nick as much as herself for all the upset. Especially when he didn't have to show his mother and daughter that video, he had chosen to. Ronnie knew she shouldn't have been surprised though. Nick had to hate the fact that Bea felt unable to give him and Gaye her blessing; that she preferred his ex over his new woman. Under those circumstances he probably saw an opportunity when he walked in that night, a chance to cause trouble between Ronnie and Bea. Ronnie took a deep breath and slowly exhaled, thinking of the games that had been played. As difficult as it was to acknowledge, she had to admit that of late, she and Nick were as bad as each other.

She heard number eight's back door suddenly open, followed by Gaye's chatter.

"But it's such a lovely evening," the woman said to the sound of clinking glass. "There's no point sitting inside when we could be enjoying ourselves out here."

And so the games continue, Ronnie thought.

As she listened to the sound of a bottle cork popping, she felt irritated. Gaye had to have seen her setting things up for that night's recital, and was making her presence known in the hope of ruining it. Ronnie took in the three chairs again, realising that Nick and Gaye could pull any stunt they wanted with PC Jack Shenton in the audience. *Jack Shenton*, Ronnie thought, her stomach doing a little summersault. She still couldn't believe she'd invited him.

"Nick," Gaye called out, as Ronnie headed inside. "Could you come here please."

Leaving them to it, Ronnie closed the door behind her and checked her watch. Instead of being stuck in the house, she would have liked to have spent a bit of time practicing her musical arrangements before her guests arrived. She might not have much of a repertoire, but *Three Blind Mice* and *London's Burning* were tricky pieces for a newbie musician like her; another couple of run-throughs wouldn't have hurt.

Wondering what to do instead, Ronnie found herself distracted when raised voices filtered in from outside. But whereas she'd usually attempt to decipher Nick and Gaye's conversation, Ronnie shook her head, happy to dismiss it. Determined to succeed at Willow and Bea's six-step plan, Ronnie refused to let anything spoil the evening ahead. And as the voices, at last, died down, she decided that whatever they were talking about, it was none of her business.

Moments later, Ronnie's front door burst open. "Ronnie!" Nick shouted. "You really are pushing your luck."

Her shoulders slumped. "Not again." She wondered what she was meant to have done. Having learnt her lesson following the man's last visit, she'd left Nick and Gaye alone ever since.

As Nick stormed down the hall, Charlie flew under the table. Ronnie reached down and gave him a comforting stroke. "It's okay, boy," she said, and in acknowledging the dog's fear, told herself it was time to change the locks.

"Where is it?" Nick asked. As he stomped into the room, his eyes darted from one corner to the next.

Watching him, Ronnie couldn't believe the man's change in behaviour of late. When he'd first walked out on their marriage, he did everything he could to avoid being in Ronnie's presence. Lately, the man couldn't stay away. "Where's what?"

"That mutt of yours. He's in here somewhere."

"Excuse me?" Whatever argument Nick had come for, she was not going to have it.

"Oh, don't play the innocent with me."

Ronnie raised her eyebrows, wondering what on earth Nick wanted with Charlie. She felt the yellow Lab secrete itself at the back of her legs.

"You probably trained the damn thing in the first place."

Ronnie looked at her ex in all his blustering glory. "You don't get to do this, Nick," she said.

"Do what?"

"Keep bursting in here, shouting your mouth off on a whim."

Nick scoffed. "I think you'll find this is my house. I'm the one who paid for it."

"No, Nick. You relinquished any rights to this property the day you walked out." Ronnie knew she was spot on morally but didn't have a clue where either of them stood from a legal position. She made another mental note, this time to make an appointment with a solicitor. In the meantime, she simply hoped that she looked like she knew what she was talking about, while holding on to the old adage that *possession was nine tenths of the law.*

"Well *that* certainly isn't yours." He pointed towards number eight's garden. "So why you're letting that excuse for a dog, that mutant..."

Ronnie pictured Charlie's muddy feet as he sprang from the Limelight Hydrangea whenever she called. He hadn't been trying to evict a hedgehog or a mouse, or dig down to Australia at all, he'd been sneaking into next door. She felt the yellow Lab shaking as he leaned further into her legs, her pulse quickening in response. Nick had no right to scare her dog like that. He had no right to be so nasty about such a beautiful loving animal. In fact, he had no right to do any of what he'd done.

Standing there watching him fume, Ronnie stared at her ex-husband, for the first time properly questioning what she ever saw in him. She silently scoffed. No matter what names he called Charlie, no matter how he mocked her, Nick personified *ugly* in every sense of the word. Ronnie just couldn't believe it had taken twenty-five years to notice.

"Like I said, you don't get to do this. You're a hypocrite, Nick. I don't know how you've got the gall to complain about anyone being on or in your property without permission, when here you are, yet again, stood in my kitchen uninvited. As for acting superior, considering your conduct, that says more about you than it does me."

"What do you expect the way you've behaved?" Nick smirked. "Then again, like mother like daughter."

Nick had seen her mother's abusiveness first-hand; he'd helped pick up the pieces when Ronnie had finally found the courage to break off contact. And standing there, Ronnie couldn't believe how low he would stoop to make whatever point he was trying to make. But whereas she knew his remark was supposed to sting, that it was supposed to shut her up, strangely, it did neither. "Yet, I was good enough to stay married to you for twenty-five years," she said instead. "Good enough to raise your daughter." Ronnie laughed. "You're an adulterer, Nick. A man who sneaks around behind his wife's back, having some dirty affair with some bint of a woman. You're not a cut above. You don't have the moral high ground. It's shocking that you ever thought you did."

"And you're not a victim."

Ronnie had had enough. "Get out."

"Sorry?"

"You heard me."

Nick opened his mouth to speak, but Ronnie wouldn't let him.

"And if you ever step inside my house again, in fact, if you so much as look at Charlie, or me... Let's say, up until now, you've only had a taste of what I'm capable of."

Nick let out a burst of mock laughter. "So, you're threatening us, are you?"

Ronnie glared in response, a steely determination in her eyes. "Like I said, get out."

Nick sneered. "I was going anyway."

Ronnie scoffed as he turned to leave. She knew his scorn was an act of bravado, that underneath it all, the man was a coward. Were he not, he wouldn't have left their marriage in the way he had. He'd have gone before he'd found another woman to climb into bed with.

"Oh," Nick said, before disappearing down the hall altogether. "Seeing as this is your house, you'll have no problem covering its running costs as of today, will you? Enjoy your evening."

Ronnie couldn't believe he still thought he had the upper hand. As if she'd be silent for the sake of a few pounds every month. She didn't care about his money; she'd manage without it. She'd have to.

She crouched down to give Charlie a hug, his adorable expression enough to make her heart melt. His tail wagged, letting Ronnie know that everything was well in his world again, enough to make Ronnie give him another embrace.

Rising to her feet, Ronnie felt a compulsion to purge herself of her ex-husband and his new woman once and for all, and she knew exactly how to do it. But with Bea, Willow and Jack due round, she couldn't just disappear. She headed for a kitchen drawer, pulling out a notepad and pen. *Sorry*, she wrote, at the same time checking the kitchen clock. She put the pen back down, realising she didn't need to leave a note. She could be there and back before her recital guests arrived.

"You stay here, boy," she said to the dog and grabbing her car keys, made her way outside.

36

R onnie's car began to putter. "Please," she said to the vehicle. "Don't let me down now." With not far to go before she reached the viaduct, Ronnie knew she'd pushed its engine to the limits. Instead of getting it to the garage, she'd ignored its problems and driven the car anyway, something she was beginning to regret. The vehicle emitted a final cough, before cutting out completely. "No," Ronnie said, using the last of its momentum to steer it to the side of the road. "Don't do this to me."

With the car at a standstill, she switched off the ignition, waited a few seconds, then turned the key again. The engine spluttered, doing its best to turn over. However, it refused to start, forcing Ronnie to repeat the procedure over and over until in the end there was nothing. She slumped forward, letting her head drop onto the steering wheel. Out of all the times her car could have broken down, why did it have to be then?

Ronnie straightened herself back up and snatching the keys from the ignition barrel, got out of the car. "You'll simply have to walk the rest of the way." She kicked the vehicle's front wheel and, refusing to even think about the cost involved, imagined the hassle she'd have to go through getting it towed to a garage.

Setting off up the road, Ronnie almost tripped. She cursed under her breath as she looked down at her kitten heels, wishing she'd swapped them for something more suited to the countryside before leaving the house. With no choice but to carry them, she slipped them off as an oncoming car slowed in its approach. Its driver gawped at her, clearly wondering why a barefoot woman in a posh frock was traipsing around in the middle of nowhere. Ronnie gave him an acerbic smile as he passed, tempted to put her tongue out at the man. "Not curious enough to stop and ask if I need assistance," she said as, just like him, she continued on her way.

She took in the fields of sheep as she walked, admired the limestone rocks dotted around and breathed in the fresh air. Marching along, it felt good to get away from Holme Lea Avenue for a while, if a little strange for not having Charlie by her side. She wondered why she hadn't thought to bring him with her. No doubt he could have done with some time out as well after Nick's outburst.

Finally, with its twenty-four arches and magnificent stonework, the viaduct came into view, standing proud against the landscape. Ronnie picked up pace as she turned off the road and onto the gravel path that led towards it, soon forced to hobble, thanks to the jagged stones and pebbles pressing into the soles of her feet.

"You really didn't think this through," she told herself as she scrambled up the grass banking until she, at last, reached the old rail track. She began following the ancient train line that made its way across the hundred-and-fifty-year-old bridge, only coming to a stop once she'd reached the viaduct's halfway point. She cautiously approached the wall that kept her from falling the thirty-two meters it would take to hit the ground, taking a deep breath, ready to soak up the long-distance view.

Standing there in the quiet, Ronnie felt a sense of freedom. She looked first left and then right, pleased to see there wasn't another living soul around. She smiled, knowing she could say what she wanted, in the way that she wanted, and equally as important, without judgement. She could curse and scream and holler to her heart's content and every word would be carried away on the wind. No-one would know.

She felt a breeze around her ears as she reflected on what had led her to that bridge, knowing she wasn't there simply because of Nick's latest tantrum, but because of everything that had happened in the months prior.

Thoughts about Nick's relationship with Gaye swarmed around Ronnie's head. She still couldn't understand why they refused to start over somewhere new and she pictured them as they mocked her, the abandoned wife, for wanting them to. She felt her resentment rise as she considered the way Nick deemed he had a right to barge into number six whenever he felt like it, insulting not only her, but Charlie, thanks to the yellow Lab's sweet disfigured face. Whatever Nick thought of Ronnie, that dog, her loving faithful friend, didn't deserve any of it.

Ronnie felt equally annoyed with herself and readily contemplated her own actions. *Operation Poltergeist* might have seemed like her last hope, but she had to admit how daft she'd been for coming up with the idea, let alone for thinking she'd get away with it. It was childish and because of it, she'd hurt the two people she cared about most in the world, Willow and Bea. Not that she was letting the two of them off scot-free.

Instead of talking to her about their concerns, they'd sulked and felt sorry for themselves. They'd more or less ignored Ronnie those last couple of weeks, which they had to know would hurt her as much as she'd hurt them. An image of Mr

Wright popped into her head, and Ronnie's stomach turned at the thought of his moist lips and sinister smile. *Poor Mrs Wright*, Ronnie thought. Why did the woman stay with that man?

As she tried to get her head around everything that had happened since Nick had left, Ronnie felt her anger simmer then boil. Feeling the urge to get it all out, she climbed onto the wall in front of her and, oblivious to the drop, unmindful of her fear of heights, began screaming into the void. She shouted profanities at Nick and Gaye, for their affair, for the man her ex had turned into, and their refusal to do the decent thing. Ronnie cursed her elderly neighbour for being a blackmailer and a pervert, for thinking Ronnie was a soft touch who could be manipulated. She swore at herself for not being the bigger woman and for not dealing with things better. Even Pete the hairdresser got a blaspheme for transforming her into Rod Stewart, as did the two teenagers who'd turned her into an overnight Internet sensation. Ronnie spewed out her frustrations over everything and everyone, at the same time wondering how she'd survived intact, a question that only made her scream some more.

Ronnie felt purging herself of such rage liberating; she felt euphoric as if the real world around her didn't exist. She continued to shout and swear as she threw her arms high into the air and turned her gaze skyward. She paused, suddenly silent, her eyes narrowing as she found herself staring at a heli-copter hovering directly above.

"Ronnie!" a voice shouted from somewhere to her right.

She let her arms drop, before turning to see who was calling her. "Jack?" she said, confused. "What are you doing here?" She looked behind him and, spotting a handful of uniformed police officers, wondered what was going on.

Jack slowed to an almost standstill, putting an arm out as if directing those at the back of him to stay where they were.

"Please, Ronnie," Jack said. Cautious in his approach, he held out his hand for Ronnie to take. "Let me help you down."

Ronnie frowned, bewildered by his concerned expression. Anyone would've thought she was about to jump such was the fuss going on around her. She froze, her eyes widening as her gaze went from him to his numerous colleagues. She swallowed hard, before turning her attention to the helicopter above – a police helicopter. "Oh Lordy," she said, realisation dawning.

Standing there, she remembered the note she'd started to write before leaving the house, pictured her broken down car in the middle of nowhere, and looking down at her bare feet, considered the fact that she was stood on a wall next to a rather big drop. Putting those things together, there was no denying the fact that she was surrounded by a search party, that everyone there thought she was in the process of ending it all.

Not for the first time of late, Ronnie realised, she cringed in embarrassment. Why did such ridiculous things keep happening to her?

37

Ronnie sat squirming in the passenger seat of Jack's car. Rather than being driven home, she wanted to find a great big hole that could swallow her up. Not knowing what to say about it, she couldn't believe the drama that had just unfolded. She pictured the helicopter above her head that had undoubtedly filmed every second of her purging, the uniformed officers racing towards her, and Jack's fearful expression. A police search party, for goodness sake. How was she ever going to live it all down?

She stole a look at Jack, wondering what he must think of her. She'd been in so many embarrassing situations of late, which was bad enough in itself. But to know the man sat next to her had witnessed most of them, she found that excruciating.

He stared at the road ahead, a big grin on his face.

"I don't know what's so funny," Ronnie said. "Those people, seeing me scream like a banshee, thinking I was about to..." She turned to stare out of the side window. "The shame of it." Ronnie shook her head, before bringing her attention back to Jack. "You're lucky I didn't jump out of sheer humiliation."

Her driver continued to smile.

"How did you know where to find me anyway?"

"The usual," Jack replied, matter of fact.

Ronnie's brow furrowed. He said that like such misunderstandings happened all the time.

"A concerned member of the public rang the station. Some bloke who'd seen an inappropriately dressed woman wandering about in the middle of nowhere, before coming across an abandoned car..."

"It wasn't abandoned."

Jack looked straight at her. "Something he wasn't to know." He faced the road again. "Anyway, he thought the woman might be in trouble and naturally your daughter and mother-in-law had already reported you as missing."

Ronnie groaned, even more mortified by the whole thing. "I wasn't missing."

"It was easy enough to put two and two together."

Ronnie let her head drop onto her chest, again asking why she kept finding herself in such absurd situations.

"Maybe next time you'll tell people you're simply nipping out, instead of leaving them a one-word apology."

Ronnie's head shot back up. "*Sorry* is hardly a suicide note."

The car slowed as Jack pulled it over to the side of the road and switched off the engine. He shifted round in his seat to face Ronnie. "To you, maybe not. But to concerned family and friends."

Ronnie scoffed, but the man's sincerity continued. She took in his earnest expression, knowing that if he'd been worried, Willow and Bea must have been frantic. Ronnie looked at the evening's events in their entirety again and felt guilty. How could she have been so thoughtless as to make everyone think she planned on ending things?

"You can't blame people for thinking the worst," Jack said.

"But none of you were meant to see that note. I intended on

being there and back before any of you landed. And if that damn car of mine hadn't broken down, I would have been."

"Ronnie, you've had a lot to deal with."

"Not enough to kill myself! People who do that have far worse problems than me."

Jack smiled. "All I'm saying is, everything considered, we're bound to panic when you disappear like that."

Ronnie clocked how he'd included himself in that sentence. It felt nice to think someone other than Willow and Bea cared, even if only a little. Ronnie stared down at her hands, thinking about the trouble she'd caused. She took a deep breath and exhaled. She felt so stupid.

"I hope you noticed I was quite the superhero back there," Jack said, clearly trying to lighten the mood.

Ronnie attempted a smile, but as she looked up at him, a tear rolled down her cheek.

"Hey." Jack leaned over and, cradling her face with his hand, used his thumb to wipe it away. "There's no need to get upset. These things happen all the time."

Ronnie found that hard to believe. The man was obviously just being kind.

"Honestly. When it comes to missing persons who aren't really missing, you'd be surprised."

Ronnie took in Jack's warm expression, his kind eyes and tender smile, no longer able to hold back the feelings she'd been doing her best to deny. A yearning came over her as she continued to look at him. "Would you kiss me?" she asked, her voice quiet.

Her question appeared to take Jack by surprise, his expression serious as he stared back at her for a moment. "Are you sure?"

Ronnie nodded. In that moment, she wanted nothing more. Her heart raced as he slowly leaned forward until their lips, at last, met. His felt soft and gentle against her own, tentative even, before settling into a wonderfully luscious rhythm. Ronnie's body stirred as she felt his tongue search for hers. He wrapped his arms around her and the urgency between them intensified. She wanted him as much as Jack seemed to want her. Finally, their kiss slowed and both she and Jack giggled.

"You don't know how long I've been wanting to do that," Jack said, pulling back slightly.

If his timeline matched hers, Ronnie had a pretty good idea. "Me too."

Jack leaned in to kiss her once more, but Ronnie put a hand on his chest to stop him. Realising that Willow had been right to say she was too all or nothing, Ronnie wanted more than a fumble around in a car. If she and Jack were to go any further, she needed a kind of commitment. She had a good idea his interest went beyond any sexual attraction, but Ronnie had to be sure and unfortunately for her, that meant being up front. "Before we do that again, there's something I need to tell you."

"Okay," Jack said, curious.

"Firstly, I can't do friends with benefits."

Jack let out a burst of laughter. "Thank you for telling me."

Ronnie noted that Jack appeared to like the way the conversation was going. There was an eager anticipation in his eyes.

"And secondly, if we're to be more than friends..."

"Yes."

Ronnie swallowed, her nerves coming to the fore. But not wanting to ruin things before they'd begun, she knew she had to be honest, and not least because of Jack's job. She told herself that as a police officer, honesty was something he'd undoubtedly respect and clearing her throat ready to confess her sins, Ronnie insisted it was only right he knew about *Operation Poltergeist* and that she'd partaken in a criminal activity.

"I've been really silly," she finally said.

Jack, too, straightened himself up. "Go on."

As his eyes searched hers, she struggled to find the right words. Ronnie told herself that he'd understand, but that didn't make owning up any easier. She screwed up her face, deciding she'd no choice but to simply come out and say it. "I've been sneaking into next door. Through the loft."

Jack cocked his head. "Excuse me?"

"To make them think their house is haunted." Ronnie waited for him to say something, but he simply looked at her.

"I know it's wrong. And in my defence, I've only done it a couple of times. Well, three in total. But I didn't cause any damage or nosey about the place, I only moved things."

Jack continued to stare; his expression neutral.

"To make them think the house was haunted. You know, so they'd find somewhere else to live."

Still Jack gave nothing away, which only made Ronnie ramble on more.

"But it's all right. When they found out about it, Willow stepped in and took the blame so I wouldn't get arrested." Ronnie fell quiet for a moment, realising that made everything sound worse. "I'm not explaining myself very well, am I?"

"I think you've explained yourself perfectly." Jack turned away from her, reached for the ignition key and started up the car engine.

"But..."

"We need to get you back." Refusing to look at Ronnie, he kept his eyes forward as he spoke. "Your daughter and mother-in-law will be worried you're not back yet."

38

W ith Charlie at her side, Ronnie tried to busy herself in her workshop, insisting that getting on with her job was exactly what she needed. Focusing on something productive stopped her thinking about Jack and his damn principles, and about the *what ifs* that yet again invaded her head. It also stopped her thinking about the kiss they shared. At least it was supposed to. She paused to let out a dreamy sigh, still able to feel Jack's lips on hers; it was a kiss like she'd never experienced.

She shook herself out of her daydream, ready to concentrate on the second of her commissions. She looked at her notes. The customer had given her a notion of what she wanted – a pale-pink rose design fabric, a big contrasting bow somewhere on the front, and rigid loop handles that enabled the whole bag to rest comfortable yet firm on the woman's forearm. As a starting point, Ronnie liked it. It gave her direction while leaving enough room to show off her creativity.

She began rough sketching a couple of design ideas in preparation of putting together a final mock-up for the customer's approval. However, Charlie jumped to his feet, immediately distracting her. He whined as he scratched at the door, causing Ronnie to get up from her seat to investigate. Looking up the garden to the house, she smiled as she spotted Willow and Bea waving at her from the kitchen and she waved back in acknowledgement.

"What do you think, Charlie?" Ronnie asked, looking down at the yellow Lab. "Is it really time for a break?" He let out a short sharp bark which Ronnie interpreted as a *yes*, before opening the door so they could head out to join them.

As soon as she entered the kitchen, Willow thrust out her hand, offering Ronnie a ready-made cup of coffee. "Wonderful," she said in appreciation. She eyed her guests, dubious of the reasons behind their visit. "Come to make sure I haven't done anything stupid, have you?"

She still cringed at the thought of being reported missing like that, but was glad of the heart-to-heart they'd had afterwards. Ronnie got the chance to properly admit how silly she'd been over *Operation Poltergeist*, while at the same time explain how difficult she'd found the situation with number eight. Of course, she thanked Willow and Bea too. Their finding out about her antics, and subsequent response, gave her the kick up the backside she'd needed.

"What?" Bea said, in answer to Ronnie's question. "Like a spot of trespassing?"

Ronnie let out a laugh. "Touché!" she said, raising her cup. Ronnie took in her mother-in-law's appearance. Bea looked weary; her smile appeared less bright somehow. Then again, Ronnie supposed it hardly surprising after the worry she'd put the woman through, something she had no intention of ever doing again.

She led the way to the table and everyone took a seat. "I want you both to know," Ronnie said, coming over all serious, "that you can stop worrying about me. After the other night, I plan on staying out of trouble and keeping a low profile." She drank a mouthful of coffee. "There's been too much excitement of late and before you say it, yes, most of it has been of my own making. But I assure you, I'll be living a quieter existence in the future."

Having finally come to her senses, Ronnie expected sighs of relief. Instead, Willow and Bea simply looked at her, their expressions full of disappointment. "What? I thought you'd be happy." As Ronnie's gaze went from one woman to the other, she found herself wondering if she would ever please those two.

"Existence?" Bea said, her tone flat. She and Willow exchanged glances; they couldn't have been more disapproving if they tried.

"And does Jack fit in with this new way of living?" Willow asked.

Ronnie watched her daughter sip on her drink, trying and failing to demonstrate the air of casualness she clearly aimed for. "Why would he?"

"No reason." Willow looked to her grandmother again, giving her a visual nudge. She obviously wanted a bit of assistance on the matter.

"It's just that having spent a little time with him the other night, before the drama, of course, he seemed like such a lovely chap and very..."

"Keen," Willow said.

"So, when he didn't escort you in..." Bea said.

"When he dropped you on the street and left..." Willow said.

Ronnie's eyes went from one to the other as her daughter and mother-in-law played verbal tag team.

"It seemed a bit weird. Up until that point, every time your name was mentioned..."

"The man's eyes lit up."

Ronnie knew what they were saying. She'd seen that light for herself. Unfortunately, she'd also seen the moment it went out. One minute they were in a passionate embrace, as if they couldn't get enough of each other, in the next they were like two strangers. She recalled the journey back to Holme Lea Avenue and Jack's blank expression as he stared at the road ahead. The silence between them felt unbearable. Not that Jack needed to say anything; the nothingness on his face said it all. It was just like her to get it wrong. When it came to PC Jack Shenton, honesty certainly hadn't been the best policy. "No," she said. "Jack will not be a part of my future."

"But why not?" Willow asked. "He's perfect for you."

Perfect was exactly how Ronnie would have described Jack too. He proved himself to be kind and caring, and he loved animals, especially Charlie. Physically, the man was gorgeous and, boy, could the man kiss... Almost whimpering at the thought of his lips, she could at least console herself in the fact that she got to taste them before he disappeared into the ether. "Because it wouldn't be fair."

"What wouldn't be?" Willow asked.

"What are you talking about?" Bea said.

Both women looked at Ronnie like she was speaking another language.

"Because of what I've done." Ronnie sighed as the two women still struggled to understand. "As in my visits to next door," she said, clarifying her point.

Finally, the penny appeared to drop.

"He's a policeman, which of course means he has principles." Ronnie thought back to the man's emptiness once she'd revealed to him what she'd been up to; how he went from hot to cold in an instant.

"I wouldn't tell him," Willow said, nonchalant. "I mean, he doesn't have to know, does he?"

"I would," Bea said. "Just not straight away. I'd wait until he was so enamoured by my presence, I could tell him I was Vlad the Impaler's love child and he wouldn't care."

"Whereas I think there's been enough game playing already," Ronnie replied.

Willow and Bea narrowed their eyes.

"You've already said something, haven't you?" her daughter asked.

Bea threw her head back in disbelief. "Why on earth would you do that?"

Despite a part of her wishing she hadn't, Ronnie knew she was right to be honest with Jack, even if it hadn't given her the result she'd hoped for. It would have been unfair to keep *Operation Poltergeist* a secret and besides, it was bound to come out at some point. If Ronnie didn't tell him, the odds were that Nick and Gaye would. "If *I* didn't mention it, we all know there are others who'd more than happily do the honours."

Willow and Bea sighed, unable to disagree.

"It's my own fault for doing what I did in the first place," Ronnie said, trying to be philosophical about it.

"Speaking of which," Willow said. She reached into her handbag and pulled out an envelope. "Step five."

Ronnie smiled, merely looking at it almost brought tears to her eyes. After step four, she was convinced her daughter and mother-in-law had discarded their plan. She thought it funny how in the beginning she'd been the one to doubt their six-step intervention, yet the nearer they got to the end, she was the one with the faith. "Thank you," Ronnie said. "For not giving up on me."

"Never," Willow replied.

"Ever," Bea said.

39

While Charlie slept at the foot of the bed, Ronnie sat on the edge, glancing around the room. As with the rest of her abode, she'd always considered it a comfortable homely space, a place to relax. She frowned; in reality it was tired and in need of an overhaul. With its pine wardrobes, plain walls and boring duvet set, the room certainly didn't compare to the glamorous décor boudoir next door. Maybe when Ronnie had sorted out her finances, she'd think about redecorating.

She let out a laugh as she compared the inside of her house to Gaye's. Each seemed to reflect their respective relationships with Nick – boring and jaded *versus* exciting and fresh.

She looked down at the envelope laid next to her. *Exorcise Nick*, the piece of paper inside it said. Something Ronnie knew she needed to do. Emotionally, she supposed she'd already begun that process; her trip to the viaduct had enabled her to offload at least some of her angst towards him. When it came to his physical presence, however, that was a different story. Six Holme Lea Avenue was still packed with her ex's belongings. Be they his tools in the loft or his aftershave in the bathroom cupboard, in one form or another, he occupied every room in the house. So much so that Ronnie didn't know where to begin.

She stared at Nick's wardrobe. "What do you think, Charlie?"

The yellow Lab looked up from his resting place, wagging his tale at the sound of his name.

Ronnie smiled in response as she rose to her feet. "I guess it's as good a place to start as any."

Opening the wardrobe doors, she took in the line of clothing. A few shirts, a couple of suits, jeans and a handful of T-shirts. It was clear none of them would suit Nick's new image. Ronnie smiled as she looked at them, her naughty side wanting to bag everything up and dump it all outside number eight. The amount of stuff Nick had left behind would certainly bring chaos to Gaye's perfectly ordered surroundings. Ronnie told herself she wouldn't, of course; that was her old way of thinking. The new Ronnie was done playing games. She'd give anything worth keeping to a local charity and take anything that wasn't to the tip.

Ronnie worked quickly. Tackling the hangers and shelving space, there was no reminiscing about when something was bought and for what occasion. Staring at the two neat piles of clothing and stack of shoes, Ronnie felt nothing. Not that there was much as attire went, but she supposed Nick had never been a clothes horse. She frowned. At least, not until Gaye had gotten her hands on him.

Ronnie moved on to Nick's bedside table where the book he'd been reading before he left still sat next to his lamp. She picked it up to look at the cover and glance at the blurb. Police procedurals weren't exactly her own preferred bedtime read; in her mind, novels about serial killers weren't conducive to a good night's sleep. Thinking about it, Ronnie supposed she and Nick had different tastes when it came to lots of things. Books, films, music, they could never agree.

She opened the novel to its dog-ear, letting out a sarcastic laugh as she clocked the page number. *Page twenty-five*, she thought. *How apt*. Her brow knitted as she recalled her foray into Gaye's bedroom, unable to remember seeing any reading material on either side of next door's bed. She shuddered, refusing to let any unwanted images enter her head. The two of them probably had better things to do at bedtime.

She considered her own sex life with Nick. Like her surroundings, Ronnie had to confess that that had been passed its best too. In fact, after her kiss with Jack, Ronnie had to wonder if it had ever been up to much to begin with. She sighed, trying and failing to put all thoughts of Jack to the back of her mind, knowing Willow had been right to say she didn't know what she'd been missing over the years.

With Nick being the only man she'd ever made love to, Ronnie had spent years telling herself that the earth only ever moved in the movies, that panting and moaning during intercourse only existed in the realms of fiction. Those things certainly didn't happen in real life, at least not to her. Then a police officer came along and looked at her like no other man had before; a situation that sadly included her husband. One wink from Jack and her whole being tingled with possibility. She felt a chemistry when she was around him that she couldn't explain; a sexual desire that she couldn't deny. As for Jack's kiss, it wasn't only her lips that had wanted more, her whole body screamed for it too.

Ronnie wondered if Nick had the same physical responses to Gaye's presence. Ronnie sighed, for his sake hoping so.

40

Ronnie stood on a dining chair, scrubbing the inside of an empty kitchen cupboard. "Almost done," she said to Charlie, who'd taken up residence under the table. Dipping the sponge into a washing-up bowl filled with what had turned into cold soapy water, she gave the cupboard another quick wipe before whipping the tea towel off her shoulder and drying off the space. "There," she said, feeling a sense of accomplishment. "Finished."

Climbing down, Ronnie's eyes scanned the room. Every unit door and drawer front sat open, revealing nothing but clean empty spaces. She sighed, the downside being that everything that once occupied those units and drawers now filled every available work surface. Baking equipment, pans, oven trays, crockery, measuring jugs, mugs, the cutlery tray, the toaster... the list went on. As for the table linen, Ronnie couldn't remember the last time she'd used a fancy runner or napkin. She took another deep breath. The room was in chaos and if Ronnie was honest, sorting through everything, ready to put some of it back, felt a tad overwhelming. Still, at least she'd made sure that everything she needed for a perfect cup of coffee was to hand.

Her phone pinged for the umpteenth time and with her mobile buried somewhere beneath the mounds of stuff, Ronnie didn't have a clue where to start looking for it. Hoping there wasn't an emergency, she wondered why she hadn't simply put it in her pocket for safekeeping. Not that there was any point worrying, she realised. Whoever was trying to get in touch would just have to wait.

As she reached for the kettle and stuck the spout under the tap to fill it with water, Ronnie glanced out into the garden. She couldn't believe how hard she'd worked. While her mornings involved working with fine silks and threads as a handbag designer, her afternoons had been spent with her sleeves rolled up, copious amounts of bleach and an inordinate number of bin liners.

She looked out at cardboard box after cardboard box and bag after bag of unwanted or unneeded items, every one of them waiting to be taken to the local charity shop or the refuse tip. Ronnie hadn't meant to go on such a mammoth decluttering mission, but once she'd started getting rid of Nick's belongings, it made sense to go through her own stuff too. Room after room, she'd blitzed them all, unable to remember the last time the house had had such a good sort out. Not that she'd stopped there. Every single inch of the place had had a thorough deep clean. She looked around the kitchen again, wondering why she'd saved the hardest space until last.

It had been a therapeutic experience, Ronnie considered, liberating even, as if she was making room for a whole different future. A picture of Jack popped into her head, but she immediately dismissed it. Having not heard a single word from the man since the viaduct fiasco, as far as Ronnie was concerned, that ship had sailed.

Continuing to look at the boxes, Ronnie still felt surprised at how everything they owned seemed to have a purpose. Nothing was frivolous, each item practical in nature. And their photographs. While they were all smiles and excitement on the outside, hers and Nick's eyes told a different story. However, equally as shocking were the things that Ronnie didn't find.

There were no love notes in their belongings, no little teddies with hearts embroidered on their chests and no cards with special messages. Ronnie realised that while some people might find such items tacky or twee, after twenty-five years there should have been some keepsakes amongst their stuff to mark the specialness of their relationship. As it was, she found nothing.

It was as if, emotionally, she and Nick had simply existed. As if they'd lived under the same roof, slept in the same bed, gone on holidays together, raised their daughter, but they hadn't loved each other, not in the way a couple should. They'd got on with it, tried to make the best of things. Ronnie heaved a sigh, resigned to the reality of it all. Under those circumstances, she supposed their relationship was lucky to have lasted as long as it did.

With the water for her coffee hot and ready, Ronnie picked up the caddy, while Charlie suddenly jumped out of his hiding place and headed out into the hall.

"Mum," Willow called out, above the yellow Lab's excitement.

"It's only us," Bea added.

Ronnie shook her head, a part of her convinced those two could smell a kettle boiling. "In here," she called back.

"I've been trying to get a hold of you," her daughter said.

Such was her tone, Ronnie couldn't tell if Willow was annoyed or excited. Still, at least she'd answered the phone pinging question.

While Charlie trotted in and headed straight back under the table, Willow and Bea suddenly stopped once they'd reached the kitchen doorway. Almost bumping into each other, they stared at the chaos that met them.

"What's going on?" Ronnie's daughter asked.

"Oh my word," her mother-in-law said.

Ronnie laughed. To say they were the ones to suggest she declutter in the first place, she found their response amusing. "I'm having a sort out. Like you told me to."

Willow appeared horrified. "We didn't tell you to do this, we only said to get rid of Dad's things." She approached the laden dining table. "And since when did *he* own a food mixer?"

Bea looked equally disturbed. "Or a tablecloth?"

"Or a…" Willow picked up an egg slicer, a piece of kitchenalia from years gone by. "What the hell is this anyway?"

Ignoring their comments, Ronnie raised her mug. "You're welcome to join me if you can find yourselves a cup."

"I think we're going to have to pass," Bea replied, she and her granddaughter continuing to survey the mess.

Willow turned her gaze on Ronnie, eyeing her from head-to-toe. "As for you, Mum. Have you got no shame?"

Ronnie looked down at her jeans and T-shirt. Aside of being covered in filth, which simply proved she'd been working hard, she couldn't see what was wrong with her outfit. It was what she always wore.

"You can't go around looking like that," Willow said.

"What do you suggest I wear to clean the house?" Ronnie replied, wondering why her daughter was creating such a fuss. "Stilettos and a ballgown?"

"Yes!" Willow said. "No! Don't worry, we'll figure it out."

"Figure what out?"

Ronnie watched her daughter head for the kitchen window and scan the outdoors, the poor woman's eyes widening even more when she spotted the numerous bags and boxes lying out there. "And what the blooming heck is all that?"

"I was going to ring you..." Ronnie gestured to the room. "Once I'd sorted through this lot. I'm going to need some help getting rid of it."

Willow looked like she was reaching the end of her tether.

"I would have done it myself, but with my car still in the garage."

Willow turned to Bea. "She doesn't know, does she?"

Bea shook her head. "Doesn't look like it."

Ronnie stared at them both. "I don't know what?"

"About why I've been calling you?" Willow pulled out her phone, pressed call, and waited until Ronnie's mobile rang.

"Good luck finding it," Ronnie said as it rang from somewhere within the mess. "Although you could just tell me what's on your mind instead of trying to show me."

"I was coming to that," Willow said.

Bea's eyes lit up. "You might want to sit down."

Ronnie laughed. "I'm fine, thank you." After everything she'd been through, from a dodgy haircut to a police search party, she doubted anything they had to say could warrant a funny turn.

"Don't say you haven't been warned," her mother-in-law said.

41

R onnie watched Willow bring up an image on her phone, before holding it out for Ronnie to accept. Ronnie put down her drink in readiness, pausing nervously. Not quite able to look at the screen, she'd been in that situation too many times already. Having watched herself flying off a treadmill and then rearrange someone else's cupboards, she didn't think she could face any more embarrassment. "Please don't tell me I've gone viral again."

Willow nodded to the mobile, encouraging Ronnie to take a look.

Ronnie did as instructed, although glancing at the picture before her, she wasn't sure what she was meant to be seeing. Going off everyone's posh outfits, the photo was of a celebration of some kind, but other than that she didn't clock anything relevant to herself. She looked to her daughter and mother-in-law for the answer.

"Keep scrolling," Willow said.

Doing as she was told, Ronnie realised the images were of someone's wedding and that she vaguely recognised the groom, although she had no clue where from. Again, she turned to Willow and Bea.

"He's a footballer. Premier league," Bea said, her excitement coming to the fore. "And the bride's an actress."

Ronnie swiped over to the next photo, one that included more of the wedding party. "They make a beautiful couple."

"You haven't spotted it yet, have you?" Willow asked.

"Spotted what?"

Willow used her finger and thumb to zoom in on a particular section of the photo.

Ronnie's heart skipped a beat. "But that's my..." She smiled, unable to believe what she was looking at.

"Handbag," Willow said.

"Wow!" Ronnie had no idea her mother-of-the-bride creation was headed for that kind of wedding.

"Only in one of the biggest celebrity magazines going," Bea said.

Ronnie felt a bit in shock. "I think I might need that seat after all."

Bea cleared some stuff off the nearest chair so Ronnie could sit down.

"So, now you see why we can't have this," Willow said, waving her hands at the kitchen paraphernalia laid about the place. "Or this." She pointed to the boxes and bags piled high in the garden. "And we definitely can't have any of this." She stared at Ronnie's attire, shaking her head as if that was the worst crime of all.

"I'm not following," Ronnie said, failing to understand what the state of her house or wardrobe had to do with anything.

"Chanel, Gucci, Prada, Fendi...You don't see any of their designers wandering around looking like the office cleaner, do you? And I bet none of them are secret hoarders either." Willow picked up the egg slicer again, as if to prove her point.

Ronnie laughed. "I'm hardly in the same league."

"And you never will be if you carry on like this." Willow pointed first to the room and then to Ronnie's attire.

"She's right, dear," Bea said. "You could be playing with the big boys now. And to get the part you have to look the part."

Willow rolled up her sleeves ready for action. "So, the quicker we get this lot sorted, Mum." Again, she gestured to the room. "The quicker we can get working on you."

"Here you are," Bea said, reaching into her bag. "We were going to wait a while longer, but now it's a case of needs must."

Ronnie smiled at the envelope being proffered.

"Step six," Bea said.

For the first time since their plan started, Ronnie had a good idea as to what was inside.

42

Ronnie stared at her reflection in the changing room mirror. The outfits Willow and Bea had chosen for her were certainly vibrant. She twisted first to the left and then right, assessing the fit of the red crepe trouser suit they'd picked. Tailored in style, she could see it gave her a flattering silhouette. The trousers were an ankle-grazer length, which according to Ronnie's daughter, were perfect for both the flat shoes and heels she'd already bought, and the single-breasted jacket had a notch lapel. It was lined with a bold floral silk fabric, giving the outfit a sense of fun. And best of all, both the trousers and jacket had pockets.

"Let's have a look then," Willow called out.

Ronnie smiled, picturing her daughter and mother-in-law sat on the other side of the curtain, eager to offer their opinion. Ronnie swished back the drape and ready to hear what they had to say, twirled around to show the suit off from every angle.

"Oh, that looks fabulous," Bea said, a big smile on her face.

Willow gestured to the numerous carrier bags at their feet. "Another one to add to the collection, me thinks."

Ronnie laughed. "And then that's it," she said, feeling

shopped out. Not only had her credit card taken a hammering, her feet ached from all the pavement pounding they'd done as they went from store to store to store. "I don't know about you two, but I could do with a drink."

"Most definitely," Bea replied.

Ronnie headed back into the booth. Closing the curtain behind her, she changed back into her own clothes. Looking at herself once more, she shook her head at what she saw, forced to admit how scruffy she'd become. Since Charlie's arrival, she knew she'd lost weight thanks to the dog walking but hadn't, until then, appreciated quite how much. Her jeans and top hung on the wrong side of loose and her pumps had seen better days. Not one for clothes shopping as a rule, it seemed step six of Willow and Bea's plan hadn't only been fun, it had come at just the right time.

Ronnie hung the trouser suit back on its hangers. "Why don't I meet you two at the coffee shop over the road?" she called out to Willow and Bea. "There's no point you both loitering by the till while I pay for this." She pulled the curtain open again.

"Good idea," Willow said, rising to her feet. "Come on, Grandmother, we'll get the drinks in."

While they headed off, Ronnie made her way to the cash desk and placed her purchase on the counter.

"For you?" the female shop assistant asked.

Ronnie nodded, taking in the young woman's fabulous sense of style. "My daughter's choice though," she said, feeling the need to explain. She indicated to the clothes she wore. "As you can see, I'm not very up on fashion."

"Great hair though."

Ronnie put a hand up to her head. No longer bald, she ran her fingers across what had turned into an overgrown crew cut.

"For what it's worth," the young girl said, placing Ronnie's suit into a paper carrier bag. "Your daughter made the right choice. You're gonna look badass in this."

Ronnie laughed as she handed over her payment. Surprised at how good the compliment felt, *badass* was not how she'd have described herself no matter her clothing. "Thank you."

As she made her way out of the store, Ronnie continued to smile, holding her head high as she walked. She knew her new positive frame of mind was thanks to Willow and Bea and their six steps. In the beginning, Ronnie might have considered their plan pure folly, but looking back, she had to admit it had saved her. She'd gone from feeling lost and abandoned, as if she was treading water most of the time, to embracing a new future and, as a result, owed her daughter and mother-in-law far more than she could ever repay.

Ronnie crossed the street and as she entered the coffee shop, spotted Willow and Bea at a table in the corner. She raced over to join them, pleased to see the cup of caffeine awaiting her. "Just what I need," she said, taking a sip. She looked at her daughter and mother-in-law, wondering what she would have done without them during those last few months. There'd been some ups and downs since Nick left and the two of them had been Ronnie's anchor throughout. "I want to say thank you. For everything."

Bea waved a hand, dismissive, but Ronnie could see she appreciated the sentiment.

"What did you expect?" Willow said. "We're the three amigos."

"The three musketeers," Bea said.

Ronnie laughed. "More like the three stooges."

Aside of any jokes, Ronnie knew exactly who they were. They were three generations of Jacobs women, supporting each other no matter what. As she watched her daughter and mother-in-law laugh along with her, Ronnie felt her smile fade a little.

Whether she liked it or not, she knew Nick had a place amongst them, but she pushed the thought to the back of her mind, not wanting to spoil the moment.

"So, having got your image sorted, Mum, and we know how well work is going..." Willow said.

Ronnie thought about the number of enquiries she'd had since the magazine article. It certainly seemed that she was going to be busy for the foreseeable future. She'd never liked the way journalists insisted on giving their readers an exact breakdown on the fashion choices of every woman they featured. To her, it often felt like a woman's clothing was more important than anything she had to say or had achieved. On that occasion, however, it had worked to Ronnie's advantage. Not only did the journo concerned describe the mother-of-the-bride clutch bag, Ronnie's name as the designer was mentioned too.

"...we need to find you a man."

Ronnie almost choked on her coffee. After PC Jack Shenton with his principles, and Nick and Mr Wright without, Ronnie needed no such thing. "I'm fine on my own, thank you very much."

"I take it he still hasn't been in touch then?" Bea asked.

Ronnie didn't have to ask who the question related to. She shook her head. "And nor do I expect him to."

Willow sighed. "I have to say I'm disappointed."

"I don't know why," Ronnie said.

"I thought he'd come around, realise you're not really a criminal, just a bit barmy sometimes."

Ronnie chuckled. "Thank you for that."

"Aren't you the one who insists we're not built for relationships?" Bea said to her granddaughter.

"Yes, I am," Willow replied. "But we're not talking about me here, are we?"

Ronnie chuckled again. "While we're on the subject, how's Mr Whateverhisnameis?"

"Who?" Willow asked.

Ronnie couldn't believe her daughter had forgotten him already. "The chap with the dog?"

"Oh, him. He's long gone."

"So, who's next in your firing line," Bea asked. "Anyone we know?"

"I wish you'd meet Mr Right and settle down," Ronnie said.

"Ooh, me too. And have lots of children. You don't know how desperate I am to join the honourable Great-grandparent club."

"Whoah!" Willow replied.

She might be laughing, Ronnie considered, but the mere thought clearly filled her daughter with dread.

"Not on the cards, I'm afraid."

All at once, Bea put a hand on the table as if needing to steady herself.

"Are you okay?" Ronnie frowned, concerned.

"Grandmother?"

"I just feel a bit dizzy all of a sudden."

"You do look pale," Ronnie said.

"Don't worry, it'll pass." Bea appeared to grip the table a little tighter.

Willow jumped up from her seat. "Let me get you some water."

"You mean this has happened before?" Ronnie said.

"At my age, funny turns are the norm," Bea replied.

Ronnie reached out to comfort her mother-in-law. "You feel a bit warm too," she said, placing a hand on hers.

"I've probably over done it with the walking," Bea said. "We've covered some miles today." She smiled. "Either that or it's excitement after talking about great-grandchildren."

Ronnie tried to match her mother-in-law's smile, but she

couldn't help but feel guilty. She'd been enjoying herself so much on the shopping front, she hadn't thought to question how Bea was coping along the way. Despite what the woman said, it was obvious Bea felt dreadful and was simply putting on a brave face.

Willow returned with a glass of water. "Here. Sip this."

Keeping one hand firmly on the table, Bea took the glass with the other and did as she was told.

"Better?" Ronnie asked.

"A little."

"Maybe we should get you home?" Willow said. "So you can rest up properly."

"Good idea," Ronnie said.

"Shall I go and get the car? It's only up the road, I can meet you outside."

Ronnie nodded.

"I'll take this lot with me." Willow gathered up the shopping bags. "It'll save the kerfuffle when I pull up and you can concentrate on Grandmother."

Ronnie watched her daughter head out.

"She's a good girl," Bea said, watching her too.

"She is."

"Takes after her mother."

"And her grandmother." Ronnie sat stroking her mother-in-law's hand. "Have you seen a doctor about these funny turns?" Ronnie waited for an answer, but none was forthcoming. "What are we going to do with you, eh?"

Bea continued to drink her water in silence, before a car horn finally beeped.

"She's here," Ronnie said, spotting Willow's vehicle at the roadside. "Do you think you can manage?"

Bea nodded.

Ronnie helped her mother-in-law to her feet, before gently

guiding her through the coffee shop and out onto the street. Willow had already opened the car's rear door by the time they got outside, making it easier for Ronnie to assist Bea to get in. Ronnie ran around to the other door and climbed in alongside Bea, Ronnie's concern fast increasing when she saw how much colour had drained from the older woman's face. "I think we need to get her to the hospital," Ronnie said to Willow. "Now."

43

Ronnie cursed her hometown for being too small to warrant having its own hospital, leaving them no choice but to drive all the way out to the next. Her mother-in-law could be really sick, but what did her local authority care? Once their emergency was over with and Bea had gotten the help she needed, Ronnie planned on complaining to anyone and everyone who'd listen. Of course, her daughter was doing her best, but the car seemed to be going nowhere fast. Sunday drivers, cyclists and wayward pedestrians seemed to be out in force. Road junctions were too busy to easily pull out of and signals were constantly against them.

"No," Willow said, her shoulders slumping as the approaching traffic lights turned red, forcing her to slow to yet another standstill. "This is ridiculous."

Ronnie kept one hand on Bea's lap, while her fingers on the other drummed on the seat. She couldn't agree with her daughter more.

"Sod it," Willow said. "Hold on to your hats back there."

Ronnie watched her daughter crane her neck as if trying to

assess the various traffic flows around them. She obviously thought going for it worth the risk as, much to Ronnie's horror, Willow suddenly rammed the car into gear, dipped her clutch and hit the accelerator. The car wheels screeched as the vehicle shot forward, at the same time throwing Ronnie and Bea headlong in their seats.

"Jesus, Mary and Joseph. Please be careful," Ronnie said. But as her daughter put her foot down even further, it was clear she wasn't listening. Ronnie tried to keep Bea secure in her seat as they were flung left and then right and back again, the poor woman whimpering throughout. With her panic rising and their seat belts struggling to keep them safe, Ronnie began to wonder if they'd get to the hospital at all.

A vehicle ahead should have been enough for Willow to slow down, but instead she sped up and pulled out for an overtake. Ronnie stared at the oncoming white van through the front windscreen, convinced they weren't going to make it back into their own lane in time. The van driver frantically beeped his horn, the poor man obviously thinking the same thing. Willow yanked at her steering wheel only just getting them back to safety, before the van got the chance to hit them.

"I think I'm going to faint," Bea said, barely audible.

The sound of a police siren suddenly blared from behind.

"Bugger!" Willow said.

Praise the Lord, a part of Ronnie thought.

As Willow pulled her car over to the side of the road and switched off the engine, Ronnie did her best to soothe her ailing mother-in-law. It might only have been seconds, but she felt herself getting impatient, wishing the police officers concerned would get a move on. She attempted to twist round in her seat so she could see for herself what was taking so long, but not wanting to unnecessarily disturb Bea, who leant against her for support, she soon gave up trying. "What are they doing back there?" she asked, noticing she wasn't the only one getting frustrated.

Willow unclipped her seat belt and jumped out of the car, clearly as desperate as Ronnie not to waste any more time. Ronnie could hear her daughter, frantic in her attempts to explain the situation, the officer doing his best in response to calm her down. "At last," Ronnie said, as footsteps finally approached.

"Jack?" Ronnie said, as the uniformed officer suddenly appeared at her window. In that moment she didn't care what issues there were between them, she was simply glad to see him. "Thank God it's you. We could do with some help here."

Jack's eyes widened at the sight of Ronnie's mother-in-law. He hastily opened the car's rear door and leaned inside to assess her condition.

"She suddenly came over all dizzy, but she's getting worse," Ronnie said.

"How long has she been unconscious?" Jack asked.

Ronnie looked at her mother-in-law, for the first time realising the woman had passed out. Ronnie's heart raced, seeing Bea appear so lifeless. "I don't know," Ronnie said, panicking. "Think, Ronnie, think... A minute, maybe more."

Jack positioned his cheek millimetres from Bea's nose, before putting two fingers against her neck, assessing her carotid pulse.

"She is all right, isn't she?" Willow asked, terrified. "She's not going to die?"

"Please tell us she's still breathing," Ronnie said.

"She's going to be fine," Jack replied. He put a quick hand on Ronnie's arm, before jumping out of the car and immediately talking on his radio.

Ronnie was too freaked out to follow his conversation; odd words like *hospital, escort,* and *eta* reached her consciousness, but nothing else. Her eyes followed Jack as he approached Willow who stood there looking helpless.

"We're not waiting for an ambulance," he said. "You'll have to follow me."

Willow nodded, instantly pulling herself together. She jumped behind the wheel and turned the ignition key. The car engine fired up as Jack ran back to his vehicle. The wail of sirens sounded again and the police car, with its blue lights flashing, pulled out to lead the way. Willow immediately put her car into gear and hit the accelerator, making sure she was almost bumper-to-bumper with Jack as they raced to the hospital.

Throughout it all, Ronnie didn't know how her daughter managed to remain so cool.

"Hang on in there," Ronnie said to Bea, her voice cracking with fear. "Don't you dare leave us." She hugged Bea tight with relief as her mother-in-law stirred.

While Willow concentrated on keeping up with Jack, unlike her daughter, Ronnie struggled to keep calm. As they sped through the streets, cars didn't seem to get out of the way quickly enough; lorries were too wide, forcing both Jack and Willow to slow down in order to squeeze past and, worst of all, arrogant drivers played chicken at various traffic lights, determined to get through before the police car hit them. *What's wrong with some people?* Ronnie silently asked. *Can't they see we have an emergency here?*

Finally, both vehicles screeched into the Accident and Emergency car park, Jack immediately jumping out of his before signalling to the waiting medical staff who sprinted over to assist.

Ronnie reluctantly climbed out from the back seat, giving the team of medics the room they needed to help Bea. Ronnie stood there, feeling powerless as they pulled her limp mother-in-law from the back seat and placed her on a stretcher. Ronnie tried to keep up with everyone as they rushed Bea into the building. Once inside though, a nurse stepped in front of Ronnie and her daughter, preventing them from going any further.

"You'll have to wait here," she said as Bea and her medical entourage disappeared behind a set of swinging doors.

"But she'll be scared," Ronnie said.

"She'll want us there," Willow added.

The nurse put a hand on Ronnie's arm. "Please," she said to them both. "Someone will be back to update you once we know more."

"Come on, you two," Jack said, appearing at Ronnie's side. "Let the doctors do their job."

Ronnie stood there silent as she watched the nurse disappear behind the swing doors too. Ronnie couldn't understand what was happening. Less than an hour previous everything had been so normal, so perfect. Bea had seemed fine. Ronnie tried to pull herself together, before turning to Willow and Jack. "Someone should ring Nick."

"I'll do it." Willow rummaged in her bag for her mobile. "Are you okay hanging on for a minute?" she asked Jack. "Until I get back."

Jack nodded as Willow smiled, her appreciation obvious as she headed outside.

"You don't have to stay," Ronnie said. "I mean, you're on the clock and I wouldn't want you getting into trouble."

"But I want to."

Feeling grateful, Ronnie wanted that too. She clearly didn't have her daughter's strength when it came to emergencies.

Jack led Ronnie over to the waiting room area and taking a seat, she glanced around. Children with various injuries sat fidgeting next to concerned parents; an elderly woman sat coughing and spluttering, her symptoms unappreciated by the thirty-something woman with a bandaged hand; and a teenager sporting a sling sat with a smile on her face, still managing to scroll through her smartphone. Ronnie smelt the mix of antiseptic, bleach and vomit. Boy, did she hate those places.

Ronnie sneaked a look at Jack, wondering what he was thinking and why he'd offered to stay. She felt an awkwardness in the air around them, as if they both had things they wanted to say, but each recognised it was neither the time nor the place. "I suppose you come here a lot?" she said, needing to break the silence. "What with the things you have to deal with."

"Goes with the territory, I'm afraid."

Recalling all the occasions she'd sat in Accident and Emergency back in the day, Ronnie knew what he meant. The police often turned up with some drunk or drug addict or domestic violence victim in need of medical attention. Of course, she was there for the same reason, having dialled 999 after her latest beating. The hours she'd spent in crowded hospital waiting rooms, the lies she'd told about walking into doors or slipping on the stairs. She took a deep breath and let out a long woeful sigh. Better that than being at home when her drunken mother woke up.

"Penny for them?" Jack asked, interrupting Ronnie's reverie.

"Sorry?"

"A penny? For your thoughts?"

Ronnie took a deep breath, pushing her memories back into the recesses of her mind where they belonged. "I'm just worried about Bea."

"She's going to be all right. You'll see."

Ronnie returned his encouraging smile, wishing she had his confidence. If only she'd paid more attention weeks earlier when Willow had said her mother-in-law hadn't been well. Ronnie knew if anything happened to Bea, she'd never be able to forgive herself.

"I thought we could all do with one of these," Willow said.

Suddenly appearing with three cups of coffee, she struggled to hand them out. "Not sure how they'll taste, but it's better than nothing."

Jack jumped up to help, passing one to Ronnie before taking one for himself.

"Dad's on his way," Willow said.

44

The swing doors burst open and a nurse stepped out from the corridor beyond. Ronnie rose to her feet in readiness of an update on Bea's condition, but the nurse kept her eyes forward and walked straight past. Watching her go, Ronnie's face fell and with no other choice, she sat down again, disheartened.

Jack smiled a gentle smile. "It won't be too long now." He checked his watch, quickly turning his attention to both Ronnie and Willow. "Are you two okay if I go and book off, let comms know I'm done for the day?" He indicated to his police radio. "I'll only be a few minutes."

Ronnie nodded. "We'll be fine."

"Won't you have to drive the police car back to the station?" Willow asked.

"I'll get one of the lads to pick it up. And hopefully get mine dropped off after they've done that."

Ronnie opened her mouth to say something, but Jack jumped in before she could speak. "No, I don't mind," he said, anticipating her very words. "And, yes, I'm happy to hang around as long as it takes." He gave Ronnie's arm a tender rub before going on his way.

Watching him head off, Willow filled her cheeks with air, as if dying to say something.

Ronnie rolled her eyes. "Spit it out."

Willow turned to face her. "I know Grandmother's sick," she ventured. "And that's where our focus needs to be, but, Mum, I'm going to say it anyway."

"Say what?"

"You could do worse."

Ronnie frowned. "You're seeing something that isn't there."

"Oh, come on. He might not have admitted it yet, but believe me, PC Jack Shenton is besotted. And, dare I say it, so are you."

"Rubbish." Having admitted her feelings towards the man once, Ronnie wasn't about to make that mistake again.

"Really? He hangs around hospitals for everyone, does he?"

"He might do. If he's personally escorted them."

Willow raised her eyebrows. "And you let *every* man you meet stroke your arm like that, do you? The bloke hasn't kept his hands to himself since we landed."

Ronnie felt herself blush. The truth was, she'd noticed Jack's familiarity too. She was glad of it, but it also scared her, and unlike her daughter, Ronnie refused to let herself read too much into things. Jack had shown her affection before, they'd kissed, gotten passionate. And then when she was honest with him, he ran. As far as Ronnie was concerned, the man was only doing his job, a bit of crime prevention, no doubt. Knowing him, he probably thought she'd go on some sort of spree if he wasn't around to keep an eye on her.

"The tension between the two of you is tan-gi-ble," Willow said. "You need to sort yourselves out, talk things through. Or at least have a shag to get it out of your systems."

"Willow!"

Her daughter put her palms up, feigning defeat. "I'm only saying."

"Well, don't. You don't know what you're talking about."

With nothing else to do except glance around the room again, Ronnie heard Nick before she saw him.

"I'm here about my mother," he called out to the receptionist before he'd even properly stepped through the doorway.

Ronnie stiffened as she looked up to spot him, unfortunately with Gaye in tow.

"Why is she here?" Willow asked.

Nick scanned the waiting area, his eyes falling on Ronnie. "It doesn't matter," he said to the receptionist.

Ronnie rose to her feet as Nick headed directly for her. As he approached, she prepared to tell him what little she knew about Bea's condition.

"What happened?" he asked, his voice demanding.

Willow jumped up, seemingly aligning herself next to Ronnie. "We're still waiting to hear from the doctors."

"I'm not talking to you," Nick replied. "And besides, that doesn't answer my question."

With both Nick and Gaye's eyes on her, Ronnie could tell that they weren't in the mood for facts, that they already blamed her for events regardless. And seeing their impatience as they waited for her to speak, she felt under pressure to explain something she knew they'd refuse to understand. "I don't know what happened. We were out clothes shopping. One minute everything was fine, then it wasn't. Bea went pale and she felt dizzy, that's when we brought her here."

"Shopping? You mean you dragged a seventy-odd-year-old woman around town so you could buy some fancy clothes?"

"No, Nick. That's not what I mean."

"Dad," Willow said. "This isn't Mum's fault."

"Seventy-three," Ronnie said.

"What?" Nick scowled, looking at her like she'd lost the plot.

"Your mother, she's seventy-three."

"Oh, here we go." Nick threw his arms in the air. "Acting like you know her better than me again. I'm only her son."

"Dad," Willow said, her tone pleading.

"It's all right," Ronnie reassured her daughter. "Your dad's upset."

"Damn right I'm upset." He trained his eyes directly on Ronnie. "You do know this is your fault, don't you? Dragging her into your stupid games to turn her against us."

Listening to him, Ronnie knew he had a point. Not because of any games she had or hadn't played. After all, she'd done her best to keep both her daughter and mother-in-law out of all that. What she was guilty of, however, was secretly liking the fact that Bea had chosen her over Nick's new woman. Because in a sense, that meant Bea had chosen her over Nick.

"Poor little Ronnie," he continued, his voice suddenly mocking. "Your son is so bad because he left me for someone better."

Ronnie felt herself redden, embarrassed that Nick could behave that way in full view of the hospital waiting room. She saw they were attracting an audience, although she wasn't surprised, considering her ex-husband had just announced to the world that his girlfriend was a marriage wrecker.

"Come on, love," Gaye said, clearly feeling uncomfortable at the dirty looks being thrown her way. "There's no point letting her get to you." She linked her arm into his.

Willow scoffed at Gaye. "And you're here because?"

"Willow," Ronnie said. "That's enough." Her daughter opened her mouth to respond, but Ronnie gave her a look warning her not to.

Nick shrugged Gaye off, obviously on a roll when it came to Ronnie. "I'm telling you, if my mother... if she..."

Ronnie's whole body tensed up as Nick leaned in until his face was centimetres from hers. "I'll..."

"You'll what?" Jack said, suddenly behind him.

45

Grateful for Jack's arrival, Ronnie finally exhaled. She watched on as Nick spun round. The shock on his face might have been fleeting, but as he looked from Jack, to her, and back again, it was there long enough for Ronnie to see it.

"I should have known you'd be here," Nick said, full of bravado. "Don't think I haven't noticed you sniffing around my–"

"Ex-wife," Jack interrupted. He folded his arms and took a deep breath, purposefully puffing out his chest. He straightened his back, instantly gaining another inch in height.

Ronnie couldn't help but notice how puny Nick looked in comparison, forcing her again to ask what she ever saw in the man.

"You do know if you carry on making a scene, I shall have to arrest you," Jack said.

Nick scoffed. "For what?" He gestured to Ronnie. "We all know she's the criminal around here."

"To prevent a breach of the peace, for starters," Jack said. "This is, after all, a hospital." He glanced around the room. "And you do seem to be upsetting an awful lot of people."

Nick fell silent as he too looked around.

"Come on, love," Gaye said, taking Nick by the arm. "Let's go and sit down."

"Good idea, madam," Jack said.

Nick hesitated, but Jack stood firm, leaving Nick no choice but to do as requested.

Jack turned to Ronnie and Willow. "Are you two okay?"

Willow nodded.

As did Ronnie. She suddenly felt overwhelmed. Not only was she worried about Bea but she had to contend with yet another of Nick's outbursts, and no-one had ever stuck up for her quite like that before.

Jack indicated she should sit down too, before taking the chair next to her.

"Thank you," Ronnie said.

Jack didn't say a word. Instead, he took her hand and wrapped his own around it.

Sitting there in silence, the atmosphere felt tense. With Ronnie, Willow and Jack on one side, and Nick and Gaye glaring at them from the other, Ronnie wished the doctors would hurry up. She felt Jack squeeze her hand, as if he'd somehow read her mind. It was the exact reassurance she needed.

At last, the swing doors flew open and a chap in a white coat stepped through.

Ronnie, along with everyone else, jumped to her feet eager for news.

"I take it you're all here for Bea Jacobs?" the doctor asked.

"Yes," Nick said, hastily stepping forward. "I'm her son."

"I'm pleased to say she's looking a lot better than when she first got here."

Ronnie heaved a sigh of relief. "Thank goodness."

"Although, she will be staying with us so we can run some tests," the doctor continued.

"Tests?" Ronnie asked.

"I'm afraid so," the doctor said. "Syncope, that's the medical term for passing out, or fainting if you like, happens for a reason. It's a symptom of something else that's going on in the body and it's up to us to find out what that is. But please don't worry too much at this stage. Whatever it might be we'll find it, and deal with it."

"Can we see her?" Willow asked, her expression hopeful.

"Now we've gotten her comfortable, yes. She's been asking if she can have a few minutes with family before she's admitted to the ward. If you'd like to follow me." He turned to lead the way.

Ronnie stepped forward to follow in the doctor's footsteps along with everyone else, but Nick jumped in front of her, blocking her path.

"Where do you think you're going?" he asked, his face contemptuous.

"To see Bea, of course," Ronnie replied.

"Oh, no," Nick scoffed. "You heard the doctor, he said *Family*."

Nick's words stung. Bea was her family. She'd been Ronnie's mother-in-law for twenty-five years, he couldn't take that away from her, pretend their marriage had never happened. "But..."

"No buts, Ronnie." He took Gaye's hand. "You're out."

"Dad, please," Willow said.

Ronnie found the shock in her daughter's eyes heartbreaking. Not that Nick seemed to care, strutting through the doors, the man was obviously enjoying the sense of power.

Instead of following on, Willow hesitated, as if not knowing what to do for the best.

"Go," Ronnie said. "Go and see your grandmother." She

could see her daughter felt torn, but the poor girl had no reason to. Ronnie smiled, encouraging her on. "For the both of us."

As her daughter reluctantly headed through the swinging doors, Ronnie stood there well after they closed. "Don't worry about me," Ronnie whispered, tears suddenly rolling down her face. She felt an arm around her.

"Come on," Jack said. "I'll take you home."

onnie stood on her front doorstep saying goodbye to Jack. No doubt the neighbours had clocked his morning departure, but Ronnie didn't care. Nick, Gaye, Mr and Mrs Wright, and even independent Mrs Smethurst... As far as Ronnie was concerned, they could each think what they liked. She took in Jack's towering frame, confident stance and kind face. Despite them all, he looked as tired as she felt. Then again, it wasn't as if either of them had gotten much sleep the previous night.

He checked his watch. "I suppose I'd better go and get out of this," he said, gesturing to his uniform. "Or at least change my shirt before the next shift starts."

"You should."

He seemed to pause before leaving, as if waiting for Ronnie to say something. But she remained quiet.

Jack leaned in and kissed her cheek, before whispering in her ear. "You have my number," he said. "Call me. Anytime."

Ronnie smiled. "Thank you." She watched him head down the path to his car, remembering the first time she'd seen him. He'd seemed so intimidating back then, nothing at all like the gentle giant she'd gotten to know. On that occasion, she'd been desperate to see him leave and never come back. *Funny how things turn out*, she considered. Standing there in that moment, she didn't want him to ever go.

He put up his hand before climbing into his vehicle, and Ronnie waved back as he drove away. She let out a wistful sigh, knowing she probably wouldn't ring him, she didn't have the guts. She took a deep breath, knowing that meant she'd perhaps never speak to the man again.

As Willow pulled into the space Jack had just left, Ronnie waved in acknowledgement for a second time. She couldn't help but smile as she clocked her daughter's expression – a confused mix of both shock and delight. *Here we go*, she thought, anticipating the round of twenty questions about to follow.

Fighting with her seat belt, Ronnie's daughter didn't seem able to get out of her car quickly enough. "Mother," she said, when she at last managed it. "Please tell me I'm right in what I'm thinking here, I mean that definitely wasn't a police car." She charged towards Ronnie. "Please tell me PC Jack Shenton stayed the night."

Ronnie stood aside to let her daughter into the hallway and, with a mischievous twinkle in her eye, closed the door behind them. "He did."

Willow gasped, putting a hand up to her chest. "You devil." She let her hand fall. "I want to know everything."

Ronnie opened the door to the lounge. "I think this should explain all," she said, a big smile on her face as she revealed a pillow and a spare duvet folded neatly into a pile on the sofa.

Willow's expression turned deadpan. "I am so disappointed in you right now."

Ronnie shook her head and chuckled.

"So, what you're saying is you spent the whole evening talking?"

"Yes."

Willow groaned.

"Because that's what we did."

It was clear Willow couldn't have been less impressed if she'd tried. "We're so not related. I'm adopted. I have to be." She sighed. "It must have been a long conversation if the man was too tired to drive home."

"It was," Ronnie replied. "We chatted about lots of things. My job, you, your grandmother and your six-step plan. Even your dad got a mention a couple of times."

Willow raised an eyebrow. "You're telling me you did all the talking, aren't you? And that Jack didn't get a word in?"

"Yep."

"You gave him your life story, didn't you?"

"Pretty much."

"That poor man."

Ronnie laughed again. "What can I say, he's a good listener."

Willow shook her head.

"Let me get my bag and we're good to go." Ronnie headed into the kitchen to collect it, knowing that a part of her felt as frustrated as her daughter. She and Jack had sat for hours the night before, while Charlie lay happy at their feet. On and on she'd prattled, Jack laughing in the right places, reassuring her in others, and knowing when to simply say nothing. Jack made opening up easy. Ronnie sighed. Not that she had disclosed everything.

On the few occasions when Ronnie had fallen quiet, she found herself looking into the man's eyes. During those moments, she'd wanted so much to kiss him; to lead him upstairs to her decluttered bedroom where they could make wild passionate love. Jack would have let her too, she knew that. She could tell by the intensity in his gaze that he wanted her as much as she wanted him. But like Ronnie had formerly explained, she didn't believe in friends with benefits.

Willow had been right to describe Ronnie as an all-or-nothing kind of person; one-night stands would never be her thing. Jack had to want to commit, to accept her for who she was, regardless of her prior antics. However, while Ronnie was happy to forget all about *Operation Poltergeist*, that didn't mean Jack was too.

Ronnie sighed, wishing she were more like her daughter. If she were, she'd have had the confidence to ask him if he'd put aside his principles, to tell him how she really felt. She smiled. She'd have had the confidence to simply go for it and ravish him.

Ronnie grabbed her handbag before scanning the room in search of Charlie. She spotted his tail poking out from under the table and smiling, crouched down to his level. Despite his permanent smile, he looked pitiful, lying there, with his head resting on the ground between his two front paws. "I feel the same," Ronnie said, guessing the yellow Lab was also wondering when, if ever, he would see Jack again. She rubbed his head, a bit of her wishing she could stay so they could feel sorry for themselves together. But she couldn't. If one good thing had come out of her wittering on to Jack, it was that she'd finally been able to put things into perspective. "You be a good boy," she said, rising to her feet. "I won't be long. I promise."

"Ready?" she asked Willow, as she headed back out into the hall. Her daughter nodded and Ronnie locked the door behind them as they made their way out to the car. Climbing in, Ronnie felt nervous. "Are you sure this is okay? The last thing your grandmother needs right now is any trouble and if your dad finds out..."

Willow laughed. "Who do you think organised it?"

Ronnie smiled to herself. It was just like Bea to find a way to circumvent hospital visiting time rules.

"You should have seen her yesterday when Dad walked in with Gaye instead of you."

Knowing Bea's thoughts on the woman, Ronnie could imagine.

"Naturally, Gaye tried to fawn all over her, but Grandmother wasn't having any of it."

"It's good to know she's back to her usual indomitable self," Ronnie said as her daughter started up the car. "I have to admit, she had me worried for a while."

"Me too," Willow replied, pulling away from the kerb. "I'd love to know what was in that drip they gave her. It's like some miracle cure."

Ronnie thought back to when she first met Bea. Ronnie and Nick hadn't been together long and her then future mother-in-law didn't seem keen on their relationship at all. Bea never said as much, but Ronnie heard it in the woman's voice, saw it in her facial expressions, and Bea was quite the expert when it came to backhanded compliments.

Ronnie put it down to Nick's dad dying so young. It had been mother and son, and no-one else for so long, Ronnie was bound to be an intrusion, a threat even. Then they had to go and fall pregnant and the prospect of breaking that bit of news felt terrifying.

That was when everything changed. Overnight, Bea went from covert dragon lady to the nicest, kindest, most supportive woman anyone could meet. She still had her moments, of course, and Bea was a lioness when it came to her family. Ronnie tried to picture the previous night's events, and while she never thought she'd say it, she had to admit she felt a bit sorry for Gaye. As mothers-in-law went, Ronnie's could be quite intimidating when she wanted to be.

As the drive continued, Ronnie listened to her daughter chatting away about the tension between everyone during the previous day's hospital visit. How Bea had struggled to look at Gaye, let alone engage with her. The way Willow told it, Nick spent the whole time acting like they were one big happy family, ignoring the fact that the medical staff popping in and out could sense they were anything but. However, while Willow laughed about it all, Ronnie struggled to raise a smile. She shifted in her seat, uncomfortable, finding the whole situation anything but funny.

47

Ronnie was pleased to find Bea sat up in bed awaiting their arrival when she and Willow tapped on the door and entered her room. Her daughter had been right to question what had been in the woman's drip, her mother-in-law appeared back to her happy healthy self. It was as if her funny turn had never happened, and Ronnie smiled at the sight of Bea's face lighting up as soon as they walked in.

She moved to give her mother-in-law a hug, before glancing around the room. "Comfortable enough," she said, taking in how bright and airy the space was thanks to its huge window. There was a sink unit in the corner, a TV screen fixed to the wall opposite Bea's bed, and a glass and jug of water sat on the bedside cabinet, which was made up of a drawer and a cupboard in which to house Bea's belongings. Ronnie turned her attention back to her mother-in-law. "So, how is the patient feeling today?"

"Ready to go home," Bea replied. "I keep telling them I feel fine now, but will they listen?"

Ronnie chuckled, glad she wasn't part of her mother-in-law's medical team. She could imagine the grief Bea was giving them. "You have to let them do their job."

"Before you even think about leaving," Willow said.

"You wouldn't be saying that if you were the one being prodded and poked every five minutes. Have you seen this?" Bea held out her arm, inner elbow face-up to reveal the biggest and blackest of bruises left behind after a blood test.

Ronnie and Willow grimaced at the sight.

"Exactly. Call themselves nurses, butchers more like."

"Yes, well, like the doctor said, dizzy spells and fainting happen for a reason. They have to do these things to figure out what that reason is."

"Hopefully this lot will cheer you up," Willow said, placing the holdall she carried at the bottom of Bea's bed. "A toothbrush, a nightie, everything you asked for with a few extras. Magazines, some sweets, that kind of thing."

"Thank you." Bea indicated to the hospital gown she'd had to make do with. "These things do nothing for a woman's modesty."

Ronnie pulled a couple of chairs up to the side of the bed and she and Willow sat down. "So, how are you really doing?"

Her mother-in-law's shoulders slumped. "If you must know, I'm feeling a bit silly. This really is a lot of fuss over nothing."

"We'll let the medical experts be the judge of that," Ronnie replied.

"I don't know what you're complaining about," Willow said. "Being able to lie in bed all day, your meals brought to you on a tray, lots of dishy men in white coats giving you special attention. Minus the illness, I wouldn't mind a bit of that."

"Now you mention it," Bea replied, a naughty smile suddenly appearing on her face. "There is this one young gentleman who pops in from time to time."

Ronnie smiled too, happy to see her mother-in-law's spirits lifting again.

"Doctor Raj, oh he does light up the room. But don't worry, I'm keeping my hands to myself. It wouldn't do to cross a line with my granddaughter's future husband."

Ronnie laughed while Willow spluttered.

"Mum, we really do need to find out what medication they've given her."

"I'm telling you, Willow," Bea said. "He's *The One.*"

"And I'm telling you, there's no such..."

The hospital room door opened, cutting Willow's sentence short.

"Doctor Raj," Bea said. Straightening herself up, she gave her granddaughter a wink. "We were just talking about you."

Ronnie let out a giggle as she looked at the handsome chap before her. Her mother-in-law was right, he did have the power to light up a room.

"I wanted to check how you're feeling this morning, Bea," he said.

"Better for seeing you," Ronnie's mother-in-law replied.

He picked up Bea's notes that hung at the bottom of her bed and began reading.

Ronnie turned her attention to Willow, who was obviously thinking the same thing as her; that the man was rather dishy. She tried not to laugh as her daughter sat there uncharacteristically lost for words. And if Ronnie wasn't mistaken, her daughter was blushing slightly. Ronnie nudged Bea, discreetly drawing her attention to Willow as well.

"How did you manage to swing this?" Doctor Raj asked, putting Bea's notes back where they belonged. "Visitors outside visiting hours." He smiled at Ronnie and then at Willow, holding the latter's gaze a tad longer than necessary. He cleared his throat, as if suddenly feeling less self-assured. "You must be Bea's granddaughter."

Willow nodded.

"She's told me all about you."

I bet she has, Ronnie thought.

Willow tried to reply, but rather than fully formed words, she seemed to speak in syllables. However, the doctor didn't seem to notice; he appeared equally as mesmerised.

He shook himself out of whatever was going on in his head. "I think I've disturbed you enough," he said to Bea, obviously trying to regain a degree of professionalism. "I'll come back and have a chat later, when there are no..." He looked at Willow again. "Distractions." He appeared to steal yet another look at Willow as he hastily left the room.

Bea leaned towards her granddaughter, excited to hear what she thought. "So?"

Willow's eyes stayed on the doorway, she seemed to be in a world of her own.

"Am I right? Or am I right?" Bea asked.

"Sorry?" Willow said, doing her best to focus.

Ronnie shook her head, both surprised by and pleased with her daughter's response to Doctor Raj. She'd never known Willow react to a man like that before and struggled to believe what she was seeing. "Oh, yes," Ronnie said, answering on her daughter's behalf. "He's definitely *The One*."

"I need some fresh air," Willow said. "I feel a bit dizzy, I don't know what's come over me." She looked at her grandmother. "I think what you've got might be catching."

Ronnie and Bea watched her get up from her seat and leave the room, the poor woman's confusion continuing as she turned to head down the corridor. Ronnie and Bea laughed.

"Looks like we'll be buying new hats in the not-too-distant future," Bea said, a big smile on her face.

Ronnie chuckled. "I think you might be right," she said, supposing time would tell.

"Then all this is worth it," Bea replied, looking around the room. She clasped her hands and dropped them on her lap, gratified.

Ronnie observed her mother-in-law's contentment, not wanting to spoil her good mood. But with Willow out of the way, Ronnie had the perfect opportunity to have a serious conversation with Bea. Things needed saying and, considering where they were, sooner rather than later. She took her mother-in-law's hand. "Can we talk?"

48

Bea smiled in response. "Of course. What is it you want to say?"

"I'll start by saying thank you. I don't know what I'd have done without you being there for me all these years, let alone the last few months. You've supported me through thick and thin, and that six-step plan you and Willow came up with has made me feel like a new woman. It took me out of my comfort zone, gave me a good shaking up, it was what I needed."

"It worked then?"

"It certainly did. You were both right, and now we've come to the end of it, Timbuktu or number eight, Holme Leave Avenue, I don't care where Nick and Gaye live."

Bea seemed pleased to hear it.

Ronnie paused. "Which brings me to my next point of discussion..."

Bea narrowed her eyes, clearly wondering what was left to say. "And that is?"

"I want to talk about yesterday."

Bea relaxed again. "I've told you." She waved her hand,

dismissive. "There's nothing wrong with me. I really am fine now."

"Maybe, maybe not. But it's not just that, is it?"

"If you're referring to..." Bea's expression turned sad. "I'm so sorry that Nick did that to you, Ronnie. Willow told me how he behaved and it's unforgivable."

"Willow shouldn't have."

"Yes, she should," Bea said, coming over rather adamant. "You'll always be family to me, no matter what that son of mine says. He had no right to treat you that way."

"No, he didn't."

Bea twisted in her position to face Ronnie. "As for bringing in that woman. You do know she tried to fluff up my pillows when I was leaning against them, don't you? How does she know how I like my pillows? I've barely spoken to the woman since the two of them got together and there she was, acting like she knew everything about me. Like she cared."

"She cares about Nick."

"Does she? Then why break up his perfectly good marriage?"

Ronnie smiled. "If it had been perfect, Bea, Nick and I would still be together."

Her mother-in-law remained indignant.

"Remember when I first met Nick. You didn't think all that much about me either."

"That was different."

"How so?"

"Because it was."

"You changed your mind though, once you got to know me."

"Because you didn't sleep with married men, for one."

Ronnie laughed. "All I'm saying is, it might be time to give Gaye a chance."

Bea stared at Ronnie, as if Ronnie had lost control of her faculties.

"We both know neither of them are ever going to make my Christmas card list," Ronnie continued. "But when I think about what could have happened yesterday, Bea, if we'd lost you."

"But you didn't."

"But if we had? And you and Nick hadn't worked through things. He's your son, Bea, you need to sort things out, for both your sakes. And mine. Whenever the time comes, I don't want to be the one responsible for coming between you. That's a big weight to have to carry around."

Bea sighed. "But Gaye isn't you."

Ronnie laughed. "She most certainly isn't."

Bea folded her arms tight across her chest. "I'll never get on with her."

"You might surprise yourself."

"You *are* different," Bea said with a sulk. "Now I wish we'd never come up with that six-step plan."

Ronnie shook her head, letting out another laugh. "It's not like I'm going anywhere, Bea. I'll always be here. You don't have to choose between Gaye and me, it isn't necessary. But you do have to choose your son."

Bea seemed to contemplate for a moment. "Say I take your advice, would you do something for me in return?"

"Of course. Anything."

"Promise?"

Ronnie crossed her heart. "Promise."

"Would you thank Jack for what he did yesterday? You know, for getting me here?"

Ronnie nodded. "I will."

"And then be honest with the man about how you feel?"

Ronnie closed her eyes for a second, letting her head drop as she realised she'd walked straight into that.

"Like you said, yesterday could have been it for me and I don't ever want to die thinking you're alone when you needn't be."

Ronnie lifted her head back up.

"Believe me, I know what it's like to have no-one and it's hard. Jack's a good man, who feels the same for you as you do him. You're just both too stubborn or too scared to tell one another."

Ronnie knew in her case it was the latter. Jack had rejected her once already thanks to *Operation Poltergeist* and she didn't want to give him the chance to do it again.

As if reading Ronnie's mind, Bea squeezed Ronnie's hand in reassurance. "No matter what happens in life, no matter how many times that heart of yours gets broken, you still deserve your happy ever after." She smiled. "So, are we agreed? I'll give things with Gaye a go, and you'll do the same with Jack?" She held out her other hand, ready to seal the deal.

49

Ronnie sat at the dining table, her mobile and Jack's handwritten phone number in front of her. Having promised Bea, she knew she had to ring him, but plucking up the courage proved difficult. Having been rejected by Nick in the most spectacular fashion, and then by Jack after an equally spectacular event, she wasn't sure she could suffer the humiliation for a third time.

But you gave your word, a little voice in the back of her head said.

Ronnie picked up the piece of paper and stared at it. She told herself not to be so soft; it was a phone call, a conversation, nothing more and nothing less. "And it is the twenty-first century," she insisted. "A time when women ask men out as much as men do women." At least that's what her daughter claimed, and she would know. After all, Willow approached members of the opposite sex all the time. She didn't care about getting rebuffed, she simply moved on to the next one.

Feeling Charlie's eyes boring into the back of her head, Ronnie turned to look at him.

The dog sat there upright, as if to attention, while at the same time willing her on. He let out a short sharp bark.

"All right, all right," Ronnie said. "I need another minute." She took a couple of deep breaths in readiness, before snatching up her phone. In a now-or-never moment, she dialled the number and waited, her heart racing in anticipation.

"Jack," she finally said. "It's me. Ronnie. I'm ringing because I promised Bea I would. She says thank you for getting her to the hospital the other day. Anyway, there's something I want to say and I'm just going to come out with it. I like you. A lot. You're gorgeous and funny and kind and a great kisser... The greatest of kissers, in fact. And I know you have your principles too and that on paper, well not on paper because I didn't get arrested, I'm probably a criminal. But I've learnt my lesson. I should never have sneaked into next door once, let alone three times. But that's over with now. I don't care where Nick and Gaye live, I don't care about them at all. And because of that, I was hoping you'd maybe want to go on a date sometime? To see how things go between us? But only if you think the same about me as I do you. Yes, I know I'm waffling, but I know if I don't tell you how I feel now, I probably won't ever—"

The line went dead.

Ronnie fell silent. She couldn't believe she'd been cut off before she had the chance to finish. She looked at her phone screen and then at Charlie. "I left him a message."

The dog stared back at her.

"What?" Ronnie asked. "You think that was a bad idea?"

Charlie slumped down on the floor, dropping his head on the ground between his front paws.

Ronnie took that to mean yes, leaving a voicemail had been a terrible idea. "How was I supposed to know? I was married for twenty-five years, I'm not an expert when it comes to these things."

As Charlie pottered around the garden, Ronnie stood with a paint bucket under her arm, frantically mixing water into ready-prepared cement with a trowel. As with her baking, it was great for getting rid of her frustrations and, pausing to check its consistency, Ronnie had to admit it resembled her cake making too. "That should do it."

Not for the first time that day, she felt desperate to check her phone, but with her hands, in fact as she looked down at herself, most of her body, covered in the grey lumpy paste, she decided against reaching into her pocket to get it. She looked up at what was left of her pruned-back hydrangea, glad to see Charlie nowhere near her makeshift fence repair. "You stay here, boy," she said, smiling at the sight of Charlie chasing a butterfly. "And don't get either of us into any trouble."

Leaving the dog to it, Ronnie closed the back door behind her as she headed inside. Trowel and bucket in hand, she made her way through the kitchen to the hall and up to the landing, and climbed up the stepladder. She'd meant to block the hole in the dividing wall up well before then, but with everything that had been going on, hadn't gotten around to it.

Plonking herself down next to the pile of waiting bricks, Ronnie smiled, glad that the hole was actually still there. After her talk with Bea, it was as if she'd somehow subconsciously saved the task at hand until just the right time. Closing it up suddenly felt symbolic, like she'd come to the end of an era. "This is it," she said, picking up the first brick. "The first day of the rest of your life."

She plunged the trowel into the bucket and scooped up a huge dollop of cement, slapping it onto the base of brick number one. Slotting it back in place, Ronnie felt a sense of satisfaction, repeating the process with bricks two, three, four and five. With her work almost done, she paused. Putting the final brick where it belonged once and for all was like closing the door on her past. She took a deep breath as she dug into her pocket and pulled out her wedding ring; a simple gold band that for twenty-five years had meant so much. Sitting on her palm, there was no sense of attachment, it no longer represented who she was. It was simply a piece of metal.

She smeared brick number six with cement and squashed her wedding ring into the mixture. "There," she said, and forcing the whole thing back in place, closed off the last bit of the hole. "Finished."

Ronnie took a moment and as she stared at the wall before her, there were no tears, she didn't feel any sadness, rather she felt a real sense of acceptance.

Sitting there in the quiet, she again considered her conversation with her mother-in-law, surprised at how easy saying goodbye to the past was, compared to welcoming the future. She thanked Nick for their twenty-five years together, for bringing Bea into her life and for their beautiful quirky daughter. And she found herself thanking Gaye for taking Nick off her hands. After all, if her neighbour hadn't, Ronnie would be stuck in what she realised was a loveless marriage. She certainly wouldn't be on the verge of embracing a life full of opportunities, all be that a scary prospect.

Ronnie jumped when her phone rang, breaching the silence. Her hands shook as she reached into her pocket and, pulling out her mobile, checked the number. Her pulse quickened as she rose to her feet. She clicked to answer. "Jack?"

As he talked, Ronnie looked around, beginning to panic. She didn't know why, but she suddenly felt guilty for being in the loft. Leaving the trowel and bucket where they were, she climbed down onto the stepladder. "Busy? Me? Not at all."

With only one free hand, she struggled to manoeuvre the

hatch back in place. Finally she managed it, before quickly descending to ground level and dragging the steps into her bedroom. "Yes, I did ramble on a bit, didn't I?" She flipped the ladders shut and laying them on the ground, shoved them under the bed. At last, she plonked herself down on the edge of the mattress and although out of breath, could finally give Jack her full attention. She steeled herself, ready to ask the inevitable. "Have you thought about what I said?"

The doorbell suddenly rang and Ronnie cocked her head, groaning at such bad timing. She ignored it, preferring to listen to what Jack had to say, but within moments the bell rang again. She grimaced at the inconvenience, and was forced to do something about it. "Sorry to interrupt, Jack, but there's somebody at the door. I'm going to have to answer, it doesn't sound like they're going away." She kept her phone to her ear as she made her way out of the bedroom and down the stairs. "You're still there, aren't you?" she asked, wanting nothing more than for Jack to stay on the line.

She opened the front door and suddenly finding herself lost for words, stared at her visitor.

Standing there, Jack smiled back at her, a giant bunch of flowers in one hand, his phone in the other. "Yes, I'm still here."

"But..."

Jack clicked his phone off and stuffed it into his pocket. He stepped forward and, placing one hand behind Ronnie's back, pulled her close.

Ronnie let her arm drop and her phone fell to the floor. Her heart raced and butterflies caused havoc in her tummy as she looked straight into Jack's eyes. "Does this mean...?"

"It most certainly does."

Finally, Ronnie's face broke into a smile.

"So, I'm the greatest of kissers, am I?" he asked.

Ronnie nodded and as he pulled her even closer, anticipation bubbled inside of her.

"I think we need to test that theory, don't you?"

Jack leaned in and, once again, what began as a sweet gentle kiss grew in passionate urgency. Feeling his arms wrap around her, the rhythm of his lips and his tongue against hers stirred Ronnie's whole body. She heard herself moan, desperate for more. Their kiss slowed and just like the last time, Ronnie and Jack giggled.

Ronnie pulled back, looking straight at Jack once more. "Would you like to take this inside?" she asked.

Jack smiled. "Most definitely."

THE END

ACKNOWLEDGEMENTS

I'll begin by thanking everyone at Bombshell Books. Fred, Betsy, Morgen, Heather, Sumaira, Tara, Alexina, Clare, Loulou and Shirley, your continued support, hard work and dedication is very much appreciated. Thank you for holding my hand every step of the way. You're all absolute stars.

I'd like to say a special thanks to textile artist extraordinaire Philippa Day. Not only did you teach me the ins and outs of handbag design, you gave up your time to show me around your studio. Without your inside knowledge and expertise, Ronnie would have had a different career and I wouldn't have taken up sewing!

Finally, my heartfelt thanks go out to you, the reader.

Lightning Source UK Ltd.
Milton Keynes UK
UKHW041044261119
354268UK00003B/496/P